The Satyr In Bungalow D

JOYCE WADLER

THE SATYR IN BUNGALOW D

Paperback ISBN: 979-8-218-60016-7
Ebook ISBN: 979-8-218-600017-4

Published in the United States.

This is a work of fiction. All incidents, dialogue and characters, with the exception of some well-known historic figures, are products of the author's imagination and are not to be construed as real.

Joyce Wadler is represented by The Joy Harris Literary Agency.

Cover by Altemus

Book design by Sarah E. Holroyd (https://sleepingcatbooks.com)

ALSO BY JOYCE WADLER

My Breast, One Woman's Cancer Story

Liaison, The Gripping Real Story of the Diplomat Spy and the Chinese Opera Star Whose Affair Inspired "M. Butterfly"

Cured, My Ovarian Cancer Story

In memory of Gussie Wadler and her sons,

Bernard, Arthur, and Herman Wadler

My grandfather came to America in the mind of the woman he loved, an Italian opera singer, and emerged, blinking, into the sunlight of a tiny resort town called Fleischmanns in the Catskill Mountains.

Entering the mind of a sleeping woman is not unusual if you're a satyr, one slips in and out all the time. What is unusual is that my grandfather traveled over the sea. Satyrs shun and fear large bodies of water. My grandfather insisted it happened after one last tryst before his lover was to leave for a grand tour; that he fell asleep and when he awoke, the ship had sailed. What I believe is she made him so love-crazy, he could not bear to leave.

Of course, you could say I would want to believe that – for my life, too, has been unhinged by love.

"Unhinged," actually, doesn't come close to describing what love has done to me. For that you need more than a flute; you need a great voice and a sax. I don't think that even Sinatra, in the worst of his three-in-the-morning, Ava-fucked-me-over-so-bad torments, could put that feeling across. Or Dylan, who I had the honor of playing with one long-ago evening in Greenwich Village, and who, I have always suspected, had some satyr blood himself.

Believe me or disbelieve me. Entertain the possibility these sixty years later, if you dare, that the charming fellow who took your virginity behind a bungalow colony and refused to take off his hat was not the med student he claimed to be, but a satyr in full August rut. That's why we were there, in the drunken green abundance of the Catskills in summer: to give the women joy.

As for me, the minute she fell down my mountain, I was lost.

CHAPTER ONE

To start at the beginning – well, I can't actually remember my beginning. Nymphs are notoriously rotten mothers. They allow themselves to get pregnant only because it's good for their skin and, after giving birth, don't stick around long, a few months at most. Sure, they're tender the first week or two after birth, when your eyes mirror their image. They'll chew up the new grass, when it's the sweetest, and put it in your mouth, and bring you the tiniest strawberries. With raspberry season, the novelty of creation has worn off, and they're distracted by their primary interest – themselves – and are studying their reflections in ponds. By blackberry season, which coincides with the time their waists are once again 28 inches and their sons can forage on their own, the mothers disappear.

Like all nymphs, the mother's season is short. Nymphs awake in early May. The moment the weather drops below delicious, usually late September, they take their winter sleep in a fragrant bush or fruit tree. That bush or tree is what gives a nymph her scent. Passing that tree, say a Japanese wisteria in full bloom, a satyr becomes sentimental and sighs, but I have never passed a tree that reminded me of my mother. I have no memories of my mother, who dumped me when I was two weeks old, and who my father refuses to discuss.

My first scents, in fact, are not floral, but scents from The Maplewood House, the hotel on my mountain, a few miles outside Fleischmanns. When my grandfather arrived in the early 1900s, the town was a mix of fine hotels, ethnic boarding houses, dairy farms, and grand estates, many owned by wealthy German Jews. The Fleischmanns family, for whom the town is named, came upstate every summer in their own railroad car, outfitted a band to celebrate their arrival, and had a deer park and baseball team, both kept freshly stocked.

By my time, the early '60s, the hotel business is in decline. The summer people are primarily working people from New York City — cab drivers, schoolteachers, people who sit at sewing machines all day. There are still, however, echoes of the old days: Viennese tea gardens with violinists and European-born guests, many of whom are refugees from Hitler. They speak German and Hungarian and Yiddish, dress for dinner and *shpatzir*, or promenade, down Main Street.

Scattered invisibly in the mountains, unknown to the humans, is the secret colony of satyrs to which Pop and I belong. Those paintings of dopey satyrs gamboling in the woods, which portray us with the ears of horses or the lower bodies of goats, are unfortunate folkloric slurs.

We are, at the risk of sounding immodest, a strikingly handsome species, differing in aspect from humans primarily because of our short, thick horns, which are easily hidden by our curly hair or a hat, and our hooves, which while dark and cloven, are not that different in size and shape from a human foot and can be covered with socks and shoes. Our lower bodies are very hairy, but from a distance that hairiness can be mistaken for pants. Outfitted in human clothing it is easy for us to pass, and in summer, when the population of Fleischmanns explodes and delectable New York City ladies take cautious but hopeful walks up solitary mountain paths, many do.

Our hotel, at the base of Halcott Mountain in the farming community of Halcott Center, originally had been a dairy farm that took in boarders and still had cows and chickens. It was not as grand as the huge hotels on the southern side of the Catskills: Grossinger's, The Concord, Brown's, which had golf courses and indoor swimming pools and were open year-round. But it was not small: there was a fifty-room main building surrounded by a dozen smaller buildings and cottages, including a bungalow for Pop, where, of course, he never spent the night. There was a fake Cuban dance instructor team and a P.A. system that blasted cha-cha and Sinatra. The kitchen was huge and noisy. The dishwashers dried silverware by shaking it in a pillowcase.

Satyrs have an excellent sense of sound and smell. The sounds and smells I remember, carried up Halcott Mountain, were of the hotel: the rooster crowing, the waiters setting up in the kitchen, the smell of stuffed cabbage, sweet and tart, the way the Eastern European Jews liked it. The secret, at The Maplewood House, was adding gingersnaps to the sauce.

I also have memories of Mrs. Belinsky, the old lady who ran the hotel with her two sons. I could always get something to eat from her in the kitchen if it was quiet and nobody but the family was around, though Pop didn't like me on the hotel grounds.

"You're there," I would tell him. "You're there all the time, hanging around the pool."

"I can handle it," he'd say. "For you, it's dangerous."

Pop could handle anything. He was built like a wrestler, short and powerful, with a cocky grin like Kirk Douglas, whose picture I had once seen in a movie magazine. Even with the thick hair on his arms and legs, Pop had no trouble passing. Playing poker with the male guests in the afternoon, he covered his short, thick horns with a porkpie hat and hid his hooves under socks and sandals like the ones all the middle-aged men wore. He radiated lust, which was the reason Mrs. Belinsky liked having him around. A satyr who keeps women satisfied is more valuable to a hotel owner than a dance instructor. I once overheard two weekday widows discussing Pop.

"He gripped me down there like a bowling ball," I heard one say.

Even though I was very young at the time and didn't understand, I knew "down there" was hot.

Winters were long in the Catskills. By the end of October, the frosts had come, our signal to withdraw into our caves for the long sleep; we emerged with the leaves in early May.

Being practically grown, I had my own cave and it was a good one: cliff-side, which gave me an excellent view, with an interior height of a young maple and cracks in the rocks to let in light. A stream trickled down a wall, giving me the luxury of running water. Outside, trailing arbutus made a carpet of flowers and a black locust tree dripped small white blossoms, perfuming the air with the scent of orange blossom honey. It also hid the entrance in case any humans wandered up. That was unlikely, because it's precarious up here, with loose slate and rock slides. The locals avoided it, but there were always the annoying Boy Scouts.

My bed, which had a frame of woven branches, was filled with straw and fragrant herbs. I had an old steamer trunk, which had been discarded behind the hotel and I had dragged up the mountain. It stood on its side and opened to form a cabinet with a small mirror – not very goat, but useful for storing the jeans and T-shirts Pop insisted I wear if I was going anywhere near the hotel. I had a stash of wine, apples, and nuts, and, of course, my flutes. Every satyr plays. We have an affinity for music, but I wanted to write my own stuff.

For snacking, I kept stacks of discarded magazines and newspapers. I also, though I didn't broadcast this, liked to read them, including Mrs. Belinsky's Yiddish newspaper, The Jewish Daily Forward. When I overheard the older hotel guests speaking in Yiddish I could understand them. It's true what they say: you start eating newspapers young enough, you absorb the language.

Most satyrs don't care to read – they're taught letters so they can pick out signs like "Hunt Club" and "Trespassers Will Be Shot"– and they're done. I read books and magazines wherever I found them; the hotel grounds at night, when nobody was around, the town dump. That included paperback sexual instruction books by Mickey Spillane and Henry Miller. From Mickey Spillane, I learned that women with unnatural hair color are always sexually available and are ready for consummation when their breasts begin to heave. Unfortunately, like praying mantises, they try to kill you immediately after. Henry Miller provided explicit detail but treated women roughly and insultingly; he was everything a satyr is not. I found his writing so repellent I threw it out, though it was interesting to learn that humans had bones in their penises. Henry Miller said his was six inches long.

My favorite book was "The Great Gatsby," which I found under a lounge chair at the pool. Gatsby loves a married woman so deeply he builds a house across a great body of water and stares at a green light at the end of her pier. It's truly sad. Satyrs cannot cry any more than goats or horses, but if we could I would cry at that part. Then Gatsby and the woman, whose name is Daisy, are reunited. I liked this book so much that I stopped eating it three pages in, so I could read it over and over again. The last chapters had been rotted in a June thunderstorm, so I was never able to finish, but I knew a story with a love so strong could only end with Gatsby and Daisy together for the rest of their lives.

Unfortunately, though I spent a lot of time thinking about love, I had never really been with a nymph. I think that's because even though I was starting my third summer, which is like being seventeen or eighteen for a human, I had yet to horn, and without horns, nymphs don't take you seriously. I had the beginnings of horns, but they were little more than bony lumps, the size of a half-lemon, entirely hidden by my hair. "Wasp stings," my best friend Ben, who has three-inch horns nearly as thick as Pop's, called them. I had hoped this was the spring they would finally come in.

Waking up from the big sleep in my third season in early May, I immediately grab the top of my head. The lumps are larger, but there are still no horns, a big disappointment. Then, the last weekend in May, I wake up late with the most erotic dream I have ever had: A naked nymph is straddling

me, legs locked around my waist, and she is slowly licking my
horns. I grab my head with both hands and there they are:
two thick, tapering knobs. Finally!

I run my fingers up the length of them, then rush to the
mirror. My hair, which is thick and curly, hides most of the
horns, but the ends are sticking out, a beautiful, dark honey,
so shiny and clean they look polished. I dip my hands in the
stream and slick down my hair to get a better look.

They are gorgeous!

Okay, maybe not as big yet as Ben's or Pop's, but excellent
starters.

I pick up the sharp stone I have been saving. The day a
satyr gets his horns, he honors his mother by exposing the
nymph mark he was born with – a birthmark, humans call
it. They're about the size of a violet. My nymph mark, which
sits over my heart, is in the shape of an apple. I lather up with
soapwort root, carefully shave it clean and admire it in the
mirror.

Then I grab my pipes, run outside, and make my morning
gratitudes to nature:

*Thank you for making me a satyr. Thank you for the abundance of
summer. May I never squander a ray of sun, nor fail to delight in the
glory of a flower, and never, ever, decline the gift of love from a lady.*

Then – as I am horned and finally entitled – I play a loud
triumphant, *Fweet*!! on my pipes, followed by the five-tone
song to summer that's as old as satyrs and apple trees:

I'm here, I'm on fire, I'm ready to love you till your toes
curl! Daughters of summer, come forth from the flowering
trees!

Those aren't the words, of course. There are none. It's a
melody that every satyr brings his own feelings to, but that's

the meaning. A few minutes later, I hear satyr pipes singing congratulations from the mountains.

Fweet! Fweet! Fweet!

I run back to the cave. I put on my newest jeans and T-shirt, that Pop left for me just last week – and a good thing he did, as the old ones were getting tight. I pull on the thick white socks and sneakers that are necessary for camouflaging my hooves. I muss my hair to hide my horns. Then, I race down the mountain to Pop's cave. Pop isn't there, which means he is probably at the hotel.

I head down to the pool, stopping to check when I cross open fields – *Sniff, look around, sniff again* – then hide in the trees and shrubs behind the changing rooms, where the humans won't spot me. Memorial Day Weekend is the beginning of the summer season and the place is packed. There are dozens of guests, mostly middle-aged as The Maplewood House attracts an older crowd, staking out their spots, but no Pop. I spot Noah, Pop's human friend who works in the music business in the city and is here every weekend, next to an empty lounge chair with Pop's tote bag and quietly call out to him.

"Pop?" I ask.

Noah nods his head in the direction of a pretty, plump woman in a black skirted bathing suit which comes halfway to her knees. She's asleep and she is smiling. I can see that her breasts are heaving, just like Mickey Spillane says. Now I know exactly where Pop is and what he is doing. He has slipped into this woman's mind as a passionate dream and is giving her the best sex of her life.

"Rabbi's wife," Noah says.

A satyr never rushes, especially with a woman who's been doing without. This could be a while. I find the thickest cover and take a nap. Sometime later, Pop wakes me. Normally he'd be pissed to find me here so close to the guests, but I see him in his porkpie hat, looking down at me, grinning.

"So, you've got quite a pair there, I see," Pop says, squatting next to me.

I sit up, proud but wanting to be cool. But I can't help it; I'm grinning, too.

"Yeah," I say. "Not as big as yours, but you know. . . . "

"Just the beginning," Pop says. "C'mon, let's take a little walk."

He picks up his tote bag and we walk through the woods, up the hill, to one of our favorite spots, overlooking the Halcott valley. The fields are crazy yellow with dandelions. Hidden in the deep woods, satyrs are lingering over late breakfasts, romancing nymphs with honey and song, inhaling the sun-warmed clover. The fragrant delights of summer rise up like the scent of a warm peach.

"You looking?" Pop asks.

"Yeah," I say.

"Are you *feeling*?"

"I think so."

"It's a big day, the day you get your horns," Pop says. "I don't have to tell you, the nymphs will take notice. The summer your horns come in – that's the summer you remember the rest of your life. But getting your horns isn't just about making love. Today you take your place among a fucking *mythic* race. Nothing alive comes close to what we are. We're creatures of summer, here to celebrate the abundance of the season: the flowers, the fruits, the grasses. There are a lot of living things in the woods, but we're the guys with the ability to appreciate what we have. We don't just grab an apple and eat it as fast as we can. We taste, we savor. We sing summer with every breath we take." He's been telling me this stuff my whole life, but today I am hearing it with horns, which I have to say, makes a difference. I nod my head, soberly. "The same goes for the nymphs," Pop says. "A satyr honors his name by his actions. Gallantry, adoration, a hand when she climbs. We *worship* female beauty and — unlike the hornless idiots — we understand that they're all beautiful. Every female, every shape, every age, gets your respect. You *listen* when she talks. Maybe you want to fool around, but the lady wants flowers for her hair. You go get her flowers — not the first ones you find, but the most beautiful ones in the woods. She's in the mood for peaches, they're three miles away, you get off your ass and get her peaches."

It's hard not to drift off into dreams when Pop starts talking about nymphs and peaches, but this is an important day, today I am a satyr, so I try to concentrate.

"And now that you've got horns, you need to be extra careful about humans," Pop says. "When you're older, when you've got more experience, you know how to pass without fucking up, different story. But right now, you stay away. The Belinsky family, okay; they're never gonna look too closely, they think they know us. Noah, special case, he's practically got horns himself. The rest of them, forget it. It doesn't matter if they're drunk. It doesn't matter if they're unconscious. It doesn't matter if they're dead. You do *not* go near them."

Horns or no horns, there are only so many times I can hear Pop's "Don't go near the humans/ they think we're the spawn of the devil/ if they spot our horns, they'll kill us" speech.

"I know, Pop," I say. "You've been telling me this since I was born."

"Right, wise guy, and I'm telling you again," Pop says. "Anyway, I got you something."

He reaches into his bag and pulls out a hat. Not a porkpie, like his, but a soft blue cap with a visor, embroidered with the letters, "N" and "Y." It's the coolest hat I have ever seen.

"It's a baseball cap," Pop says. "I had Noah bring it up from the city, I figured this would be the month you horned. 'NY' – that stands for New York Yankees. That's a big New York team. Baseball. You'll have to start eating the sports pages."

He gives it to me and I put it on, excited.

"It's great, Pop," I say.

"Yeah," he says. "Looks good."

I'd love to see my reflection, but there are no ponds nearby. I also realize that I'm famished. I've been so excited about my horns, I haven't eaten even a handful of grass. Some French toast would also be great.

"Pop, I'm starving," I say. "Can I go to the kitchen and get something to eat?"

Pop checks the sun.

"Well, it is a special day," he says. "I guess you've got time. But don't stay too long. The help will be in in an hour."

There are humans who have such a lust for women and wine and the pleasures of summer that they have an affinity with satyrs and can spot us. They're rare, but they're out there. Pop's friend, Noah, who tries to seduce every woman he sees, is one. Musicians, if they are very gifted, can occasionally sense us also.

Mrs. Belinsky, a plump, gray-haired woman who was born in Russia and now seems to live in the hotel kitchen, is blind to satyrs. She thinks Pop is a widowed New York City professor, raising his son on his own, and with no grandchildren, she's always happy to see me. She's standing at one of the big wooden tables in a man's white apron. As usual, she gives me the impression of being dusted with flour. She's making Linzer tarts, cutting cookie dough into circles with a drinking glass, and layering them with raspberry jam. A half dozen trays are cooling. I smell the vanilla and berries. Enough checking the premises. I go inside. Mrs. Belinsky hugs me so hard I lose my breath.

"*Oy, meyn mlakh,* my angel," she says. "Such a beautiful boy."

She switches to English, which is so heavily accented it sounds like Yiddish. "But there's something different, I think . . ."

I wish I could show her, but of course, I can't.

"I got a hat," I say.

"Aah, yes," Mrs. Belinsky says. "That must be it. But still too skinny. Sit, I'll make you something."

She goes to one of the big steel refrigerators, pulls out food, and starts piling it up on the table. A big bowl of sour cream, bananas, stewed prunes, honeydew. Then she makes me French toast. Soon, there's a half-moon of food spread out in front of me. That's how Mrs. Belinsky is, too much is barely enough.

"You know, Mrs. Belinsky," Pop once told her, "They're making a special refrigerator just for old ladies. You open the door and you wheel the kids in."

Not even a satyr could eat this much food, but it makes me feel loved.

Mrs. Belinsky is as happy watching me eat as I am eating. I'm helping myself to more sour cream and bananas, when Mrs. Belinsky's younger son, Artie, walks in.

Artie is the son who does the heavy work around the hotel; fixing the stone fences and the roofs and plumbing, setting up the green army surplus tents the family uses when there are so many guests that they give up their rooms. He makes me a little nervous. He's a former Marine sharpshooter who enjoys picking off woodchucks with a pistol when the guests aren't around. He's also extremely strong — I once saw him lift the front of a pickup truck to impress a girl. He's never been mean to me, but he's never been friendly either. I have the feeling he wishes I didn't exist.

Artie walks into the kitchen, sweaty and wearing a torn T-shirt with grease stains, and grabs a chicken leg from the refrigerator.

"Artie," Mrs. Belinsky says, in Yiddish. "Wash first the hands!"

Artie ignores that. He's looking at me in a way that makes me feel like a woodchuck.

"Danny," he says. "So, you're a Yankees fan, now?"

"Uh, well, yeah," I say.

"So, who you think's gonna hit more homers this season, Maris or Mantle?" Artie asks. "Seems to me Mantle can't even run."

I have no idea what he's talking about.

Mrs. Belinsky interrupts.

"Let the boy eat," she says. "Mantle's mother can worry about Mantle."

Artie grins, gives his mother a squeeze, and leaves, going back to whatever engine he's tearing apart with his teeth.

I can tell by the light that the waiters will be coming in soon for lunch. Mrs. Belinksy, who never lets me leave without some treat, gives me a paper bag with cookies. I head back to my place, lost in thoughts of nymphs cooing over my horns.

The wind shifts; I smell Ben only as he jumps me. If I got the satyr gift for music, Ben got the wrestling moves. It takes him no time to wrestle me to the ground and pin me with his knee on my chest. Then he tosses off my Yankees cap, exposing my horns.

"Would you look at this?" he says. "Finally! Maybe this year you'll get some action. You know where to put it, right?"

He's not getting away with that. I get a surge of strength, toss him off, and pin him.

"Say 'vanquished,'" I say. "Say, 'Those are the most beautiful horns I have ever seen in my life.'"

Ben is laughing.

"I can't," he says. "You've got your knee on my throat. I can't breathe."

"If you can talk, you can breathe," I tell him. "I want to hear it: 'Your horns are beautiful. Beau-ti-ful.'"

"You'll have to tell me you love me first," he says.

I start laughing, which makes me forget about holding him down. He throws me off and we both collapse on our backs, looking at the sky.

"Really, they look good, Danny," Ben says. "Very studly. They ought to make you more confident. And if you'd like to practice, there are some very affectionate sheep over at Olivera's farm."

That's a coarse bit of human folklore goats use to razz one another. I give Ben a sharp elbow in the arm, which doesn't slow him down one bit.

"Hey, don't knock it," Ben says. "Those sheep are probably really nice to hold on to. Cushy."

We crack up again but don't move. We just lie on our backs, watching the clouds move by, inhaling the black locust and the white-pink blossoms of the trailing arbutus. The ground is sweet with violets and tiny, white strawberry blossoms.

"You know what, Ben?" I say. "This is the summer I'm going to meet a nymph and fall in love. I know it."

"*Dozens* of nymphs," Ben says.

CHAPTER TWO

Memorial Day might mark the start of summer for humans, but for me and my guys it's Arrival Day, a few days later, when the young nymphs fly in.

You've probably seen the paintings: nymphs and satyrs frolicking in a flowery glade with a fancy spread of wine and bread and grapes. You think all that stuff just happens to be there, that grapes are ripe in the Catskills in early June and roses braid themselves around swings?

The truth is, Arrivals take a tremendous amount of planning. And if the nymphs don't like what they see when they do the float-down, they just keep flying and blame it on an updraft. Nymphs are not easy. They are mercurial and demanding, and I have yet to meet one who has a low opinion of herself. Nymphs are the blossoms of summer, and they know it. Treat a nymph with indifference and you're going to be one lonely goat.

The place we choose for the Arrival this year is Slippery Rock, a small meadow deep in the Halcott hills with a stream and several flat boulders, which nymphs like for posing. It's also deep enough in the woods for safety.

I'm getting dried fruits, nuts, and grapes from The Maplewood House. Ben will steal the wine from Silberstein's liquor store in Fleischmanns. All satyrs steal but Ben is a truly outstanding thief.

Mario, who lives in a cave near the Di Benedetto farm, will swipe some of their cheeses. I don't want to say anything against Mrs. Belinsky, but when it comes to cheese, the Italians ace the Jews hands down. Pot cheese is just not a recipe for romance.

Thor, whose cave is under the Belleayre Mountain ski slope a few miles from here, and who is good with his hands, will put up the swings. There's no end of deserted, collapsing hotels outside Fleischmanns; finding lumber and cable is easy.

Dante, who lives up the mountain from the sprawling Takanassee Hotel in Fleischmanns, which has a pool so vast it has a raft, will do the flower arrangements. Dante is something of a klutz; his nose was broken last season when he fell out of a tree, which is unheard of for a satyr, but he has a talent for making a beautiful tableau. He collects Architectural Digest magazines and drags furniture from deserted hotels to his cave. I've always suspected he prefers guys.

I'll be the lead for the music, which is extremely important. You have to make a nymph feel she's the most glorious creature on earth before you so much as bow over her hand, Pop says, although, given the speed with which he operates, I don't know how he has the time. The Catskills are full of music in summer: the hotel PA systems play love songs and show tunes all day; the bands play cha-cha and mambo at night. My favorite songwriter is Lorenz Hart. I can play all that stuff – a satyr hears a song once, he knows it – but I've always wanted to write my own. But I'm having problems. The morning of the Arrival, I'm sitting outside my cave, trying to find words for a melody that keeps going through my head, the one I think of as the "Stay With Me" song.

Be my spring, be my song,
Keep me close, all night long,
Stay with me . . .

"Song," "Long," – there's an original rhyme. Pathetic. I'd be laughed out of the colony.

Suddenly, I hear the voices of two humans, a guy and a girl. They're way above me, near the cliffs.

"I know de Beauvoir is supposed to be this brilliant, independent woman who doesn't need a man," the girl is saying, "but when you read her letters, Sartre is always playing around and telling her about it and she's jealous and pissed off. She's just another woman putting up with some guy's bullshit."

"Could we discuss this some other time, Diane, when I'm not worried about falling to my death?" the guy says. "We don't even have the right shoes."

"Oh, don't be such a pussy, Jeffrey," the girl says. "It's not that far. It's the best view in the Catskills."

I freeze. They must have taken a back way up the mountain, behind my cave. From the sound of their voices, they're on a dangerous patch.

I hear a man curse and a girl scream. Moments later, stones are cascading down the mountain. A girl is half stumbling, half running, trying to get out of their path. I see her fall and go limp, but she keeps sliding, in a flurry of stones, towards the edge of my cliff. I grab her just as she starts going over. She's much heavier than a nymph, I feel like she might drag us both down. I strain, get my knee behind a boulder to steady myself and pull. It feels like forever, but I manage to drag her up and onto the ground, where I collapse next to her, panting. I'm so exhausted that it takes me a few seconds to realize I am practically lying on top of a human girl. I've never been so close to one before.

I have never smelled a scent as powerful as the one that's coming off this one, either. It's musky, like a doe in autumn, interlaced with a riot of blossoms: the pink bergamot that drives the hummingbirds wild; nectar and lily and rose and flowers I've never smelled before. Nymphs carry only the scent of the bush they winter in. This human is a floral cornucopia, I want to inhale her for hours.

I lean back and study her. She's beautiful, but in a different way than the nymphs are beautiful. Her jawline and nose are sharper, her body more angular and substantial. Her long, straight hair is so dark brown it's almost black. I have never been attracted to a nymph the way I am to this girl. I'd love to kiss her. And her breasts are right under me.

I rest myself on my arm, torn between the good satyr and the one who has just gotten a raging hard-on.

You don't touch a lady without a sign that she's interested, every satyr alive knows that. But what would be the harm if I stole one kiss? Or touched a breast? I would do it with the greatest respect. An homage, really. And she's a human, a different species. I'm dying to know what they're like.

I reach out with the tip of my finger and very lightly trace the outside of her breast. It's firm and full and I can feel the warmth of her coming through her shirt. I'd love to take a peek underneath, but that would really be crossing the line. The girl opens her eyes.

I'm too stunned to move.

"You have horns," she says.

"Yes, uh, no, not actually –," I say.

"I can feel your dick, creep!" she says, her voice getting louder. "Get the fuck off of me!"

She brings up her knee and kicks me in the balls. I howl.

"*Pervert!*" she hollers. "*Jeffff-rey!*"

Oh, crap. I completely forgot – she was with a guy. I take off, running as fast as I can into the woods, and hide. My heart is still pounding a few minutes later, as they come down the mountain.

"There's a lump on your head, you were knocked out, you were seeing things," the man is saying. "You probably have a concussion. "

"Don't give me that second-year med school crap," the girl is saying. "I know what I saw. It was a pervert wearing horns. And he was feeling me up."

I'm scared. It sounds like Jeffrey Med School doesn't believe her, but I don't want to be the satyr who blows fifty years of cover. I try to slow down my breathing and wait for them to pass. Then I take a back route to my cave, where I sit as far from the entrance as I can, still terrified. A few minutes later, Ben arrives.

"What's going on?" he says, putting down his pack. "Are you sick?"

"I was sitting outside when some humans were on the mountain," I say. "The girl saw my horns."

"Oh shit," Ben says. "You sure?"

"I was closer to her than I am to you," I say. "I was right on top of her."

"*What?*" Ben says. "You're telling me you jumped a human?"

"No, what? Are you crazy? She was climbing with some guy and she fell down the hill and knocked herself out. Nothing happened. Well, almost nothing. I might have kind of touched her breast when she was out."

"No!" Ben says. "You dog. You get your horns and the first thing you do is cop a feel from a human. Were her nipples pebbles, like they say?"

"I have no idea," I say, annoyed. "I didn't see them. I barely felt them. It was more a brush. Then she woke up, saw my horns, and started screaming. The guy who was with her came running, but I had taken off by then."

"The guy didn't see you?" Ben says.

"No. I'm sure of it."

"We're okay then," Ben says. "Nobody up here has ever spotted us. She hits her head, she says she saw a guy with horns, people will say she's seeing things. The worst that'll happen is they'll think some pervert is running around wearing devil's horns."

"That's the word she used, 'pervert,' " I say.

"Don't worry about it," Ben says. "I get that it shook you up but it doesn't matter. We don't exist for them. Look, I have something to show you."

He reaches into his pack and brings out a white box with a transparent top, with a large white flower inside. He opens the box. The scent is extraordinary. It makes me think of pictures I have eaten in travel magazines. It's a scent that could make a satyr drunk.

"It's a gardenia," Ben says, passing it to me. "They fly them in from Georgia – that's one of their territories that's like a thousand miles away. I swiped two of them from the flower shop in Arkville. Be careful; they bruise. I also got a bottle of wine at Silberstein's: Mouton Rothschild. Very expensive. If you buy it."

I put on my Yankees hat – not that I think any humans will be in the deep woods, but that girl has made me nervous – and put the box with the gardenia carefully in my pack. We cut through the woods to Slippery Rock.

Dante has outdone himself. There are two flower-decked swings; a maypole; private lounging places strewn with cushions and brocades and silks. Nymphs love silks.

We don't have a huge colony in this corner of the Catskills, maybe eight or nine goats our age, and almost everyone is here. I check out the competition. Mario has tipped his horns with gold pollen – I wish I'd thought of that. Thor, who has blue eyes, which are rare in a satyr, and looks like the blond ski instructors on Bavarian travel posters ("Come to the Alps! Sleep with Thor!"), has been working on his tan, which makes his curls even sunnier. The handsomest goat is Ben, who's got the body of a discus thrower and is just flat-out great-looking. I have to admit, it's not always easy to have a guy who looks like that as your best friend.

I'm happy to see that Nico and George, the rowdy twin brothers who are a year older than me, live near The Acropolis Hotel in Halcott Center, and often celebrate holidays with a Greek colony south of Roxbury, are not here. Those guys love an excuse for a fight. My first season, Nico's big thing was jumping out of a tree, wrestling me to the ground and stuffing stinging nettles down my throat. Mario claims that once when

George saw a bear going after a hive of honey he wanted, he kicked the bear in the tail and sent him whimpering into the woods. The brothers love sports, they may be off somewhere playing soccer. Their hooves are enormous, so they're perfect for the game.

I stuff my hat in my bag, surreptitiously slick down my hair to make my horns stand out and say hello to the guys.

Then I take out my flute. I cue the guys with a few phrases of "Let's Do It," a Cole Porter song. Cole Porter is very big with satyrs. Dante and Ben join in. The air is charged with excitement and the promise of love. We anxiously scan the sky.

Three songs in, we see what looks like a cloud of supersized butterflies. The satyrs cheer and wave. The nymphs float lower and we can see their diaphanous gowns in flower-petal pastels, their long, wavy hair.

The first nymph, toes pointed like a dancer, touches down on the large rock overlooking the glade. Several more follow. The nymphs smile and preen, curvy, fresh, and absolutely delicious.

A painting can't capture a nymph in spring. A painting has no fragrance, which is literally the most intoxicating thing about a nymph – it's like burying your face in a field of flowers. A nymph's skin is as smooth as milk. Their toenails are real seashell, whorls of cream and pink, and their fingernails are semi-precious stones: emerald, pearl, amethyst. Their hair is saturated with their scent. When I have love dreams, I am grabbing handfuls and inhaling.

All the nymphs who've touched down this morning are gorgeous, of course, but I like the one whose pale pink gown is so fine, I can see the outline of her thighs. She's got lavender hair and a behind like a fat apple and she smells like crushed raspberries; ten feet away, I am inhaling her. Ben is focused on a nymph in an aqua gown, with bright red hair. She is standing at the front of the group and must be the senior.

"Dibs on the redhead," he whispers to me, as I put down my flute.

Thor, the oldest satyr here, falls to one knee and we all follow.

"Ethereal ladies, welcome," he says.

The redhead looks down at Thor and gives him a cool smile. I have the impression she knows how to get exactly what she wants, but was there ever a nymph who didn't? There's no extended exchange of courtesies, the redhead gets right down to it, negotiating the handicap for the stone toss.

"Forty seconds," she says, firmly.

"Ten," Thor counters.

The senior nymph doesn't even pretend to consider his counter-offer, she just picks up a small stone.

"Flat," the redhead says.

"Rounded," Thor says.

The redhead tosses the stone in the air, catches it and flips it. It's a pretty silly tradition; the nymphs always claim the win, and we always let them.

"What a surprise," the redhead says. "Flat."

And to the ladies around her, "Fly!"

The nymphs race into the woods. Thor counts down, shaving off time.

"Forty," Thor begins, loudly. "Thirty-six. Thirty-four. Twenty-nine. Twenty. Eleven, three, two, one, GO!"

The satyr pack takes off.

"C'mon," Ben yells to me over his shoulder. "Trot!"

I put my strength into it. Pink Gown is agile, slipping around trees, jumping brambles and, unlike a satyr, she has the advantage of being able to go airborne. I stay with her. Maybe my new horns have given me a boost, because I am finally so close I leap and grab her ankle, tumbling us both to the ground. Her raspberry scent is so delicious, I don't know whether I want to make love to her or devour her. But I manage to recite the ceremonial words, pant them, actually:

"Ethereal Creature, it's an afternoon in summer. Make it perfect. Be with me."

She looks up at me and gives me a playful smile. Gods, she's adorable.

"Well, it *is* an afternoon in summer, made for our delight," she says, "My name is Thalia. Do you truly long for me?"

There is no ritual script for this part; you have to wing it.

"Oh, yeah," I say. "I mean, yes."

Thalia waits for me to continue. Her skin is so glowy it's like she's swallowed the moon, but I can't say that, it's stupid. I can see her raspberry nipples through her dress. Raspberries, satyrs believe, were created in tribute to the nipples of a nymph. I'm not super religious, but that's one bit I'm down with.

"My name is Daniel, Danny," I say. "You've got incredible eyes."

What I'm really thinking about are her breasts, but you're not supposed to get to the sexy bits that fast. She really is beautiful. So fresh, a new rose. I remember the gardenia.

"I brought you a present," I say.

"*Me?* But you've only just met me," Thalia says.

What would Ben say? I need something from Ben's greatest hits.

"I've been dreaming you," I say. "All winter."

I bring the box with the gardenia out of my pack and open it. Thalia gasps and buries her face in it.

"Oh, my goddesses," Thalia says. "I've never smelled anything like it. Where does it come from?"

"The colony of Georgia," I say. "It's very distant."

Maybe I need to sell it a little more.

"And savage," I say.

Thalia puts the gardenia in her hair. She is a flower herself and seeing that waxy white gardenia against her lavender hair is like discovering an enchanted garden.

"It was meant for you," I say, which may not be poetry, but I mean it.

I am now enveloped in a cloud of crushed raspberries and gardenia. If there is anything more erotic than those two scents, I can't imagine it. I stand up and offer Thalia my hand. She takes it, stands, then takes my arm. It's a little thing, but it makes me feel like the king of the satyrs. I find myself standing taller. We walk back to the glade, where Ben has found a secluded spot under a weeping willow. The redhead, who has the scent of ripe peaches, is next to him. From the way she's looking at Ben, he has already won her.

"Glynnis," Ben says, introducing her.

I bow and kiss her fingertips. Ben opens his pack.

"You know, you ladies are so beautiful it is going to be impossible for me to eat," Ben says. "But maybe a little wine?"

He brings out the Mouton Rothschild. The girls are impressed. It's a funny thing with nymphs, I have never heard one mention a book; most of them can't even read, but they sure know wine labels.

Ben passes the wine to Glynnis, giving her the honor of the first drink. Then I offer the bottle to Thalia. She smiles at me, tilts up her head, and swallows. A trickle of wine dribbles down her chin. I want to lick it off. Thalia passes me the bottle. Wine works on me quickly; I feel it down to my hooves. It *is* a glorious afternoon in summer.

"So," Glynnis says to me and Ben, "What's your calling? Do you write poetry? Paint? Compose?"

"I steal," Ben says.

Thalia and Glynnis giggle, not certain he's telling the truth, but charmed. Nymphs are always charmed by Ben.

"Seriously," Ben says. "There's something you want, I can snag it. Just point."

Glynnis looks interested. I have the feeling she's already drawing up a list.

"What about you?" Thalia says to me. "Are you an artist? I would love to be immortalized. I have a sister who's in a very famous painting in a restaurant in New York City. She never shuts up about it, actually."

I can't believe it.

"You've been to New York City?" I ask.

"No, silly, of course not," Thalia says. "She showed me a picture. It's in a restaurant called Café des Artistes. My sister is the one in the swing. *Naturally.* Do you paint?"

"I play pipes," I say.

"Well, you all do that, don't you?" Thalia says, teasing.

I hope it's teasing.

"I also write songs."

That impresses her.

"Oh," she says. "Would I know any?"

"Well, no," I say, "I'm just starting, and – "

A war whoop pierces the air.

"*Attack and pillage!*" a satyr screams.

The Greek jerks, Nico and George, are running at us. They're wearing loincloths and carrying nets and tridents, which is just ridiculous. They've also got the element of surprise. They throw nets over me and Ben, so we're thrashing like fish. Nico grabs Glynnis and George grabs Thalia. They toss them over their shoulders, which is not hard because nymphs have bones like birds. Thalia and Glynnis are screaming their heads off. I wish I could say it's with outrage but it sounds more like delight. George grabs the wine. He's a moron, but he knows wine, too.

"Mouton Rothschild. Thank you, brother goats," he says. Then he takes off.

Ben and I sit there, covered in net.

"I feel like such a shmuck," I say, finally. "And what makes it worse, the girls liked it."

"Yeah," Ben says. "It's that bad goat thing."

He stands up.

"What the hell," he says. "Want to go pick up some sheep?"

CHAPTER THREE

Most people don't know this, but there was a time in the early 1900s when this part of the Catskills was very big with composers, artists, and singers. That's how my grandfather got here, with his opera singer. This singer, who Pop hates so much he doesn't let me say her name, was Amelita Galli-Curci. She was the biggest star in opera, next to Caruso. They named a movie theater for her not far from here, in the town of Margaretville.

Galli-Curci's favorite aria was "Musetta's Waltz," from "La Bohème." She sang it so often that the birds picked it up and passed it down from generation to generation so even now, if you hike up Belleayre Mountain in summer, you can hear the yellow warblers and the gray catbirds and the indigo buntings singing it.

When I'm happy, it's the song I start the morning with. The trill of the pipes is perfect for the way it soars.

Quando m'en vo. . . .
When I go walking down the street,
People stop and look at me . . .

You might not think I'd be in the mood to play it the day after a human woman had seen my horns and a nymph was stolen away. But both those ladies were so beautiful, I get high just thinking about them.

So, I'm standing outside the cave with my flute, putting my heart into this song to feminine beauty, and somebody starts playing the contrapuntal. I know without looking that it's Ben, we've played together all our lives. The melody drifts down the mountains. If music were visible, you could see it bouncing off the trees down to the valley. Three miles down the road at The St. Regis Hotel, a busboy, doing the lunch set-up, is probably humming it right now.

"Not bad," Ben says when we finish. "Now, want to go get the girls back?"

Enchanted as I am with Thalia, I don't know if that's a good idea.

"I don't know," I say. "I really like Thalia, but those girls didn't seem all that upset getting snatched by Nico and George. Maybe they like them better."

Ben bursts out laughing, grabs me, and kisses my cheek.

"Oh, Danny," he says. "They're *nymphs*. They're as selective as bees."

"I don't know about that," I say. "And Nico and George are pretty tough."

"Also pretty stupid," Ben says. "Look, if we find some other girls on the way, we'll hang with them. There are nymphs all over the place now. They're in season. You eat?"

"Not yet," I say. "We can swing around the back of the hotel and I'll grab us something from the pantry."

"You have it so made, living on a hotel property," Ben says. "It's like you've got your own bungalow – Bungalow D. The closest food operation I've got is the cauliflower farm."

I can't argue. Having the run of a hotel is pretty sweet. And it's all because of Pop. He told me how it happened.

A guest from The Maplewood House, an older woman, had taken a walk up Halcott Mountain one morning. Her legs were swollen from standing all day in a candy store in New York City, her hair was streaked with gray, by human standards, she was dumpy. But Pop, when he was in the mood, saw only a woman's charms. This one, he said, had such a deep and commodious double chin that he was overcome by a desire to dive in and nuzzle her neck. And it was coming up on noon and he was hungry for love.

Afterward, the woman was so giddy she had to talk to someone and that someone was Mrs. Belinsky. She is sunning herself on the mountain, the guest says, when a strikingly handsome man walks out of the woods and says he has been intoxicated by her beauty. Did you ever hear such nonsense, the widow says, in the city, she would have thrown him out of the store. Now, it's as if she has inhaled a magic potion. The guest allows the man, a complete stranger, to make love to her. She is a mother of five, she knows what goes on in the bedroom, but never has she experienced the euphoria that sweeps over her or understood her erotic power. The man makes her realize she is beautiful.

"A Hungarian," Mrs. Belinsky thinks, because in the mountains they have a reputation, particularly when it comes to widows with property. And if this woman is beautiful, the sacks of potatoes in Mrs. Belinsky's pantry are movie stars. Still, this guest, who had been complaining about everything, now has a contented glow which, Mrs. Belinsky realizes, she has seen popping up on other weekday widows. And she extends her stay. Mrs. Belinsky takes a walk up the mountain: not for love, which ended when her husband died but strictly for business. Next thing you know, Pop is an honored guest of The Maplewood House.

Now Ben and I pick our way through the woods to the hotel.

He stays in the woods while I make us some peanut butter sandwiches, peanut butter being our favorite fancy food. I also get us a bottle of milk. We eat on the hill overlooking the pool, under a protective overhang of willows, passing the bottle back and forth and checking out the guests. The recreation director, Howie, a nephew of Mrs. Belinksy, is a fourth-grade English teacher in New York City, who has illusions of being a big-shot entertainer. He is leading the guests in a game of Simon Sez.

"Simon says, 'Jump in the air!,'" Howie hollers.

Thirty guests, bellies bloated from breakfast, jump in the air.

"Simon says, 'Clap your hands.' Simon says, 'Touch your toes!' 'Jump!' "

"Does it ever strike you that humans are morons?" Ben says.

We head northwest to The Acropolis, in the thickly wooded area of Halcott Center which the locals call the West Settlement, with Ben keeping an anxious eye out for dogs. One bit him on the ass last summer and he drove me crazy for a month, worrying about it.

"My mother always told me I had a great ass, the nymphs

would go crazy for it," he said. "Just take another look. If it scars, I'm going to murder that dog."

"I am *not* going to keep checking out your hairy ass," I told him. "And it's a weird thing for a mother to tell a little kid."

"She's European," Ben said. "They're much more sophisticated about this stuff."

The hotels around Fleischmanns are mostly Jewish, but you've also got a few other ethnic boarding houses sprinkled in the hills: Spanish, Italian, and at least two Greek hotels in Halcott. No Irish places, they're northeast of here in what they call the Irish Alps.

The Acropolis, run by the Pavlos family, is a pink stucco three-story hotel, which advertises berry picking, badminton, and clean country air. They don't even have a pool. But if you go far enough into the property, they do have something special, a waterfall. Nymphs love waterfalls. They're up there with arbors and swings, and while there are a lot of streams and ponds in this part of the Catskills, there aren't that many falls. If Nico and George have Thalia and Glynnis, that's where they'll be. The problem is, we have to get past the hotel, which has a lot of open property.

Sniff, look, sniff again . . .

"Stay low," Ben says, crouching down.

I follow him past the veranda, where two old guys in short-sleeved shirts are napping, to the back of the building. Then I smell it, coming off an open kitchen window on the side of the house.

"Baklava with apple blossom honey," I whisper to Ben. "They must have just made it."

"For the gods' sake, how can you be hungry? We just had breakfast," Ben says.

"I love baklava."

"Don't even –" Ben is saying, but before he can finish the sentence I have snagged the entire thing, cooling on wax paper.

"Great," Ben says. "You wonder why you never get laid. You're too busy stuffing your face."

I ignore him, wrap the baklava in the wax paper, and put it carefully in my pack. We head to the tall, swampy grass near the waterfall, keeping low. The Catskills may have terrible farmland – two stones for every dirt, the locals say – but it is beautiful. We see a small waterfall dropping into a pond of pale pink lilies, but there are no nymphs and no Greek satyrs. I smell Japanese wisteria, to my mind far more delectable than lilac, though I don't see the tree. Then I see movement in the branches of a tree near the waterfall. A stupefyingly beautiful nymph in a short white gown steps out.

"Holy crap!" I whisper to Ben, "Is that a freaking toga?"

Ben is staring, too.

"Oh, great god Dionysus, thank you," Ben says. "Now can you get her dress off?"

The nymph is tall, with the broad shoulders and muscled arms of an Amazon. She has blue-black hair, held up and away from her face with coils of white ribbon. She wears a style of sandal I have never seen, laced to her knees.

"Y'know," I whisper to Ben, "I don't think she's from around here."

"Shhhhhh!!!"

The nymph, who I can now see is older than us, definitely mature but prime, takes off her sandals and unties her gold-rope belt. Then she pulls her toga over her head and tosses it on the grass. She is completely naked. Her breasts are small and perfect and the patch of tightly curled hair between her legs, what we call the flower of the woman, is a shiny blue-black. It's magnificent. I want to bury my face in it and inhale. The nymph scoops up a lily and walks into the waterfall, slowly washing one breast with the flower. The yellow stamens streak her breast with gold. The nymph tilts back her head and opens her mouth to the spray of the falls.

"That's it," Ben says.

He stands up out of the tall grass to what I call his "Full Irresistible," giving the nymph time to spot him and check him out. It's annoying what a perfect body he's got. He's built like the sculpture of a dozing satyr I once saw in a magazine, the Barberini Faun: lightly muscled body, legs splayed so he could show off the goods even when he was sleeping. Satyrs are growers, not showers, and the dark hair we have between waist and hooves pretty much hides our equipment. But if a satyr is trying to make an impression on a nymph, he may flash it a little to pique her interest. This is called "Displaying." It's what Ben is doing now. Ben holds his pose for a few minutes, taking care to look confident but not cocky, giving the nymph time to consider.

Then he walks to the edge of the water, where the nymph is openly studying him, and kneels. If I were a girl, I'd probably fall for Ben, though the nymph he's kneeling in front of is a lot older than a girl.

"Ethereal Creature, it's an afternoon in summer," Ben says. "Make it perfect. Be with me."

The nymph could dismiss him with a wave of her hand and Ben would have to retreat with full courtesy, bowing and backing away, but she doesn't. She doesn't try to cover herself, either. She looks Ben over with the expression I've seen on humans when waiters wheel out a dessert cart. I have a strong feeling this is a nymph who has been around.

"Well, it *is* an afternoon in summer, blah, blah, blah," she says, with what I think is a Greek accent. "Are we going to recite the whole holy scripture here? *My name is Melena. Do you truly long for me? More than you long for grapes? Than summer wine? Than the nymph who blew you off ten minutes ago?*"

For the first time I can remember, Ben is thrown off his game. But only for a moment.

"If that's what it takes to get next to you, absolutely," Ben says. "I'll recite it backward if you want."

Ben lifts Melena's hand to kiss it. From where I'm standing, the nymph's fingernails appear to be blue sapphire. Melena snatches her hand back.

"You *are* a nervy kid," she says. "Here you are flirting and you haven't even brought me a gift."

Ben stands.

"No gift?" he says. "I bring the gift of fresh baked baklava, the finest in the mountains. Watch. I'll conjure it out of the air for you."

Ben lifts his hand.

Damn. I had plans for this baklava.

I take the carefully wrapped pastry out of my pack and toss it over. Ben catches it and offers it to Melena.

"Wasn't Mrs. Pavlos making baklava this morning?" Melena says.

"You don't like it? The hell with it," Ben says, throwing it into the woods.

I groan.

"I also bring the gift of song," Ben says. "Just let me cue the orchestra."

I stand up in the soggy grass and pull out my flute. Melena, who I suspect knew we were here all along, smiles. I'd do anything that nymph asked if she gave me that smile. Ben sings a song I've often heard coming up from The Maplewood Hotel at night, "A Fine Romance."

I pick it up. Ben's singing to a naked nymph; my ass is soaked from squatting in the swampy grass, but what the hell, that's what friends are for. He does have a beautiful voice. He's just gotten to the part about never giving the orchids he sends a glance when I hear a satyr screaming across the hill.

"Ben, you prick, what the fuck!" Nico screams.

"Oh, shit," Melena says.

She snatches her toga, Ben grabs her sandals and belt, and they tear off into the woods.

"You know that guy?" I hear Ben say.

"He's my son," Melena says.

CHAPTER FOUR

Now it's true that if Nico and George are pissed at someone for putting the moves on their mother, it should be at Ben, not me. But when those brothers are itching for a fight, they're likely to start it with whoever they find first. I decide it's safest to lay low for a while in Bungalow D.

I re-read "The Great Gatsby," my favorite part, where Gatsby is reunited with the woman he loves after pining for her for five years.

I sneak down to the pool at night to look for more sex instruction books and find a copy of Playboy Magazine, with guaranteed pick-up lines and sex tips, like blowing into a lady's ear. For how long it does not say, but I figure at least half an hour. I find a book "The Group" by Mary McCarthy, which suggests to me that if I ever work up to humans, I should hit a temple of learning called Vassar, because these women are definitely into it. I also pick up "Advertisements for Myself" by Norman Mailer. That one is very informative. Mailer talks about doing it in the butt, which I was not even aware was an option. The woman he is doing it with, his German maid, tells him "no" at first, but then she loves it. She tells him afterward that she doesn't know why he has problems with his wife, he is a *genius*.

I am getting a little depressed, though, because it is obvious that everybody in the hotel has someone to love but me. Artie is having sex with New York college girls in his truck. The waiters meet girls from the Fleischmanns hotels in the break between lunch and dinner. Ricardo, the male half of the hotel's fake Cuban dance instructor team, Ricardo and Lucia, is banging the weekday widows in the dance studio. All the dance instructors in the mountains are Jews pretending to be Cuban or Italian. Ricardo and Lucia are really Richard and Lucille, cousins from New York City who hate each other.

Pop is jumping in and out of women's dreams at the pool or taking them into the woods or his bungalow when he wants to do it flesh-on-flesh. That's how it is for old goats; they've got no end of options.

Pop has already got a few regulars: there's the rabbi's wife, who I had noticed when Pop entered her mind at the pool at the beginning of summer. When she first got here, she was your usual depressed New York City woman, pulling down the skirt of her bathing suit to cover her legs, worrying about her various veins, which is something older women at the pool talk about a lot. Pop has made her blossom; now she wears a bright bathing suit with flowers and pulls the front down to show herself off.

Pop is also making it with a dark-haired kindergarten teacher I think of as Harder Jake, which is what I heard her hollering when Pop had her on her back near the Frog Hollow rhubarb patch. Harder Jake lies by the pool all day and is tanned almost brown. Neither she nor the Rabbi's wife go into the pool. This is not unusual for human women, who sicken if their hair gets wet.

Pop can't limit himself to women who are unhappy in love, either. The hotel business in the northern Catskills is hurting; Pop has to handle all sorts of problems. Memorial Day weekend, a new guest, who smokes instead of eats and wears heavy, turquoise eyeliner, had found mouse shit in her room and was so angry I could hear her hollering from my cave. Pop does a mind-drop on her that afternoon at the pool when she is dozing right next to Harder Jake. When Turquoise Makeup wakes up, she stretches out like a contented cat.

"I just had the best nap of my life," she says.

Pop's friend Noah Yablonsky, the music guy from the city, is having a thing with Magda, a 40-year-old Austrian refugee. Hunting for books near the pool one night, I hear her saying, "No, Noah, not there!" A few moments later it's, "Yes, God, yes!" This makes me wonder: is Noah doing the Mailer thing? Is there some trick that makes them go from "No!" to "Yes?"

I'm in Bungalow D, flipping through my Norman Mailer book to research this, when Pop walks in. He takes the book, glances at the cover, and sneers.

"Mailer," he says, tossing it. "Amateur. What are you doing inside on a day like this? You should be out in the woods with a beautiful nymph."

"I'm hiding out from Nico," I say. "Ben put the moves on his mother and he wants to kill both of us."

"Melena?" Pop says, surprised. "What's she doing here so early? But you can't hide all summer."

"I'm just waiting a few days for Nico and George to cool down," I say. "Anyway, Nico got the one I liked."

"The *one?*" Pop says. "Where do you get these crazy ideas? Do you drink just one kind of wine? Do you eat just one kind of pear? I saw a whole flock fly in this week. Enjoy 'em all."

I can't tell Pop I don't need a flock. I want what Gatsby had, the one deep love you build your life around. And limiting yourself to just one woman? Pop would think I'd lost my mind. Still, I'm annoyed.

"Why don't you ever make it with nymphs if they're so great?" I say. "Why are you always doing it with those old ladies around the pool?"

"*Old?*" Pop says. "Women in their 40's and 50's? Do they look like crones to you?"

"No, not exactly," I say. "But they're all human."

"Well, as you might have noticed, it keeps us in comfort," Pop says. "When was the last time you had to worry about finding a decent piece of fruit? And these New York City women are starved for a little appreciation. You see how pale and miserable they are when they come up. The way they slouch into their bodies like they want to disappear. I hear them talking: 'My breasts are too big'; 'My breasts are too small'; 'My ass is fat'; 'My ass is flat.' How can any part of a woman be too big or too small? It's like they've never been celebrated in their lives. Anyway, the nymphs around here are too young. What am I going to talk to them about?"

"You talk in there?" I ask.

"Not always, but we have common memories, kind of like background music," Pop says. "The day the radio announced V.E. Day. Hires Root Beer. Sinatra."

"I listen to Sinatra," I say.

"You're an unusual kid," Pop says. "Now go out and meet some nice nymphs."

Pop has given me advice about how to behave with women since I was a kid, courtesies and courtships and gallantries, but we never talk about the actual sex. I think he figures that since I'm a satyr and his son I'm a natural, and I've always been too embarrassed to ask. If I have a question about something, I look for the answers in my books or I ask Ben. But the question that's been on my mind jumps out of my mouth before I can stop it.

"Pop, when you're with all these women, how do you know it will work? The, you know, sex part?"

Pop laughs.

"What, are you kidding? You can breathe, you can fuck. You're a satyr," he says.

The truth is, I've got something on my mind I could never discuss with Pop: Diane. I can't stop thinking about the exotic, musky scent of her. I have a dream in which she is coming up my mountain, looking for me, and when she sees me, she tears open her shirt and I kiss her breasts and we fall into a pink cloud of rose and musk. Sometimes I just think about hanging out with her, talking. Diane's not stuck in the woods, she's out in the world. She's seen stuff I can only read about.

But Diane is human. Humans might enjoy paintings of inane satyrs frolicking in the woods but, as Pop never gets tired of telling me, historically humans have not looked kindly on creatures with horns. Sooner or later, they get the pitchforks and run you out of town.

It's true that human women are drawn to satyrs, even if they don't recognize what we are. It's why they come to the mountains year after year: for the love they'll remember when they're ninety. Satyrs are romantic, respectful, sensual, and, as we live an average of 200 summers, extremely experienced. We do not, despite the legends, ever take a woman against her will. Lying in the summer sun with a woman, a satyr will stroke the outside of her thighs for hours. That isn't because it can lead to something, it's because it *is* something.

But a human female, particularly in territory devoid of woods and greenery, can sap a young satyr's strength and sicken him. A young satyr, it is said, also risks damage to his most intimate. parts; growth may not be merely delayed, it might even be reversed. There was a satyr of two seasons, several mountains from here, it is whispered, who lay with a human and woke up the next morning with the genitals of a newborn.

You have to be a goat of prodigious experience, like Pop, to safely make love to a human. Transporting yourself into a woman's mind, like Pop does all the time, is especially risky. It's like a swamp; you might be unable to pull yourself out. All things considered, I figure I better try to forget Diane and concentrate on nymphs.

They can be anywhere in the woods in summer, but what they really like are picturesque ruins that serve as a backdrop for showing themselves off: mountain houses with gardens gone wild, grand hotels near collapse. There are a lot of those in the hills around Fleischmanns. Many are the large hotels that went up in the 1900s and were doomed in the 1950s when the Ulster and Delaware Railroad stopped running and cheap airplane travel came in.

The most magical ruin is Crump's Castle, a few miles south of my cave. It was built by a New York City surgeon named Walter Crump in the early 1900s as his country house and abandoned in the 1940s after he died. It wasn't a castle with a moat and an iron gate, but it was pretty impressive: a rectangular three-story stone house looking out at Belleayre Mountain, with wrought-iron doors, stained glass, a pool, statues, and gardens. Dr. Crump also used discarded advertising batten board from the Ringling Bros. and Barnum & Bailey Circus for insulation, why I don't know. For sure, Dr. Crump had a satyr soul: at the entrance to the main house and in the windowsills, welcoming words and bits of poetry are engraved the way every poet wants them to be, in marble:

Whoever you are, whatever you believe, you are welcome here.
My home, my hearth, my castle in the sky is yours.

"Yours to shoot at," is how the local teenagers have interpreted that because the place is riddled with bullet holes. The castle has been reduced to stone walls and floors and rusting wrought iron. A gargoyle whose teeth are crumbling glares protectively out of a wall; iron planters too heavy to steal are upended in the garden. I don't know what it is about a once beautiful property lying in ruin, but it tears my heart out.

One of my favorite spots is a small stone building, which might have been a guest house. It has a wall that has crumbled down to the batten board, a circus poster of a woman bareback rider in a short red dress with a cinched waist. She's standing on one leg on a white horse, arms outstretched like she could fly.

I always stop to admire her. Where are you now, beautiful lady? Are you even alive? Do you have any idea that you can stop a satyr in his tracks? I bend one knee in homage: exquisite creature, if your spirit is visiting this mountain, welcome and thrive.

I move on to the castle, climbing the stairs to the roof, and sit there awhile, savoring the view. I am a lucky goat, to live in these mountains.

I go back downstairs.

Now, I smell something new: crushed raspberries, Thalia's scent. My heart starts pounding. Thalia is a very pretty nymph, but if she is here, there's a good chance George or Nico are, too. Of course, nothing reeks like a satyr on the prowl, and I don't smell the Greeks. I peek outside and take a long time sniffing and looking. I see no satyr.

I come out of hiding.

The crushed raspberry scent is stronger – like a jar of jam that's been left out in the sun. Thalia is sitting on a stone wall in her wisp of a pink dress, head thrown back like she's posing for a picture. There's a round, copper compact beside her. Thalia opens it, studies herself as well as she can in a little mirror, then adjusts the top of her dress so more breast is exposed. She angles her body slightly and rearranges her lavender hair.

Then she spots me. If somebody had seen me primping like that, I'd be mortified, but Thalia isn't a bit bothered.

"Danny, what a nice surprise," she says.

I'm pleased. She remembered my name and she's happy to see me.

"Say something cool," I'm thinking. *"Playboy Advisor: 'The martinis here are excellent.' 'That's a stunning dress, Paris?' 'Have you read the new Norman Mailer?'"*

"Hi, Thalia," I say.

"I don't suppose you have anything to eat?" Thalia says. "I've been here all morning, and I'm starving."

"No, sorry," I say.

And, before I can stop myself, "Are you waiting for somebody?"

"Why, would that bother you?" Thalia says. "Wouldn't you fight for my favor? Or should I say, *favors?*"

I can feel my face turning red.

"Joke!" Thalia says. "Don't be so serious. Come on up and hang out."

I'm feeling a little whip-lashed, but okay.

I climb up, courteously kiss Thalia's fingertips, and sit down across from her. Her breasts are almost all exposed, though she wasn't doing that for me. But if not me, who? Do they like to air them? Do they need sunshine to stay fresh? If Thalia didn't like me, wouldn't she cover them up? I'm pretty sure this is what Playboy would call a come-on.

"Ethereal Creature, it's an afternoon in summer – " I begin.

"Oh, Danny," Thalia says. "You're so old-school."

She grabs me by the shoulders and pushes me down on the wall. Then she straddles me and starts licking my neck. I had no idea there were so many nerves in my neck. And that they were directly linked to my dick. I have the fastest boner of my life. I've got to slow it down.

The delay, what are the words to the delay? I've had it memorized since my first season. Oh, right:

Agrimony,
Anise root,
Aster,
Bee balm,
Bergamot . . .

"Don't move," Thalia says. "Do not move one inch."

A craggy rock is digging into my back. I don't care. I've got a hard-on like an oak.

Canada mayflower – no, that's not it –
Bird's-eye Speedwell,
Bishop's cap . . .

Nymphs are supposed to be into it, but I didn't know they were this fast. We've skipped the ear-blowing and are right into, "Darling, take me *now*." I've got my hands on Thalia's fat apple behind, which I'm thinking might be even better than her fat apple breasts when she pulls back.

"What am I thinking?" Thalia says. "Let's try it like this."

She sits up and opens her dress to her waist. Once, in the hotel kitchen, Mrs. Belinsky opened a freezer, and there were round cardboard containers of ice cream, mounded up high. Thalia's breasts remind me of that. I dive in, licking a breast. I've never done this before, but the body must know.

"Much better," Thalia murmurs. "Much, much better."

I'm dimly aware of new scents and voices, male and female, coming up the path. And the male is human.

"Absinthe, absinthe makes the heart fonder," the man is babbling. "I am *so* loaded. I hope I remembered my paints."

"Got them," the female, who is definitely a nymph, says.

I panic, trying to lift my head.

"Thalia, there's a human here," I say.

Thalia grips the back of my head.

"Do *not* move," she hisses. "I've been waiting for him all morning.

"*What?*" I say, fighting to get back up.

"The artist," she says. "He's a very big deal. Just gaze at me longingly. Make that worshipfully. And *do not* touch the hair."

The human comes into the clearing. Glynnis, in a frumpy human dress, is behind him, schlepping his easel and paint box. These girls must want this portrait a lot because one thing nymphs do not do is schlep.

"A nymph! An actual fucking nymph with a satyr!" the artist says. "I must be hallucinating. I hope I never stop. Get me my easel!"

Humans, of course, think that when an artist paints nymphs and satyrs he's imagined it, but I still don't want my face in a painting. And I don't want to be around a strange human, no matter how drunk he is. I wrestle with Thalia. She's got a lot of strength for a nymph. She also must really want to be famous because she's not letting go. I hear somebody screaming my name.

"Danny, you little prick!" Nico is hollering. "What were you doing spying on my mother? I'm gonna kill you."

"Holy Christ, there's two of them!" the artist says. "And the big one has hooves like a bull!"

It must be the surge of terror that gives me the strength to break loose from Thalia and jump off the wall. It's unfortunately not enough to outrun Nico. He catches up to me in about six feet and pins me down in a half nelson. The good part is we're on the grass, so he can't bash my head against rock.

"My money's on Bigfoot," the artist says, sitting down heavily.

"I'm gonna mash you into a pulp!" Nico is hollering. "Then I'm going to mash the pulp. You're going to be fertilizer, goat!"

"Listen, Nico, it's not what you think," I manage to gasp. "I didn't mean to see your mother like that."

"That's right, Nico," Ben says. "But I did. Then I took her into the woods and fucked her so hard the trees shook."

Nico bellows like a bull, jumps up, and lunges at Ben.

Ben knows how to take a punch. He actually enjoys fighting. Right now, he and Nico are hoof to hoof, trying to take one another down. I'm still on the ground, trying to catch my breath, hoping that nothing is broken.

"I can see why they outlawed it because what it does to your brain is crazy," the artist is saying. "I think I just blew out three years of art school. One of them was in Paris."

He pulls a bottle of absinthe out of his jacket and takes a slug.

A chorus of girlish voices drifts into the clearing.

I love to go a-wandering,
Along the mountain track.
And as I go, I love to sing,
My knapsack on my back..

"Girl Scouts!" Glynnis hisses to Thalia. "Those bitches . . ."

We all take off in different directions, except for the addled painter. The Scout leader is yelling at him so loudly, I hear it through the woods.

"Drunk in the middle of the morning, you should be ashamed!"

"Awww, sweetheart," the artist is saying. "Show me your tits."

CHAPTER FIVE

"So, tell me," Ben is saying the next morning when we're in the woods overlooking Lake Switzerland, just outside Fleischmanns, where the humans swim and boat, "Exactly how far did you get with Thalia?"

"C'mon," I say. "You know we're not supposed to talk about it like that."

"Oh, please," Ben says. "Since when did you get religion?"

"There's a human on the raft in a suit that's showing her belly button," I say. "Let me look in peace."

"Thalia," Ben says. "Details."

"She sucked my neck, which was insanely hot," I say. "Then she opened her dress and let me kiss her breast. Then your girl Glynnis arrives."

"Not my girl, we're satyrs, remember?" Ben says. "But a very lovely nymph. I'm seeing her later."

"What about Melena?" I say.

"Sensational," Ben says, "The coolest nymph I've ever been with, but she's flown. Listen, I don't think you should give up on Thalia."

"I have no interest in Thalia," I say. "To tell you the truth, I think she's kind of a bitch."

"But she turned you on, right?" Ben says.

"Look," I say, "Can I tell you something – strictly between us?"

"Lurid and filthy?" Ben asks, hopefully.

"Chaste and private," I say. "You've got to keep it a secret. The one I can't stop thinking about is the human who climbed up the mountain the day of the Arrive and saw my horns. Diane."

Ben is so stunned he says nothing, which for him is unusual.

"Let me get this straight," he says. "You've never made it with a nymph and you're thinking about doing it with a human? Do you have some kind of a death wish?"

"You sound just like Pop," I say.

"That's because it's insane," Ben says. "You gotta have years of experience before you can do that. There was a young goat in Roxbury who shacked up with a human in a motel for three days. They brought him back to his cave on a stretcher. He had to hibernate in moss for a year before he could walk. And what about your hooves and horns – you gonna do her in socks and a hat?"

"Well, no . . . I don't know, I hadn't worked it out that far," I say. "There's gotta be a way. The old goats have it figured out. Anyway, this isn't about doing it. There's just something really different about this girl. I got the impression she knows stuff. Thalia is pretty superficial."

"I'm not talking to you about having deep conversations," Ben says. "I'm talking to you about *fucking*. It's summer. I'm your friend and I hate to tell you this, but goats are beginning to talk. You're a three-season satyr and you've never been laid."

"Thalia has no interest in me," I say. "She was just using me to get a painting starring Thalia. I was a prop."

"Thalia's a *nymph*," Ben says. "She's perpetually horny."

"More like perpetually ambitious," I say, although the idea that I might have a chance with Thalia is making her sound much nicer.

"Believe me, you can reel this one in," Ben says. "You just have to mount a seduction. Think about the things nymphs cannot resist: mirrors, sparkly things, silks, waterfalls."

"Pastry!" I interrupt. "Cream-filled or with pink frosting. What do you call them? Éclairs. Artie, at The Maplewood House, brought some home for his mother once, and she saved one for me."

"They have them at Wizner's Bakery, at the end of Main Street," Ben says. "All you have to do is go into town and get them. I can grab us clothes and money."

"And you're saying *I'm* crazy?" I say. "You want me to stroll through a town filled with humans in the middle of the day? It's not happening. And Pop would kill me. You know he's never let me go into town."

"Oh, Danny, please, nobody will spot you," Ben says. "We look just like humans when we're covered up. I'm meeting Glynnis over at Murmuring Brook. There's a good chance Thalia will be with her. If not, she'll know where she is. All you have to do is go into town and get the pastry."

"Why don't *you* get the pastry?" I say.

"I'll be stealing Champagne," Ben says. "Much harder. Now we just have to sneak into the changing room down there and swipe some clothes."

Lake Switzerland is not large – I've seen humans swim it in twenty minutes. But the changing rooms are across the lake, which has a dam on one side and swampy woods on the other. Swamps make me nervous.

"Forget it," I say.

"You want to be the only satyr in the Catskills who's never been laid?" Ben asks.

Fifteen minutes later, we're inside the men's changing room. It's not fancy. It's a big room lined with benches, which smells of Clorox, mold, and rotting wood. Pants and shirts are hung on nails.

Ben moves fast, first snatching hats, then sneakers and socks and clothes.

"I'd say you're a size 'Goat,'" Ben says, grabbing a pair of chinos and a shirt and tossing them to me. He takes some clothes for himself and then spots a pair of pants with a conspicuous bulge. Ben takes out the wallet.

"Oooh, trusting fellow," he says, removing several bills and passing them to me.

Dressed, our hats pulled tight over our horns, we step out onto the road to town.

"Okay, pal," Ben says, "Go get 'em!" and disappears into the woods.

I'm scared, but I'm also excited. I've spent a lot of time looking down at Fleischmanns from the hills, wondering about it. And who knows? Maybe Diane is there. I stop for a minute in front of The St. Regis, a four-story, faded orange hotel overlooking the lake, where they have bands every night whose music drifts up the mountain. I pass The Hotel Mathes, where the nightclub is said to have windows that look into the big outdoor pool.

The closer I get to town, the more humans there are. A lot of the guys wear hats. Now and then, I see an older man tip his hat to a woman, not completely removing it but tilting it forward while dipping his head in respect. It's a form of courtship, I think, and, it occurs to me, something a goat could do without exposing his horns.

Nobody seems to notice anything unusual about me although a human girl, walking with a friend, takes a quick sidelong glance at me, smiles, then turns away. Could she have been flirting? The girls walk in twos or threes and smell alike: lemony, with bergamot, lavender, and nine or ten other scents. This must be a human thing: to anoint yourself in as many scents as possible. I do not see Diane. It was stupid to think I would. This is a tourist town; people come and go. I should have kissed her when she was knocked out and I had the chance.

At Main Street, I turn right, to the heart of the village.

The scents are dizzying. I smell roasted tomatoes, garlic, and onions as I walk past a pizza store; yeasty beer from Monahan's Bar; dill, brine, and lox outside Nat Israel's Herring; a sickeningly sweet animal flesh I think is pig outside a luncheonette. You rarely smell pig in the hotels here, since the Jews don't eat it.

Main Street is bustling with humans. I sit on a bench in the center of town to try to take it all in: kids from Camp Ta-Ri-Go, who we sometimes spot in the woods and who are as annoying as Boy Scouts. Women in bright sundresses carrying straw handbags embroidered with large flowers. Refugees from World War Two, who speak different languages and sometimes have numbers tattooed on their arms. I know all about World War Two from stories in Mrs. Belinsky's Yiddish newspaper.

But now, I'm smelling love. A plump, contented-looking woman in her 50s in a flowery, rumpled dress, is walking down the street arm in arm with – oh shit! – an old goat. The satyr is wearing a porkpie hat like Pop's, a stretchy short-sleeved shirt that shows off his broad chest, tan pants with a tan belt, and bulky tan shoes. The woman's face is jowly, she wears glasses and has a misshapen nose, but she is carrying herself as if she is the most desirable woman in the world. As they pass, I see a grass stain on the back of her dress. The satyr she is with looks back over his shoulder at me, winks, and nods at my hooves. I look down. One of my sneakers is unlaced. I quickly fix it, hoping to the gods the satyr is not a friend of Pop's. It's time to pick up the pastries and get out of town.

At Wizner's Bakery, there's a wonderful selection; bowties, seven-layer cakes, black and white cookies, Linzer tarts with a little hole on top, fancier than the ones Mrs. Belinsky makes. A glass case that's cool to the touch holds cheesecakes, whipped cream cakes and éclairs topped with caramel and chocolate. I've never spoken to a human other than the Belinskys and Pop's friend Noah, but I manage to tell the old lady behind the counter what I want, though my voice comes out like a mouse.

"Éclairs, please," I squeak. "Chocolate."

"How many?" the old lady asks.

I have no idea how many it will take to get a nymph in the mood.

"Eight," I say.

The old lady puts the eclairs in a white box and ties it with a piece of string.

"Straight home, into the ice box," she says.

A half-hour later, I'm at Murmuring Brook, in the woods beyond Camp Ta-Ri-Go, near a lovely grove of white birch. Ben and Thalia and Glynnis, the flirtatious redhead, are lounging on the grass with a bottle of Champagne. When I bow to Glynnis, the hand she lifts to be kissed is weighted with a thick gold bracelet in the shape of a snake, with an emerald eye. I understand immediately what one of Ben's errands was. In one of the nicer hotels, a rich woman is in meltdown.

"Beautiful bracelet," I say.

And then, just to break Ben's chops, "There's a necklace that goes with it, isn't there?"

I bow to Thalia and kiss her hand. Her gown today is orange and yellow. It's flounced like a parrot tulip and she's woven buttercups in her hair, much more to my taste than a gold bracelet.

"Danny," Thalia says, "I have to tell you, I'm really sorry about yesterday. I just wanted to be in a stupid painting, like my sister. I never asked if you were okay with it, and I should have."

I don't think I've ever heard a nymph apologize. I'm also remembering what happened yesterday when Thalia nibbled my neck.

"It's okay," I say. "I could see it meant a lot to you. Anyway, I brought something."

I give Thalia the box.

"Éclairs!" Thalia says. "How did you know? My favorite!"

Thalia takes a bite and moans. Pop says if a woman loves to eat, a woman loves to make love, and if she licks her fingers, you're a lucky goat. I can see from the way Thalia is eating, it's going to be an epic afternoon. We drink Champagne and eat the éclairs. Thalia loves them so much, that I give her my second one, which brings her éclair intake to three. This nymph is going to do it for hours.

Ben and I take out our pipes.

"Play one of yours, Danny," Thalia says. "No, you know what? Make one up just for me. With my name."

Even with the Champagne giving me a buzz, I clutch up.

"Right now?" I say.

Ben, never at a loss, jumps in.

"Thalia," he sings, "I'd love to nail ya."

"Oh, really?" laughs Thalia.

"I'd walk through rain and hail for ya," I sing. "Until you loved me, too."

We laugh. I'm as happy as I've ever been. I've written nothing that can match this moment, so I start playing "Musetta's Waltz." Ben picks up his pipes and joins me. Life is exactly as it should be. Satyrs on an afternoon in summer, playing for a pair of delectable nymphs.

Thalia stands and sings.

Quando m'en vo,
When I go walking down the street,
Everybody stops and looks at me . . .

I am dazzled. Thalia's voice is so beautiful that the birds stop singing and listen. When we finish the song, Ben and I drop our pipes and applaud.

"Thalia," I say. "You have an amazing voice."

Thalia beams at me.

Glynnis takes Ben's hand, and they disappear into the woods. I look at Thalia, glowing with cream and praise and Champagne, and fall to one knee.

"Ethereal creature, it's an afternoon in summer," I say. "Make it perfect. Be with me."

"Danny," she begins, "Danny . . . "

And then she pukes all over me.

CHAPTER SIX

A s a satyr, you can eat everything. Newspapers, weeds, clothing – not the flesh of animals, of course; that's barbaric. Nymphs apparently have more delicate systems. Thalia is barfing so much she is too weak to walk, let alone fly. Glynnis has to order a bird to call in a squad of nymphs to carry Thalia home. They are pretty pissed off. Four gorgeous nymphs are glaring at me like I meant to make Thalia sick. That's really going to help me socially.

Then, as I'm hoofing it back up the mountain, I start feeling queasy myself. Champagne and cream on a hot day might be the one thing goats can't digest. I start puking just up the hill from The Maplewood House. Unfortunately, this is not far from where Pop has been making it with a woman from the hotel. He's got her over a log, something city women especially like. If you don't hump a guest against a tree, Pop says, they don't feel they're getting their money's worth for a mountain vacation. Luckily, the woman has just gone into that post-sex swoon where they're semi-conscious, staring into space. Pop takes one look at my new outfit and knows the whole story. Two hours later, when I'm laid out in Bungalow D, determined to never eat éclairs again, he storms in.

"You went to Fleischmanns?" he hollers. "How many times have I told you to stay the hell out of Fleischmanns? Why don't you just carry a sign: 'Satyr colony in Halcott. Come on up and chase us with pitchforks.' "

"I only went to the bakery, Pop," I say, weakly. "It was fine. It was just like you at the pool. I passed."

"The clothes?" Pop says.

"Ben swiped them at the lake," I say.

"I don't want you hanging out with that kid anymore," Pop says. "He's reckless."

"That's crazy," I say. "Ben's careful. I'm telling you, nobody looked twice at me. It was just like hanging out here on the mountain with Mrs. Belinsky and Noah."

"Mrs. Belinsky knows nothing and Noah is a friend of the family," Pop says. "You think the mountain is so safe? Two farms away from here, a satyr was shot dead."

I'm stunned.

"You never told me that," I say.

"It happened before you were born," Pop said. "I don't like talking about it."

"But what happened? What was he doing?"

"He was eating tomatoes," Pop said. "On the Smithers farm. The wife grew Jersey tomatoes in the back yard, he'd go there after dark and grab the ones that were ripe. We told him it was stupid, but he'd say he could smell a human a mile away, there was nothing like a good Jersey tomato and if he got shot, it was worth it."

"He was a friend?" I ask.

"He was my best friend," Pop says. "Like you and Ben. His name was Seth. But Smithers is a hunter. He's seen Seth's hoof prints, which he can't identify, but he thinks he's on to something special. He covers his scent by stepping in cowshit and waits, and when he sees movement in the vegetable patch, he shoots. Then he sees Seth's horns and hooves, strings him up like a deer, and goes into Monahan's bar in Fleischmanns and starts shooting off his mouth about the horned man of the mountains. Luckily, the guy is a drunk who also claimed he'd seen Bigfoot, so nobody pays any attention. And Noah gets to him. There's this special kind of work some humans do, they're called press agents. You wouldn't know about it."

"Is it like . . . grape pressing?" I ask.

"Not even close," Pop says. "A press agent is a bullshit artist. He makes up stories to make people look good. That's what Noah does in the city, for musicians. Noah tells Smithers he represents this museum in New York, Ripley's Believe It or Not. He says they'd be willing to pay a lot of money for this dead freak hanging from his tree but only if the farmer shuts up about it because Ripley's wants it to be their discovery. Then Noah calls up Ripley's and tells them about Seth and they come and get him."

When a nymph or satyr dies, they're buried at the foot of a tree or cremated so their spirit returns quickly to the forest. Otherwise, they are doomed to the Nowhere World, with no chance of rebirth.

"And you let them do that?" I say. "Why didn't you just cut him down and take him away?"

"Too risky," Pop says. "The farmer was sitting out there with his gun. He'd also put his dogs out. And this Ripley's place was known for fakes; they put the top half of an ape on the body of a horse and called it a centaur when there hasn't been a centaur in North America for eight hundred years. Nobody took anything they said seriously; nobody was going to believe there was an actual satyr in the Catskill Mountains."

Pop is upset.

"Noah went for the installation," Pop says. "He said they have Seth in a very nice woodland exhibit with river nymphs. He would have liked fucking a river nymph; you never find them around here. But *stuffed*."

"I'm sorry, Pop," I say.

"Yeah," Pop says. "Me, too. I loved that guy."

That night I have a nightmare about the shooter, only instead of Pop's friend Seth in the tomato patch, it's me. A man in the window of a house is shooting at me, and I'm trying to run, but my hooves are glued to the ground on sticky pads like the ones humans use to catch mice. I wake up in a cold sweat, panting.

I make a decision to stay away from humans. I'm also going to take another shot at Thalia. She wanted a song, I'll write her a song. Years ago, there was a summer camp in Highmount called The Weingart Institute which the songwriters Lorenz Hart and Oscar Hammerstein and Richard Rodgers attended as teenagers. The camp is gone, but it will be an auspicious place to work.

I tuck my pipes into my pack and head over. Perhaps, if I show enough dedication, I will attract a muse.

A muse is the most enchanting of nymphs, so intoxicating and inspirational she can make an artist of a satyr or a human. Like nymphs, muses have no interest in human males sexually – they find them vulgar and sensually inept and are repelled by their body odor, which is rather sour. But muses – again like nymphs – enjoy adoration and impassioned supplications, especially when accompanied by gifts. I should have stopped off at the kitchen of The Maplewood House this morning and picked up something with jam.

I think about my music. My mind, as I walk through the woods, keeps going back to the "Stay With Me" song, even though the lyrics are dumb. I like the melody and the song won't get out of my head. It's like it wants to write itself.

Be my spring, be my song,
Keep me close all night long,
Stay with me.
Be my moon in the night,
When it's dark, be my light.
Please, stay with me.

"Please?" Like I'm begging. That's really the picture of a confident lover. And if it's a song for Thalia, shouldn't it include her name? It's just such a miserable name to rhyme.

I'm almost at the Weingart, when I spot Ben and Thor, the goat from Belleayre Mountain. Thor is doing one-armed pushups, which he's turned into a drinking game. Every ten pushups, Thor stops and has a drink of chianti. Ben is playing the game too, only for every ten pushups he doesn't do, he has a drink. They're both a little high.

"Hey Danny," Ben says.

He picks up his pipes and starts playing.

Oh, Danny Boy,
The pipes, the pipes are calling . . .

"Very original," I say.

Thor resumes his pushups. I sit down and take a drink.

"Danny, I'm glad you're here. We were just talking about you," Ben says. "We got Venerable Mother's Day coming up, and we need you for the music."

"I hate that idiotic holiday," I say. "And if you remember, I have no mother."

"Yeah, I know," Ben says. "But we're desperate. Everybody else will be busy with the homage. And I was thinking: you know the way these nymphs are always into each other's business. Maybe one of them knows your mother."

"They don't," I say. "I've tried."

"Well, do it to help your pals," Ben says. "We really need you."

"I'll think about it," I say, to get them off the subject. "What do you guys have on for today?"

"Big decision," Ben says. "We were planning on going over to the lily pond and watching the nymphs bathe. But Thor just told me he saw some new talent, playing on the chair-lift."

"They were out in the open?" I say.

This is important enough for Thor to stop the pushups.

"Summer on the slopes, man," says Thor, who, though he's careful to avoid humans, picks up their slang wintering under a ski slope when their words are absorbed into the earth. "Nobody's there. You should have seen these nymphs. They were doing splits on the lift line. Made me want to drop trou."

"You don't wear trou," I say.

"It's a tough call," Ben says. "Guaranteed naked nymphs, versus nymphs who may only be passing through. Hell, maybe we can do both. Want to come?"

"Thanks," I say, "But I need to work on a song for Thalia."

"Hot chick," Thor says. "Totally blew my mind this morning."

I feel like somebody sucker-punched me.

"You were just with Thalia?" I say.

"Danny really likes her," Ben says.

"Well I get that, man," Thor says. "Thalia is hot. Let's drink to her: to the glorious Thalia. And her magical middle finger."

"I gotta get back to my place," I say.

I head back to my mountain, bummed. I thought I had something special happening with Thalia. And this Venerable Mother's Day thing sucks. Some gig: the only guy at a Mother's Day party without a mother.

Ben always says I make too much of the family thing. We're grown, he says, we don't need them, family is a pain in the ass. He says that, I think, because his father Gerhardt, who lives on Hunter Mountain several mountains from here, is a jerk. He came over from Germany on a freighter on an extended drunk and he's a beer drinker who likes to pick fights. There's a boxing training camp on Gerhardt's mountain and once Gerhardt called out a human he'd heard was a heavyweight champ. He decked him with one punch. Gerhardt calls Ben "Pretty Boy" and whenever he sees him, he insists Ben hit him in the stomach, which is like a slab of granite. Then he punches Ben in the gut so hard he doubles over.

"Not so tough as the old goat yet, Pretty Boy," Gerhardt says and sends Ben to get beer.

Why Ben's mother, Zolie, who was so sweet to me my first season I wished she was my mother, went for Gerhardt is a mystery. She jokes that it was her minotaur problem.

I know Pop tried his best for me after my mother left. He mashed up fruit and peas for me; he bundled me in his cave next to him under a heavy army surplus blanket; he told me stories about giants who devoured kids who didn't listen to their fathers and wandered out of the safety of the woods. The scariest ones were the Cyclopses: one-eyed monsters who swallowed bratty satyrs in two bites. They always ate the lower half first so the kid could yell, "Pop, you were right!" before he was devoured. Once in a while, if the kid had been very bad, the giant spit him out after one bite and the kid spent the rest of his life with no lower half, shitting through his mouth. When Pop told me that part he'd always pause and we'd yell, "Yuuuccch!" together.

Pop was never far away. When a copperhead, which generally pays grudging respect to satyrs, slithered near where I was clumsily trying to make a chain of daisies and aggressively flicked its tongue, Pop picked it up by the throat.

"I see you near my kid again, I'm going to put my hoof so far up your ass you'll be tasting goat for a month," he said and flung it into the woods.

Satyrs grow quickly, it takes only a summer for us to be able to fend for ourselves. When my first summer ended, and Ben and I decided to share a cave, as is traditional for first winter, Pop made sure it was well hidden and well stocked, bringing in extra stores of apples and cider and sweet potatoes. Ben, I noticed that first winter, slept with his hands clenched and held high, like a boxer. What he noticed about my sleeping habits, he never said, but when Venerable Mother's Day came the next year, he sat me next to his mother.

I'm certain I was so slow to horn because I was abandoned by my mother. It's probably also the reason I'm a lousy wres-

tler and not as strong as the other guys. A mother's atten-
tions give a satyr his confidence and success, it continues after
you're grown. At the Venerable Mother's Lunch, you can see
the satyrs growing more handsome.

Even his own mother is a painful subject for Pop. Her
name was Saris, she wintered in lilac and she was killed when
the humans were clearing the trees on state property to make
the Belleayre Mountain ski slope. Now, every spring, Pop
takes the first lilacs from our mountain and puts them on the
spot where she died. His nymph mark, once a bright purple
lilac blossom which humans mistake for a tattoo, has faded,
as happens when a mother dies. I think his mother's death is
what made Pop such a worrier. If you're not safe in a shrub on
protected land, where are you safe?

And then Pop has me and my mother walks out, leaving
me with what? A nymph mark in the shape of an apple, which
gives me no clue to her identity at all. Ben, whose mother
Zolie came to America while sleeping in a shipment of roses
from Budapest, was born with a St. Elizabeth of Hungary
rosebud. Melena marked her sons with a Greek laurel leaf on
their calves.

I get why Pop doesn't like to talk about my mother. But
it's not right that I know nothing about her or what made her
leave. I've thought about it a lot. What I think is, she must
have been temperamental, like all nymphs, and something
pissed her off and she impulsively flew. She regretted it immediately, but by then it was too late. She was carried away by
a storm to a far territory and kept there by angry gods, who
were punishing her for walking out on her newborn. It's quite
likely she was injured, which made getting back even harder.
For all I know, she could be two mountains from here, aching

to see me, but scared about what Pop might do. I've got to get him to talk.

Pop's not at the hotel pool, so I stop in the kitchen. Mrs. Belinsky likes me, at least. It's between meals and quiet. Mrs. Belinsky is sitting at the family table, having a glass of tea and reading The Jewish Daily Forward. Artie's got his head in an oven, fixing something. At the Maplewood House, something always needs to be fixed.

Mrs. Belinsky spots me.

"My darling, my angel, why the long face?" she says in Yiddish. "You're hungry? Maybe some scrambled eggs? A sandwich?"

When I am sad there is only one thing I want, even in the middle of the morning.

"Ice cream?" I say.

Mrs. Belinsky brings me a big bowl of ice cream, a plate of sugar cookies, and a bottle of Bosco chocolate syrup. I am probably the only satyr in the world who knows what Bosco is, for all the good that does me.

She sits down next to me.

"So, what is it?" she asks. "Your girlfriend makes you miserable?"

I have an image of Thalia with Thor so lurid they wouldn't even put it in *Playboy*.

"Kind of," I say.

"You shouldn't worry," Mrs. Belinsky says. "At your age, there are plenty of girls. A new one will come along before you know it."

She sounds like a satyr.

Mrs. Belinsky's older son, Bernie, who's usually in the office dealing with reservations and bills, walks in and grunts at me. Grunts, for Bernie, constitute a language: *"What do you expect?" "They're idiots." "It's the son-in-law."* If there are grunts for, *"It's a great day"* or *"Things couldn't be better,"* I've never heard them. Seeing the plate of cookies, Bernie grabs one and polishes it off in two bites. He's like me, he eats when he's upset.

"I just got a call from a woman who wants to know if we have a heated pool," Bernie says.

"In summer?" Mrs. Belinsky asks in Yiddish, confounded.

"Yeah," Bernie says. "Where do they get these crazy ideas?"

Artie pulls his head out of the oven.

"From the owners who don't have their heads up their ass," Artie says. "The other side of the mountain, they're putting air-conditioning in the rooms. The Concord's got an indoor pool where you can swim in winter and look outside and see people skiing. We're dying over here. Yesterday when I went to the bus station, The Roaring Brook picked up two people. *Two.* Labor Day, you're gonna see smoke coming up from that property. Bet your ass on it."

I know what Artie is saying: On Labor Day, the owners are going to secretly set fire to their property to collect the insurance money. This happens so often around Fleischmanns that the humans have a joke about it: It was a case of spontaneous combustion. The insurance papers rubbing up against the mortgage papers started a fire.

Bernie grunts. I'd interpret it as an *"It's the son-in-law,"* grunt.

"What about the shingles for the barn?" Bernie says. "The green cottage could use some too."

"I can't go into the city till I get the truck fixed," Artie says.

I head to Pop's cave, the place he actually lives, though the odds of finding him there in the middle of the day are not great. It's the time disappointed women are brooding about the night before and need cheering up. But Pop is home, sitting beside his stream, eating watercress and having a bottle of the maple sap he keeps in his cave and never lets me touch – a young goat doesn't need it, he says.

"I don't know what's got into women this summer," Pop says. "They're a lot more aggressive than they used to be. I'm exhausted."

"The nymphs?" I ask, hopefully.

"Who has time for nymphs?" Pop says. "The humans. It's like they put something in the water. I never thought I'd say this, but they're wearing me out. You're eating your greens every day, right?"

"Sure," I lie.

"Well, eat more," he says. "A kid in summer, you need your strength."

I sit down next to him, disinclined to tell him his kid is still a virgin. He passes me a handful of watercress.

"Pop," I say, "How come we never talk about my mother?"

He scowls.

"You've got no mother," Pop says. "Your mother is dead to us."

"I'd just like to know something about her," I say.

"Would you like some dill to go with the watercress?" Pop asks. "Artful change of subject, huh? I find the watercress today a little bland."

"Just a few things," I say. "What did she look like? What did she like to do . . . ?"

"Why did she dump us?" Pop interrupts.

"Well, yeah, actually," I say.

"She was gorgeous, what she liked to do was break my balls, and I don't want to talk about it," Pop says. "*Two weeks.* Who the fuck dumps a kid after two weeks? A rodent with a litter sticks around longer."

I feel bad because now I've upset Pop. Not in the way he gets upset when I get too close to the hotel, some other way that I'm not used to.

"I'm sorry, Pop," I say. "I know you don't like to talk about it. I just want to have a family."

"What are you talking about?" Pop says. "You have more relatives around than any goat in the mountain. You see me all the time, you have a grandfather."

"Some grandfather," I say. "I've never even met him.

"He came to see you when you were little, you just don't remember," Pop says. "He's in poor health, he has to sleep a lot. Sometimes he doesn't get up till June. You know why he's in poor health?"

How could I not know? It's the story I've heard all my life.

"Gramp sleeps a lot because he almost killed himself with a human," I recite, sing-song.

"Right, smart-ass," Pop says. "He also travels, which doesn't help."

That's something new. Goats rarely travel. Cars, railroad trains, planes – complicated machines of any kind – are not good for our health.

"Gramp travels?" I say, excited. "Where does he go?"

"Too far," Pop says.

"C'mon, tell me," I say.

"The far territories," Pop says. "A place called California. He's probably out there right now. It's a bad place. The earth shakes so hard out there that sometimes the ground opens up and people fall in and they never see them again. They're buried alive."

That's terrifying.

"So why does Gramp go there?"

Pop is losing patience.

"Why does my father do any of the shit he does?" Pop says. "He doesn't think things through. You know what he brought you when he came to see you? A rose petal cradle. We had goddamn rabbits all over the place."

I think I remember that. I remember one rabbit, anyway, a ball of fluff who nuzzled my neck and slept with us.

"Thumper!" I say. "I loved that rabbit."

"'Shitter' was more like it," Pop says. "I was picking pellets out of the cave all summer."

He gets up.

"Dredging up this old crap is making me sick," he says. "I'm going down to the pool. You're not going to sit in your cave on a beautiful day like today, are you?"

"I thought I might work on my music."

"I heard there were some cute nymphs up on Belleayre this morning, swinging on the chair-lift," Pop says. "If I were you, I'd get up there. I'll give you a tip: look for the one that swings the highest. She won't disappoint."

CHAPTER SEVEN

I'll tell you one thing about nymphs: when it comes to mothers, they have a much better deal than satyrs. Nymphs raise daughters in a collective, so they grow up surrounded by mothers and other new nymphs – this is why nymphs are so sociable and chatty. At the end of their first summer, nymphs are not abandoned by their mothers; they winter with them, so if they awaken anxious, their mothers are right there with them, in their flowery shrubs. And when they're grown, nymphs see their mothers whenever they wish, to lunch and gossip.

Satyrs can count on seeing their mothers only once a year, on Venerable Mother's Day. Why Melena has been around so much, I have no idea. And preparing for mothers, satyrs go totally nuts. This year, Dante has gotten it into his head that we should have place cards. Since I'm the only guy who can write, I'm roped into doing them. Which is when it hits me.

"Nico and George will be coming here this year," I say to Ben. "And Melena."

"Yeah," Ben says. "Awkward."

"Well, how are you gonna handle it?" I say.

"I thought I'd take her into the woods and do her with my mouth," Ben says. "They love that. It doesn't mess up their hair."

"No, c'mon, seriously," I say.

"What I'm going to do is pretend nothing ever happened," Ben says. "And so will George and Nico. I have my own mother to look after. Wait till you see what I got her. A jade bracelet. I stole it from Lustig's jewelry store. Remind me to teach you how to pick a lock."

It's strange how satyrs go crazy trying to win the love of mothers who likely had them only to improve their looks. Pregnancy, to a nymph, is a beauty treatment. The moment conception occurs, their skin glows, wrinkles disappear, and their butts and breasts plump up. If they carry to term, it takes decades off their lives. A nymph of 100 summers can still look great. Dante's mother, Esme, is rumored to have been the model for the green fairy on the absinthe bottle, which was designed in the 1860's in France. She also may have been a muse for a famous French writer.

Giving birth does, however, thicken a nymph's waist and ruin her breasts for a few months, which is why nymphs rarely do it. As soon as they get the desired cosmetic result from a pregnancy, they brew a tea of cat's claw and sage, squat behind a bush, and that's it, end of problem. The fetus roots where it falls and grows into a pale pink violet which no satyr will pick. And when we see one, we bow our heads respectfully.

"Hello, little brother, little sister," we say and if there are weeds, we clear them away.

The weather, this Venerable Mother's Day, is excellent: mid-70s and cloudless, which creates a clean blue backdrop. I kick the music off with "The Most Beautiful Girl in the World" – an upbeat, jazzy version.

Nymphs who've given birth have a neat trick: they can flick their fingers and throw silk like spiders; only theirs is fully woven, in their most flattering color, and billows about them as they descend. When the mothers touch down, they toss the silk over their shoulders like an opulent scarf; when they sit, it becomes their backdrop, so a mother is always shown off to best effect. It makes young nymphs, who have to make do with found silks or beg them from the flowers, crazy with jealousy.

The colors, as the mothers approach, are stronger and bolder than the young nymphs: flaming orange red, vivid emerald green, violent purple, midnight blue. The wind is strong, the gowns and silks are rippling like flags in a storm but mothers know how to ride currents. They touch down one at a time. No mother is going to share a stage.

Melena, in a royal blue gown that picks up her violet eyes, is the first to arrive, trailing yards of midnight blue silk and the scent of wisteria blossoms. Nico and George are like anxious little kids. Even though she was on the mountain recently, they're jumpy with excitement. It was silly to think they would be thinking of Ben. Their focus is their mother, who tosses her silks over her shoulder and hugs the two thugs.

"My darlings, my beautiful boys," Melena says. "Is it possible you've gotten more good-looking in two weeks?"

And the biggest bruisers in the colony are goofy with happiness.

Ben's mother, Zolie, touches down next. Her silks are a palette of powerful reds. I love inhaling Zolie, who smells like roses on a hot afternoon after rain. She treats me like I am family, though her Hungarian accent is so heavy I have trouble understanding her.

"Sweet Venus, the crosswinds," I hear Zolie say to Ben, as he steps out to her. "I thought they were going to blow me back to Budapest. And then I would never see my bad boy."

She kisses Ben three times, alternating cheeks, then hugs him.

"*Dràga*," she says, in Hungarian. "Let mother look at you. So handsome. The most beautiful goat on the mountain. Of course."

I am busy playing but Zolie blows me a kiss. It feels like a drop of warm honey on my cheek.

On they come: Dante's mother, Esme, whose white-blond hair is streaked with strands of real gold, signifying her as over 150 seasons. Thor's mother, Ingrid, whose hair is silvered and is probably almost as old.

Ingrid makes the most sparkling touchdown. She is covered with a head-to-hip ivory veil, embellished with silver butterflies. It is so fantastic that the other mothers gather around to admire and examine it.

"Bridal veil," Ingrid says. "Do we love it? I saw it in the bedroom of some stupid girl. The shrieking when she saw it was gone! But imagine, this craftsmanship wasted on a cow."

Thor, a worrier when it comes to humans, is concerned.

"Isn't it bad luck to play tricks on them on their wedding day?" he asks.

Ingrid laughs.

"Her bad luck," she says. "Get Mummy a drink."

Nymphs love tormenting human women, the party is off to a good start. The mothers and sons are laughing and drinking, the satyrs are glowing with their mother's attention. Ben may be a little too happy. Walking past Melena, he gives her butt a quick squeeze.

I'm trying to figure out who the gossips are in this crowd. A nymph in a hot pink gown looks like a good bet. Her son is Micha, a new member of the colony who just drifted in from Downsville, southwest of here. When Micha goes to freshen his mother's drink, I take a break from playing and introduce myself to her. She's talking with Esme and Ingrid.

"Daniel, son of Jacob," I say. "I don't think we've met."

"Oh, you've got to be kidding. Jake, son of Maximillian?" she says. "I thought I saw the resemblance. I'm Cynthia."

And to Esme and Ingrid:

"I spent one of the craziest weekends of my life with this goat's father. He took me to a waterfall and did *terrible* things to me. Over and over again. You will remember me to him, won't you? And your mother?" she asks. "Did I miss her?"

"She's away," I say.

"Oh?" Cynthia says. "Well honestly, I'm not surprised."

"You knew her?" I ask, trying to keep it casual.

"Lunch!" Ben interrupts.

Micha takes his mother to the luncheon spread, arrayed on the grass on beautiful white linens – where Dante got them, I have no idea. I'm dying to grill her, but I'm seated at the other end where Ben wanted me, with him and his mother. Last year, being the charity case at the lunch depressed me. Now, finding someone who seems willing to talk about my mother, I'm psyched. I've also arranged the seating so that I'm next to Esme. I've got two goals today. To finally get some intel on my mother and to learn how to attract a muse. As soon as the first round of toasts is over and we're enjoying the cheese and grapes, I turn to Esme.

"Exquisite creature, there's a rumor you were once muse to a famous writer in France," I say.

I don't mention the century or the writer's name, because it is discourteous to allude to a nymph's age. I've also heard there may be non-disclosure agreements.

"Yup, you heard right," says Esme, who has been drinking steadily and seems pretty buzzed. "Guy de Maupassant! What an exhausting man! Three hundred short stories, six novels – I never should have gotten him started. Writers are such children."

Esme pauses to give Dante's hand a squeeze.

"Not that I don't love my children," she says. "How many do I have now? Eight? Nine? But writers, the whining and the demands: *Look at what I did. Do you like it? No, do you really like it? How can you like it, it's shit!*"

"Wasn't he a great writer, though?" I ask.

"Couldn't say," Esme says, reaching for a piece of Stilton blue. "I never read him."

"You didn't?"

"Of course, not," Esme says. "It's not necessary to read them. It's just necessary to tell them they're fabulous. *Exceptionnel! Nonpareil! Extraordinaire!*"

She speaks with an exaggerated moan.

"*Over* and *over* again."

I hit Esme with my big question, hoping I'm not being obvious.

"So, how did de Maupassant find you?"

Esme takes a sip of her cocktail and thinks about it.

"Well, it was Montparnasse, definitely," Esme says. "I honestly can't remember what he was doing. What a pain in the ass that man was. So needy."

The conversation has caught the attention of the group. Melena looks amused, as if she knows something she's not saying. With the powers she's rumored to have, maybe she's a muse, too.

"Why are you so interested, Danny?" Esme teases. "Is your muse playing hard to get?"

I'm embarrassed. I don't want everybody to know I'm having problems. Zolie jumps in and saves me with a story.

"I did hear something funny," Zolie says. "There is a young novelist, Philip, quite good-looking. He spends all his time in" – she turns to Ben – "what is the word, *maszturbáció*?"

"Whacking off," Ben says.

"Just so!" says Zolie. She makes a lewd motion with her hand, and the other mothers crack up. When it comes to filthy stories, mothers are much raunchier than satyrs.

"He does it in the morning, he does it in the afternoon, the poor man simply cannot stop," Zolie says. "He is in such a state that one evening he looks at a piece of liver he intends to prepare for dinner, an exceptionally *seductive* piece of liver, as organ meats so often are, the sluts . . . "

The other mothers are screaming with laughter.

"It was supposedly very *juicy*," Zolie says. "How could he resist? Anyway, a muse – Sofia, do you know her? – whispers to him there is most certainly a book in this. And now he is writing it."

"*Exceptionnel! Extraordinaire!*" yells Esme.

"There is only one question," Ingrid says. "Will he be able to *pull it off*?"

Nico and George, who are actually being helpful, have gotten up to bring the next course. I see George whisper a compliment to Dante.

"Great party, Dante," he says. "Beautiful."

Dante blushes.

I never suspected George even knew the word "beautiful." Maybe the hug from his mother increased his brain cells.

At the third-course stretch, when I really should be making music, I find Cynthia. She's definitely smashed.

"So, you knew my mother?" I say.

"Well, not exactly, but I knew *of* her," Cynthia says. "She bewitched your father. He actually stopped sleeping around. In *May*. It was a bit of a *scandale*."

There's a sharp crack and a large branch falls on Cynthia's head. She drops like a rock. I kneel beside her, as her son and a crowd quickly gather round. Cynthia is conscious, but blood is oozing from her scalp.

"Poor darling," Esme murmurs, throwing a silk tissue from her fingers and dabbing Cynthia's head. I see a wisp of smoke drifting away from her hand. Not one of the mothers mentions it.

"The winds *are* ferocious today," Ingrid says.

"No harm, thank gods," Zolie says. "Danny, darling, could I ask you to play?"

I go back to my pipes, trying to process what just happened. That falling limb was no accident. These nymphs did not want Cynthia talking about my mother. But why? Was she a dark nymph who delighted in creating chaos? Did she do something so horrible the nymphs want to erase her memory?

It's now my least favorite time, when mothers and sons find private spots to talk. I glance over at Ben and Zolie, sitting under a tree. She is stroking his hair. Ben grows more handsome with every stroke. I find myself playing "Quando me'n vo," the aria so beautiful that the birds took it for their own. Could I ever write a melody so beautiful that the birds would pick it up and carry it to my mother, wherever she is? That would prove to a nymph I am worthy of love?

The party is breaking up.

George drops to one knee and gives Melena a leg up to catch the breeze. Ben squeezes his mother and helps her aloft. Then he disappears. I don't know if he's off for a tryst with Melena and I don't care. I keep playing until everyone is gone and I'm alone in the woods.

Then I allow the "Stay With Me" song, which been nagging me all afternoon, to take over. I play a few verses and when I've enticed a warbler to pick up the melody, I put down my pipes and sing the new words:

I'm not fast, I'm not brave
Meeting beautiful nymphs not sure how to behave
But I know, I just know
You're the one. . . .
So when dark comes tonight
Hold me close, make it right
Greet the stars, sing the sun
Stay with me.

CHAPTER EIGHT

The attack of the yowling frog takes place the next morning as I'm strolling through Highmount on my way to the Weingart camp, dressed as a human so I can take a shortcut past some hotel grounds and maybe, later, look for books.

It's a sound so awful it shouldn't even be called music: a nasal male voice, accompanied by a guitar and a grating harmonica, sing-shouting. I wonder if some nymphs are playing a trick on me, but they would never sing this; it's so ugly it would ruin their looks. The poor creature must have a disease of the vocal cords. Perhaps this is his death wail although, given the intensity, I'm afraid it won't be anytime soon.

The song is so unlike anything I've ever heard, I have to see where it's coming from. I follow it to Barley Road, to a small fieldstone house with a green porch and an unusual crisscross railing. There's a dusty black car in the yard and an old lady in a shapeless housedress is dozing on a heavy wood chair on the front porch with a copy of The Jewish Daily Forward on her lap. How she can sleep through this grating wail, I don't know.

I walk around the side of the house to an open window, where the sounds are stronger. A dark-haired girl, wearing a white short-sleeved shirt, white shorts, and sneakers, is sitting on the floor with her back to the window, smoking a cigarette and listening to a record. On the floor, there's an album cover of a guy with curly hair like mine walking down a street. A girl is clutching his arm and snuggling up against him. I squint, but I can't read the name of the album. Then the wind shifts and I smell it: that unnaturally strong musk, the bergamot, lily and rose that keeps haunting me. Diane.

I move to another window so I can see her face. Diane's eyes are closed and she's humming along with the horrible singer. I would be embarrassed to open my mouth and have a sound like this come out, but this guy is joking around with the musicians who are accompanying him and he seems to be having a fine time. The song, about a guy begging a woman to allow him one more chance, to fly her airplane, to ride her passenger train, is pretty stupid too.

It does, however, have a happy, bouncy beat and I got to admit that, right now, it's speaking to me. Human, just allow this little goat one more chance. Diane thinks this guy is good; I'll show her some real music.

I pull my Yankees cap tight on my head, take out my flute and join in with the song, complementing the melody line, then lifting up and away from it.

Diane gets up and takes the needle off the record. She's heard me. I keep playing. Pop would be throwing a fit if he saw this. But now that I've found Diane, I can't move. I don't want to move.

Diane spots me at the window.

I smile at her, forcing myself to be bold, and look into her eyes as I play, giving the song flourishes, adding a fast, playful coda. Showing off again, Ben would say, and he'd be right.

Diane walks to the window.

"That was wild," she says. "You're really good."

She is so close, I can see the colors of her eyes. They're green, with a circle of black around them.

"Thank you," I manage to say.

"You look familiar," Diane says. "I'm Diane – Diane LeVine. Do we know each other from the tennis courts?"

"No," I say.

"NYU downtown, maybe?" she asks. "I just finished my first year."

I have no idea what she's talking about.

"You are a musician, though," she says. "Woodstock?"

Woodstock is maybe forty miles from here and is supposed to be loaded with artists and musicians. I've never been. I don't even know if they have a colony.

"Yeah," I say.

"I *knew* it," she says. "Fleischmanns is a drag. All these old people, talking about Europe. I'm only here because of my grandmother. She loves it up here. Woodstock is where it's at. A friend of mine saw Dylan and Peter Yarrow at the Café Espresso. I would give anything to see Dylan. Do you ever play with him?"

I'm guessing Dylan is the dying frog.

"No," I say.

Then, as I see her disappointment, "I know him, of course."

From the other side of the house, the doorbell rings.

"Coming!" Diane yells. "That's my friend, Jeffrey. Why don't you come inside and meet him?"

"Sorry," I say. "Gotta get back to Woodstock. I'm working tonight."

"But some other time?" she asks.

"Sure, absolutely," I say.

Great, jerk, I think, now she thinks you're a professional musician who lives forty miles away. And who the hell is Dylan?

But I'm also thinking, I *found* Diane. I found my Daisy. This is it, my love story is finally happening!

I race over to Slippery Rock to find Ben. Only Thor and Clea, a blond nymph I met last summer, are there. Clea had taken one look at my hornless head and decided she couldn't be bothered with me. There are nymphs like that. They have the idea that horn size reflects dick size, which is of course ridiculous. She's probably one of the nymphs gossiping about the three-season satyr who's never been laid. Now she lounges on the grass, as Thor threads daisies through her toes.

"I don't know, I think I liked the violets better," Clea says, ignoring me and lifting her foot. "They picked up the pinks in my toenails."

Important decision. Too bad I have to interrupt. I make a point of taking off my hat before I do.

"Good morning, Ethereal Creature," I say, kissing Clea's hand because even if you loathe a nymph, you greet her courteously and bow to her beauty. I also want to make sure she sees my horns.

"Oh, Danny," Clea says. "Your horns came in. You must be so *relieved.*"

I ignore that.

"I'm looking for Ben," I say to Thor. "Have you seen him?"

"Probably shacked up with Melena," Thor says. "You know, a guy told me she's a sorceress; she once fried a toad by just giving it a dirty look. I wouldn't tap that, no matter how hot she is. But good luck telling Ben anything."

It's like that with satyrs; a nymph intimidates them, they turn her into a dark nymph. I'm not interested in debating it.

"Yeah," I say. "Listen, I don't suppose either of you has heard of a human named Dylan? Who's a big deal?"

"Sure, man, Dylan Thomas," Thor says. "'*Now as I was young and easy under the apple boughs, about the lilting house and happy as the grass was green . . .* ' Pretty goaty, right? He was a human poet who drank too much and croaked. That happens with them. They can't hold alcohol."

I never would have expected this.

"You read poetry?" I say.

"I ate one of his books one day," Thor says. "It must have stuck with me. It was good going down, but an hour later I was really bloated."

"Not the same human," I said. "This Dylan's alive, and he's a singer. He's got curly hair like mine and a terrible voice."

"Never heard of him," Thor says.

I leave, trying to figure out how to learn something about Dylan. I don't remember reading about him, but you miss a lot sleeping six months a year. Then I remember that Pop's friend Noah works in the music business. I head to The Maplewood House and sneak through the brush to the changing shack behind the pool. Noah is lying in the sun in a loose plaid bathing suit, wearing sunglasses, with a maple leaf covering his nose. There is no sign of Pop.

"Noah," I whisper loudly.

Noah sits up and looks around.

"Danny, behind the shack," I say. "It's important."

Noah gets up and ambles over. I gesture to come deeper in the trees.

"You're taking some risks these days, *boychik*," Noah says, following me. "You know your old man doesn't like you down here. What's going on?"

"Noah," I say, "I have a music question. It's important. Who's Dylan?"

"Why?" Noah says. "You want to be a beatnik?"

Beatniks, I know from newspapers, are humans who do not work, go barefoot, and play tall drums called bongos.

"I just want to know why a girl would like him," I say.

"One of your, uh, woodland girls?" Noah asks, surprised.

"Yeah," I lie.

"They know about him in the woods, he must really be big," Noah says. "Dylan is Bob Dylan, sort of a folk singer. The beatniks love him. He wrote this song, "Blowin' In The Wind," it just hit number two on the Billboard charts. That means it's selling a lot. People are calling him the voice of a generation, which means nobody knows what the hell he's talking about. '*The answer my friend is blowing in the wind.*' What the fuck does that even mean? Do yourself a favor and stick with Sinatra."

"What about Peter Yarrow?"

"Another beatnik folk-singer," Noah says. "'Slack your rope hangman, slack it for awhile . . . ' 'There once was a union maid who never was afraid.' Though why they're into unions in the woods, beats me. I guess the times really are changing."

CHAPTER NINE

I guess I should explain more about clothes and satyrs: when we're by ourselves, they're totally unnecessary. Pop is insane about covering up, but that's only because he hangs out with humans all day.

The truth is, from a distance, a satyr's body looks a lot like a human's. We do have hairier legs and lower bodies than human men, but if you got a glimpse of us when you were hiking in the Catskills, which you probably have, you'd think we were humans in dark pants, hiking shirtless. You wouldn't notice our horns or dark hooves because you wouldn't be looking for them and anyway, we're as fast as deer, so we'd be out of there in a flash. Also, most of our horns are hidden by our hair. When we're in areas that humans might stumble into, we usually do wear hats to be on the safe side. But even I, who love my baseball cap, have to admit that a hat on a satyr is like a fedora on a deer. It's silly.

When courting a human, however, you've obviously got to wear clothing. My wardrobe is not large, but for my first outing with Diane I decide to wear the chinos Ben stole and a shirt with short sleeves. This is called a polo shirt and is more respectful than a T-shirt. I grab a bottle of wine from my stash and score a picnic lunch of sandwiches and cookies from Mrs. Belinsky. The moment I use the word "picnic" she knows I have a date and gets excited. Then I put together a bouquet of flowers – the most beautiful ones, not the closest ones – and head to Diane's house.

The old lady, who I figure is Diane's grandmother, is on the porch reading. I walk around to the side. On the second floor, I see an open window and a bathing suit drying on the sill. I take out my flute and play the "Honey, just allow me one more chance" song that Dylan was yowling.

Diane sticks her head out the window.

Bergamot, nectar, lily, rose, musk . . .

"It's you!" she says, excited. "I knew you'd be back. Hold on, I'll be right down."

I walk around to the front porch. The old lady looks at me and seems startled. Then she mutters something to herself in Yiddish. I have a bad feeling about this. Is she another one of those humans who can spot satyrs?

"So, who is this bargain?" the old lady says to Diane, in Yiddish. "Do we know his people?"

"Muklh mir far nischt bakenen zikh," I say. "Pardon me for not introducing myself. *Ich bin Daniel, zun fun Jakov."*

"You're Jewish?" the grandmother asks, switching to English. "Where are your people from?"

"Europe," I say, which is pretty much all I know.

"Of course, Europe," the old lady says. "Where in Europe?"

Diane jumps in to rescue me.

"Grandma, please don't give him the third degree," she says. "He's a friend. And before you ask, he doesn't drive a Volkswagen."

Diane looks at me.

"You don't, do you?" she asks.

Extended time in a mechanized vehicle gives a satyr heart disease.

"Absolutely not," I say.

The grandmother grunts and returns to the paper.

I give Diane the flowers, which surprise and please her – human men must not often bring flowers to women, I think. While she goes to put them in water, I worry about the grandmother. Did she spot me? Were satyrs ravishing Jewish women in Europe? I know from The Maplewood House that Jews don't like their daughters dating non-Jews. Is the grandmother going to alert the witch hunters?

It's a relief when Diane comes down.

"So, where to?" she says. "Where's your car?"

Ooops, I didn't think of that.

"A friend dropped me," I say. "I thought we could just go for a walk. You ever hear of Crump's Castle? It's this great old ruin. It's got 'No Trespassing' signs all over, but it's beautiful."

"Sound great," Diane says. "I love going where I'm not supposed to go."

We head through the woods.

"So where in the city do you live?" Diane asks, as I pull some blackberry brambles out of our path. "I don't know a thing about you."

"I don't," I say. "I live here. In the mountains."

I might as well have told her I have two heads.

"Year-round?" Diane says. "I've never met anybody who lived up here year-round. What about school? Where are you going to college?"

I know about college from my reading. It's where young humans go to talk about books all day and drink beer and throw up all night. I'd love that, except for the beer and puking.

"I don't go to college," I say.

That seems to stun Diane even more than living here year-round.

"I'll go to school eventually," I say, "But for a musician, it's more important to be working. Where did you grow up?"

Diane stops walking and turns, showing me her profile.

"Can't you tell?" she asks.

"Huh?" I say.

"It's a Dr. Diamond nose," Diane says. "Everybody in Great Neck has it. He's a plastic surgeon in Manhattan. When you're sixteen, your parents make an appointment and he fixes your nose. You know. . . . "

Diane makes a chopping motion at the end of her nose.

"Thwack!" she says.

When I've seen thwacking at the Maplewood House, it's because Mrs. Belinsky is lopping off the head of some poor chicken. I must not be getting this.

"He chopped off the end of your nose?"

"Yup," Diane says. "My mother also made me get electrolysis, so I'd have a heart-shaped hairline."

She pulls back her long bangs. Her hairline does resemble the top of a drawing of a heart.

"See?" she says.

"But your hair covers it," I say.

"Well, it *is* my head," Diane says. "I'll tell you the truth — I don't get along so great with my mother. She's always on my case. For my fourteenth birthday, she bought me a bathing suit. And a *scale*. She thinks the only reason a woman needs to go to college is to find a rich husband. My sister did, she's engaged to an orthodontist – that's like a Jewish mother's wet dream. I think she comes every time she hears the word. My sister's getting married in August. She spent three months finding a dress."

I'm stuck back at the part where Diane said "wet dream."

"Really?" I say, trying to catch up.

"Yup. Shoot me if I ever turn out like that," Diane says. "I'm going to do something with my life. Like Barbara Walters or Margaret Mead – I've got a double major in journalism and anthropology. I think journalism is winning out; anthropology seems to be a lot of dysentery and snakes. But you know how Margaret Mead went to New Guinea to study tribal people? Well, I had a professor who said she married one of them for research. Can you imagine? Having sex with somebody who went around the jungle naked and had never even heard of planes or television? Totally primitive screwing. It would be wild."

I have never heard of Barbara Walters or Margaret Mead. But Diane's attitude about sex with creatures who go around naked is promising.

We're in a rise, now, with a clear view of Belleayre Mountain.

"Let's stop here," I say. "It's a great view of the mountain. See, on top, there's still a little snow."

Diane looks to where I'm pointing.

"It is beautiful," she says. "But I still can't get over that you live here year-round. How did your family end up here, anyway?"

"My grandfather fell in love with an opera singer who had a house here," I say.

"Wow," Diane says. "That's pretty romantic."

"There are a lot of love stories in these mountains," I say. "For instance, Big Indian, that's the town you drove through just before Pine Hill. It was named for a seven-foot-tall Indian who fell in love with a white girl 300 years ago. Her family didn't want her to be with an Indian guy, so she ran away with him. The white people hunted them down and shot him and he died somewhere in the hills."

"Yeah, I get that," Diane says. "If I ever dated an Indian my parents would shit a brick."

The sun grows stronger and so does Diane's scent.

"I love your scent," I say.

"Kiehl's, Original Musk," Diane says. "Most guys don't notice."

"I'm good with scent," I say.

We walk on to the Crump property. It's especially pretty today. Roses, gone wild, have colonized the walls.

Diane is smiling.

"I get what you like about this place," she says. "It's pretty wild."

We go into the castle. Diane is intrigued with everything: the design of the spiral staircase; a single small room on top of the roof; the poetry engraved in the windowsills.

" 'Linger here, among the beautiful foolishness of things,' " she says. "I wonder whose room this was."

"That's what makes it interesting; we'll never know," I say. "Who do you think?"

"A woman who spent too much money on shoes," Diane says. "Probably a member of my family."

I laugh.

We go back outside. I find a spot near the wild roses, open my pack, and bring out the sandwiches and wine. I've never understood why humans go indoors to pray; a summer sky is a satyr's cathedral. To be in the green grass with a woman, enjoying food and wine; that's how you worship.

Although, I realize, for a human, something is missing.

"I'm sorry, I forgot about glasses," I say.

"That's okay, I'd rather have it straight from the bottle," Diane says. "It's more real. We could be Jack Kerouac."

Another musician I've never heard of. I pass Diane the wine and ask her about a singer she mentioned last time.

"So, Peter Yarrow," I say, "What do you like about him?"

"Oh, I've never heard him alone, just as part of Peter, Paul and Mary," Diane says. "They were okay, but what I really like about them now is that they're doing a lot of Dylan's stuff. Those folk songs they did where the guy would rather be hung than say he was sleeping with his best friend's wife? That was ridiculous. Would anyone let himself be killed rather than causing a scandal? It would be fun to cause a scandal."

The wine is making her loopy but it's cute loopy.

"Who do you listen to?" Diane asks.

"Frank Sinatra, Tony Bennett, really anybody doing Rodgers & Hart," I say. "I think Lorenz Hart is the best songwriter who ever lived."

"You're kidding!" Diane says. "Those are the people my parents listen to."

Great, now she's lumped me in with people she thinks are idiots. But if she doesn't know Lorenz Hart, she should.

"Lie back on the grass and close your eyes," I say.

"Okay," Diane says, "But don't try anything that will get you hung."

I take out my pipes. I look at her dark hair against the grass and think about the heart hidden behind her bangs. Then I sing the exquisite Rodgers & Hart song, "The Shortest Day of the Year."

I finish the song with my pipes. When I am done, Diane sits up and kisses me on the cheek.

"That was beautiful," she says. "But I should tell you, I have a boyfriend."

CHAPTER TEN

Okay, I guess there are satyrs who'd say that if a human girl tells you she has a boyfriend, you should just shove off. Mating for life is a very big thing with humans. I have a drawing at my place called "The Satyr's Family" by a human artist named Fragonard. It shows a satyr and a nymph in a cave, holding up their twin babies and smiling. It's my favorite picture, though I keep it hidden under my pile of jeans.

But obviously, if Diane kissed me, this boyfriend doesn't mean a lot to her. She's like the married women Pop messes around with, who are hoping for something better. I also know from my reading that if love is meant to be, a boyfriend doesn't matter. Gatsby waited five years to be reunited with Daisy. And when he finally found her, she had more than a boyfriend; she had a husband, and that didn't slow him down one bit.

It also turns out that Diane's boyfriend, Jeffrey, is a waiter. Waiters don't have a lot of time off. That will give me space to operate.

A few days after she's kissed me, I pop over to Diane's house. She looks really happy to see me, which proves I'm right – this so-called boyfriend is not important. I tell her I've picked up so many gigs in Fleischmanns, I'm hanging out here for a while. After that, I stop by her house every other day or so. We go for long walks, listen to music, and hang out in the ruins at Crump's. I become much more familiar with rock 'n' roll. Diane also plays me a lot of Bob Dylan, whose music and voice I actually start to like, and Peter, Paul and Mary, who mourn the loss of their pet dragon. We also listen to Pete Seeger, who is what is called a protest singer. He believes that when people get on a bus, they should not have to sit in the back, but should sit wherever they want. I had not realized this was a problem, but I absolutely agree.

Interspecies friendships do have their challenges. I need a story for Diane about why I don't have a car. (It died, so I'm hitchhiking around.) I need a story about why I won't go swimming with her. (Rotator cuff injury. I don't know what that is, but I've heard guests complain about it.) I need a story about why I don't have a phone. (I'm moving around too much.) Not having a phone does make it hard to plan. When I want to see Diane, I often just show up and hope she's free.

The grandmother who, like Bernie over at The Maplewood House, has a vocabulary of grunts, doesn't seem to trust me one bit. One day, when I come over and she's sitting on the porch, she mutters something in Yiddish, spits three times, then grunts – an annoyed grunt, I'd say — and goes inside.

"What was that about?" I ask Diane.

"The spitting?" Diane says. "It's to keep evil spirits away. Gram's got it in her head you were touched by a demon. I wouldn't worry about it."

This is getting a little too close for comfort.

"Where is your grandmother from again?" I ask.

"Austria, Poland – I'm not sure she knows, the borders in those days kept moving," Diane says. "She's got these superstitions. Like, she tied a red string around my crib when I was born to keep dark spirits away. I told her you were much too good-looking to be a demon."

Diane thinks I'm good-looking? I'm high all day.

Diane's grandmother is the only family member I meet. They're all home on Long Island, where her father has a big business building houses and her mother and her older sister, Ruth, are preparing for Ruth's wedding.

"My family is so fucking *bourgeois* I could puke," Diane says.

Bourgeois is a French word that means "obsessed with wealth and blind to literature and art." Diane uses it often when she speaks of her family, who have made her life so stressful that she sees an emotional health doctor called a shrink. Her *bourgeois* father wants to tear down every tree on Long Island and put up houses that look exactly alike. Her *bourgeois* mother and sister are going nuts over her sister's wedding. Is it that important that the napkins match the flowers? Diane asks. Will the goddamn democracy fall if the napkins are pink rather than dusty rose? How many fucking shades of pink are there?

One day when I come over I find Diane sitting on the steps of her porch, looking miserable. Her eyes are red and puffy. I have seen this sometimes with Mrs. Belinsky, after she has read letters from her family, and I know what it means.

"Diane," I say. "Have you been . . . crying?"

"My sister said I'm fat, and I'm going to ruin her wedding," Diane says. "My mother agreed with her."

This is the New York City women's fat problem that Pop has told me about. They worry about it night and day, sometimes eating nothing but carrots and celery. I can't believe someone as smart as Diane would have it, too.

"You're perfect," I tell Diane.

"They want me to lose ten pounds in a month, which is impossible," Diane says. "They were yelling at me on the phone about it for ten minutes. They said I was selfish because I don't want to go into the city to watch Ruth pick out her veil. My mother says it's an important moment for a bride and she should have her family around her. Like she's *taking the veil*. Like she's a nun. She's been fucking her fiancé ever since she got the ring."

"Are you going to go?" I ask, already missing her.

"It's either that or being guilt-tripped for the rest of my life," Diane says. "I'll be back Tuesday. We can go for a hike. I'll need to get all the pink out of my head."

Tuesday afternoon, I go over to Diane's place with my pipes – I might as well work on my music there, I think – and settle in on a stone fence that runs along her property, next to the road.

Except for the day outside her window when she was listening to Dylan, I've never played for Diane. It's one thing to accompany a guy somebody loves; it's another to do your own stuff. I know Diane likes protest songs, but I can't think of anything to protest except her boyfriend. I try something out, in a blues style Diane has turned me on to:

Dump that idiot, baby.
He can't love you like I can.

No, Diane likes the guy. That insults him. I try it again, singing the lyrics in my head.

There ain't nobody, baby,
Who can love you like I can.

A white convertible, top-down, blasting rock 'n roll, comes roaring up the road, drowning out my music. It's Diane. She's wearing sunglasses and grinning. She pulls into her yard without shutting the car down.

I hop off the fence, tuck my flute into my shirt pocket, and run over. The car is beautiful. The inside is tomato red; red leather seats, a red steering wheel with silver accents.

"Pretty sweet, huh?" Diane says. "T-bird. Hot off the lot. Hop in. I'll show you what it's got."

This goes against everything Pop has told me. *Machines are dangerous. Cars can make you sick.* But how dangerous can this car be when it's completely open to nature? And I'll be able to sit right next to Diane. I fumble with the handle. Diane leans over and opens the door. I get in.

Diane drives the car backward a few feet – that's kind of a weird feeling – then turns it around and heads down her road, across busy Route 28 and up the mountain to Belleayre. I'm used to seeing cars speeding down the road, but being inside one is entirely different – I cannot believe how fast they go. Or how complicated they are.

The driver's side has a panel of instruments shaped like clocks. Diane is steering the car with one hand with one hand

and moving a lever with the other and moving her feet between the pedals on the floor.

"Zero to sixty in 8.9 seconds," Diane says, as we head up the mountain. "Three-forty horsepower. Can you feel it? That's *power.*"

I am too overwhelmed by the speed we're going to talk. I'm also a little nauseous,

"Yeah," I manage to say.

"My father got it for me," Diane says. "It was my present for putting up with two days in Pinksville. I would have liked something smaller – this is a little *bougie* – but it does move. And what the hell, you don't have to worry about luggage. You could put a body in that trunk."

I'm starting to feel the way I did the day I ate éclairs and champagne. This machine might be getting to me, after all. Or maybe it's the way Diane is taking the turns.

"Diane," I say. "You think we could do that hike some other time? Something I ate isn't agreeing with me."

Diane looks confused for a moment, as if she's forgotten all about it.

"Hike?" she says. "Oh, right. No problem."

One thing I do know about machines: You can build up an immunity. I used to get dizzy if I stood too close to the refrigerators in The Maplewood kitchen, but after coming to the kitchen a while, they didn't bother me.

I do the same thing with cars, pushing myself to get used to them fast. If I see a car in a deserted hotel parking lot next to the woods, I stand next to it for a few minutes. When I'm no longer queasy – which only happens the first two times – I hold my hand on it. I throw up the first time I do this, but within a few days, I'm fine. As a final test, in the middle of the night, I go to Diane's house and sit in a spot where no one can see me, leaning against the car. I stay there till just before sunrise. When I get up, I'm fine.

I hang out with Diane, hiking and listening to her stories: About Paris, where she lived when she was exchanged for another student, and French existentialists, who are like beatniks, but cooler, because they are French. About Greenwich Village, where there are coffee houses and folk singers and you sit around all night, talking and listening to music.

Diane's house is loaded with books, which she lets me borrow. Unfortunately, she doesn't have "The Great Gatsby," which I'd really like to finish. I do read one of Diane's favorites, "Coming of Age in Samoa," by Margaret Mead, who asks everyone how much sex they're getting and who I think would benefit from an afternoon with Pop.

One book that especially interests me is "Another Country" by James Baldwin. It's about the problems of colored humans interacting with white humans. I have seen a colored human only once; a dishwasher outside a hotel kitchen who was a lovely shade of chestnut. The white humans look down on the colored humans, unless they are in the field of jazz, where the colored humans are recognized as superior. Romantic relations between white and colored humans are discouraged and often incite rage. It reminds me of the situation with satyrs and humans, though I can't tell that to Diane.

I can, however, feel her out on it.

"So, this white woman who goes out with the colored musician – is this something that you would do?" I ask Diane one day, when we're returning to her house from a walk up the mountain.

"Sure," Diane says. "I had two dates with a Negro guy in my French Existentialism class. Then he got distracted by a redhead in my dorm. The one we called Flaming Bush."

"Huh?" I say. "Why?"

"You know," Diane says, pointing in the direction of her crotch. "Her bush, her pussy. What do you call it?"

I'm suddenly feeling awkward.

"Uh . . . " I begin.

Diane starts laughing.

"You know, Danny, for a musician, you're very uptight about sex," she teases. "C'mon, you must call it something."

"Same things you call it," I say. "Or sometimes . . . her flower."

"No kidding?" Diane says. "I never heard that. It's very sweet. It must be a Woodstock thing."

Chapter Eleven

The friend game with Diane is not easy. There are a dozen times, when I am with her, that I want to kiss her: When she piles so many books in my hands that I don't know how I'll carry them home; when she grins with pleasure listening to a new record album; when I take her to a special spot in the mountains and she beams.

I'm always thinking about ways to get close. I don't try to hold Diane's hand when we're walking, which would be boyfriend behavior, but I do choose especially rocky paths, where she needs to reach out to me to steady her. When she grabs my hand, my whole body tingles. Sometimes Diane tells me how nice it is to be with someone who loves music and who really listens when she talks and I know my plan is working.

Ben thinks this is nuts.

"You're living in dreamland because you haven't gotten laid," he says one morning when we're foraging in Halcott Center, seeing what's ripe. "If you spent some time fucking, you'd forget this dumb human."

I am more interested in getting to the abandoned cherry orchard than having this argument for the millionth time.

"Stop breaking my chops," I say. "You go off and see Melena every chance you get."

"Melena is different than the other nymphs," Ben says. "She's not all giggly, chase me, bring me stuff. She's more, I don't know, like a guy. I can sit with her and shoot the shit. And she's incredibly strong. We ended up wrestling the other day and she pinned me. Which was very hot."

"Okay, then you should get it," I say. "That's just like me and Diane. She's not like the nymphs either. She's been out in the world."

"It's nothing like you and Diane," Ben says. "One, I get to make love to Melena. Two, I don't sit here pining when I can't. I go out and enjoy the nymphs I find. I fuck Esme, I fuck Glynnis, I fuck Arianna. I fuck every woman I can and I love them all. That's how it's supposed to be, Danny. You can't limit yourself to one woman for life. That's insane."

"Yeah, well, see, I've been thinking about that," I say, "And I'm not sure."

"*What?*" Ben says.

"There's this book I have, "The Great Gatsby." A guy – this human, Gatsby – loves a woman so much he builds a house across from where she lives, just so he can stare at it."

"And that's how he gets off, staring?" Ben says.

"No, let me finish," I say. "He has no interest in other women, none. And because the love is all concentrated in one woman, it's much more intense. The woman's got a husband, but she's going to get rid of him and when she does, it will just be her and Gatsby for the rest of their lives."

"They're gonna go crazy with boredom," Ben says.

"No," I say. "The love is going to get deeper and deeper."

"I think you better throw away this book," Ben says. "It's warped your brain."

We've now hit the cherry orchard – Montmorency cherries, the only ones that can make it with the cold up here. There's also a lone peach tree. It's a straggly little tree. One season I saw some blossoms but I've never seen it bear fruit. I always wonder how it got here, the only peach among the cherries. I feel a little sorry for it.

"Hang in there, tree," I say, patting it.

Ben has spotted some cherries on a high branch and is pulling it down.

"You always talk to the trees in July?" he says. "You know nobody's in there. Or if she is, she's dead."

"Ben!" I say. "Respect!"

And to the peach tree, "I apologize for the manners of my idiot friend. And I wish you a joyful and abundant summer."

Ben just laughs and grabs a handful of cherries. I do the same. We sit in the sun, eating, happy, soaking in summer.

"You know," Ben says, "I have a theory that nymphs are like the trees they sleep in. Sexually, I mean. The Montmorency, they're a little tart, a little bitchy and —"

"Ben," I interrupt. "Can we for once talk about something besides your sex life?"

"Like your sex life?" Ben says. "Why not? You switch to the left hand?"

I spit some pits in his direction.

"In fact, I happen to have a date with Diane this afternoon," I say, trying not to show how excited I am. "I'm taking her up to the old fire tower. I think the view will knock her out."

"Let's hope so," Ben says. "Since that's the only way you're going to get a hand on her again."

Wrong. I've planned this out. The hike up to the tower on Belleayre Mountain is steep. Diane will certainly need my help. I'll be practically pulling her at the top. There will be times her exhausted body falls against me . . .

But that's not the way it works out. Diane, as we head up the trail in late afternoon, is actually ahead of me. It's a sweet view — she's wearing pale pink pedal pushers — but not what I had in mind.

"You're really strong," I say, as we come to the tower. "Most people coming up here get winded."

"You mean most girls?" Diane teases. "Your little musician groupies? You bring a lot of them up here?"

Then, as I'm trying to figure out how to answer, "It's the tennis. A few weeks into summer, I can feel the difference. I can climb anywhere."

Diane pauses.

"Okay, confession: It's not just the tennis. My mother got me these diet pills — you know, so I wouldn't be a tub at my sister's wedding. And the energy they're giving me is incredible. I feel *unbeatable* on that tennis court, now. I'm, like, homicidal. We should play sometime."

She glances up at my baseball hat.

"Or are you too busy listening to your beloved Yankees?"

In fact, I know nothing about the Yankees. I tried eating the sports pages, like Pop told me when he gave me my Yankees hat, but it was boring.

"You're always wearing that hat," Diane says. "You're not one of those guys who thinks if he takes his hat off his team is going to lose, are you?"

Quick as a fox, she reaches out to snatch my hat off my head.

I'm panicked. I grab her wrists, realizing too late I'm hurting her. Diane looks at me, shocked. Then, before I have time to think about it, I pull her to me and kiss her on the mouth. I can't believe I'm doing it; it's like some outside force has taken over me. I feel Diane's body stiffen, then relax, those beautiful breasts, those other-worldly *human* breasts pressing into me. I don't want to let go, but I've moved too fast, without a single courtesy. And I am not supposed to be the boyfriend. I give her lower lip a little nip – where did *that* come from? — and release her.

Diane steps back.

"Wow," she says. "That was unexpected."

I nod, having no idea what to say.

"I have a boyfriend, you know," Diane says.

"Yeah," I say. "I know. I'm sorry, I –"

"Do you want to stay for supper?" Diane asks. "Gram is making blintzes. These pills are supposed to be cutting back on my appetite, but blintzes may constitute a cholesterol super-power."

Dinner with the spitting, suspicious grandmother? I try to keep my distance from her. But Diane and I have just moved to another level; there's no way I'm turning this down.

"Danny's gonna have supper with us, Gram," Diane says, sticking her head in the kitchen as we go inside the house.

"The one who's always with the hat?" the old lady says in Yiddish. "Fine. Put down another plate."

Diane looks embarrassed.

"'Scuse us a second, Gram," she says, leading us back out onto the porch.

"Danny," she whispers, "You got to take off your hat."

I'm confused.

"But why?" I ask. "I always wear my hat."

"Yeah, yeah, I know," Diane says. "But that's hanging out in my room. This is dinner. You can't wear a hat at the table."

"Why not?" I say.

Diane looks exasperated.

"Why *not*?" she says. "Were you raised by wolves? Because it's not done. It's like an insult to my grandmother. Unless you just turned into an Orthodox Jew."

Oh damn and double damn.

"But I can't," I say. "The, you know, the custom. The Yankees are having a tough time right now."

"Oh, please," Diane says. "You really think a baseball team is going to lose if you don't wear their stupid hat? That's idiotic. Just take off the hat."

"I can't," I say.

"Children!" the grandmother is hollering. "Come to the table!"

I'm cornered. There's only one way out.

"I'm sorry, Diane," I say. "I gotta go."

"*What?*" Diane says.

"I'm leaving," I say. "Tell your grandmother there was an emergency and I had to go."

"Good idea," Diane says. "Here's a better one: never come back."

CHAPTER TWELVE

"I get why some goats chase them," Ben is saying, as we're crouched down in the woods behind the Takanassee tennis courts, watching two girls and two guys all dressed in white and wearing white floppy hats, in a fast-moving game. "Those butts look hot under those little skirts. Not hot enough to risk having your heart stop after you fuck 'em, but hot."

"I keep telling you, this isn't about sex – not right away, anyway," I say. "I just want to be able to hang out with her again. Now can you steal me that stuff – a few hats, the clothes, a racquet?"

"I can steal anything you want," Ben says. "But it's a dumb-ass idea. You kissed her one time, then she told you to get lost. I don't think a game of tennis is going to get her back."

"She loves tennis," I say. "She plays it every chance she gets. And it's a game where it's okay to wear a hat. See, they're all wearing them."

Ben grabs my arm.

"Stop talking!" he says. "Just look."

I look where he's looking. A human girl, who's been chasing a ball, is bent over, flashing pink panties with frills on the back.

"Check that out!" Ben says. "That ripply stuff on the underwear. It shakes when they bend over. Like they don't want you to miss it. Maybe this game is not so dumb."

"So, you know what I need?" I say.

"Abso – do you smell that?" Ben says.

He doesn't have to ask twice. It's hit me at the same time.

"That is some powerful love," I say. "Human."

"*Half*-human," Ben says. "There's a goat at work here. Let's track them."

We slip into the woods. The woman's love scent is so strong it's like a fog and it gets thicker as we follow it. The satyr's scent, while muskier, is even more powerful. We spot the couple off a barely visible path in the woods, in a clearing. We kneel down, hiding behind the trees.

A satyr – five or six seasons older than us, horns covered with the white tennis hat, wearing the whole dumb tennis outfit — is kneeling behind a girl in tennis clothes who looks about eighteen. He's nuzzling her neck, and she's leaning back against him, eyes closed. Her panties are on the ground. The satyr moves his hand to her skirt.

The girl puts her hand on his.

"No wait," she says. "I'm all naked."

The satyr's voice is soft, but we can hear him.

"That's the way you should be," the satyr says, lifting her skirt. "Natural and beautiful. Lean back into me. Let it happen."

The satyr's hand is now hovering over the woman's flower. He's gathering her heat, compounding it and reflecting it back to her. He's making her want him, teasing her until the want becomes unbearable, which he knows it will. A satyr's powers become more concentrated with age and experience. A satyr who is an accomplished lover can arouse a human woman with a look. A deep kiss will give her pleasure no male of her species will ever match.

The satyr touches the girl, exposing her even more.

A breeze stirs the leaves.

"You feel that?" the satyr murmurs to the girl, holding her firmly around the waist. "That's summer kissing you. Fall into me. Give yourself to summer."

I've never heard anything like this. The satyr's voice is hypnotic. Ben's impressed, too.

"The goat is good," he whispers.

The satyr is touching the girl harder, still holding her upper body against him.

"That's me loving you," the satyr says. "I'm going to love you all day long. I'm going to love you when the moon comes up. I'm never going to stop. You're too beautiful. How could I stop?"

The girl's eyes are closed, but her body is arching up, she's traveling to the land of Eros.

"But somebody walking by. . . . they'd see everything," she manages to say.

The satyr nibbles her neck.

"And would you like that?" the satyr whispers. "Would it make you very, very hot?"

Forget what it's doing to her. It's making *me* very, very hot. I've got to get some place private and –

An arm presses me across the throat so hard I can't breathe. I manage to look over at Ben. A satyr with a barrel chest, also in tennis clothes, has Ben's arm twisted behind his back.

"Hey, punks," Barrel Chest whispers. "You know these courts are Dunraven turf."

Ben's in pain, but he manages to speak.

"Disputed," he says. "Tennis courts: June through August. Shared territory."

Another satyr, in whites with a gold chain around his neck, materializes. I see an insignia on his white shirt: Bacchus, carrying a tennis racquet. That's kind of funny: wine, women, tennis. The look in the satyrs' eyes as they drag me and Ben into the deep woods, not so much. Three of them, two of us. And one of us has never hit anyone in his life.

"Not the face," Ben says, as Barrel Chest pins his arms behind him and Gold Chain grins nastily at him. "I'm too pretty."

Then – by the gods, he's good—Ben kicks Barrel Chest's leg out from under him and knees Gold Chain in the balls. Gold Chain moans and falls to the ground. The goat holding me throws me to the ground, gives me a fast kick in the gut and goes after Ben. I'm trying to catch my breath when I see something flying through the air: a wasp's nest, which scores a direct hit on the satyr who'd had me in a chokehold.

The nest shatters and the wasps attack. The Bacchus satyrs take off, howling. Ben yanks me to my feet and we run in the direction the nest came from, which is where Dante is standing.

"C'mon," he says, taking off.

We run, following Dante through the woods, over a stream, and into his cave. It twists deep into the mountain like a cavern and it's the wildest cave I've ever seen. It's stuffed with furniture covered in fabrics with exotic leaves and flowers; it's filled with weird vases and hanging things with shiny glass. Magazines with houses on the covers are stacked all over. We collapse on a fat, flowery couch that drips tassels.

"I'd prefer Swedish Modern," Dante says, bringing out a bottle of wine and seeing us staring. "But you're not going to find any of that in these old hotels. *Moderne* they are not."

He gives the bottle to Ben, who takes a long drink.

"But the tennis courts?" Dante says. "Why were you guys out there? Didn't you know it's where the Dunraven colony trolls?"

"Danny's hung up on a human," Ben says, more annoyed about Diane than I've ever heard him. "He thinks if he puts on a cute little white hat, she'll fuck him."

Dante is stunned.

"You're fucking humans?" he says. "You're only three seasons. Didn't you get sick?"

"I am *not* making love to her," I say. "It's not about that. I did kiss her once."

Dante wants every detail.

"Tongues?" he asks.

"Good question," Ben says. "Are you guys up to tongues yet, Danny? Or is she waiting for August?"

"Lay off, Ben!" I say, yanking the bottle away and taking a big drink.

"There's this human girl I like," I tell Dante. "Her name is Diane. Nothing's happened between us – not yet. We got into a fight because I wouldn't take off my hat. Obviously. But tennis – that's a place it's okay to wear a hat."

"He just got his horns and now he's trying to cover them up," Ben says. "If he could chop them off for this girl, he would."

"That's so not true, Ben!" I yell.

"Yeah, it is," Ben says. "You meet her and you're ashamed of being a goat."

"Guys, please," Dante says. "It's okay, I get it. But Danny, it can't be that tough to find some other way to hide your horns."

Dante is looking at my head like I'm a woodland glen he's deciding how to style for a feast.

"Human women use glue to hold their hair in place," Dante says. "They spray it with a potion called Aqua Net, it comes in a can. I see the cans all the time at the dump. But I'm not sure that would work with horns. They could still still poke out. You need to camouflage them somehow."

"You're going to help him with this?" Ben asks. "Covering his horns? If he told you he wanted to chop off his balls, would you help him with that too?"

"Oh, Ben, stop being so dramatic," Dante says. "He's not chopping off anything. He just wants to spend a little time with a human he's curious about."

Dante walks over to me, checking out my horns.

"May I?" he asks, parting my hair, peering at the base of my horns. "One thing you've got going is, they're thick, but they're not that long yet. And your hair is thick too. We just have to fix it so it all blends together . . . y'know what might work? Pine resin!"

Pine resin is easy to get. It seeps out of the trees, forming ugly little misshapen lumps. It's also nothing you would want on your body.

"But that stuff hardens like a rock," I say. "And it's yellow."

"And you want to stick it in his hair?" Ben says. "You guys are both fucking crazy. I'm out of here. Mind if I take the bottle, Dante?"

"Take it," Dante says, preoccupied with his new design project, which is me.

"You warm the resin and mix it with charcoal and water and it turns into glue," Dante tells me. "The charcoal will also darken it. I use it all the time to fix things. We wrap some of your hair around your horns, so it makes them look like curls, then add the resin it to make it stick. Maybe add a little to the rest of your hair so the fake curls don't stand out. Of course, you wouldn't want her running her fingers through her hair, but it doesn't sound like that's a problem."

I flash on those rock-hard resin lumps.

"But how do I get it out?" I ask. "I don't want to be stuck with hairy horns."

"Warm honey," Dante says. "I use it to get glue off my fingers all the time. You just sit in the sun for half an hour to warm it up, then you wash it out. Or olive oil, if you can get some."

I'm not sure which one of us is more excited by this project – or surprised when it works. Checking myself out in Dante's mirror, my curls look stiffer than usual but my horns are gone. The tips of my horns are now just the tips of my curls.

"Remember, sleep on your stomach," Dante tells me, sending me home with a little pot of dark brown resin glue. "And when you wake up, check that nothing's come loose."

I'm too excited to sleep very well. I get up early the next morning and gather two bouquets: For Diane, wisteria and white roses, which grow wild around an abandoned farmhouse and have a spectacular perfume; for the grandmother, blue iris and yellow daisies.

Diane, when I arrive at her house, is sitting on the porch in her tennis clothes, her racquet by her side. She glares when she sees me coming, but I put the flowers carefully on the ground, do a slow, deep bow, and when I stand, Diane is grinning.

"You got rid of it!" she says. "You're not wearing the hat."

I hand Diane her bouquet.

"I'm an idiot," I say. "And I'm sorry. I had a lot going on that week and I was just nuts. I don't know what I was thinking."

"*Two* bouquets?" Diane asks.

"For your grandmother," I say.

"Danny, you are too sweet," Diane says.

Then Jeffrey drives up. Diane jumps up and passes me her flowers.

"Gram's in the kitchen," she says. "Go on in. She'll love them. And would you put these in water for me?"

CHAPTER THIRTEEN

Getting resin out of my hair is not as easy as Dante has made it out to be. First, I have to beg the honey from the bees, then I have to sit in the sunniest spot outside my cave for half an hour, with the glop on my head. Which is just when Pop arrives, carrying a spikey plant with long green leaves.

"What's that crap on your head?" Pop asks. "If you're thinking it's going to make your horns grows faster, leave them alone. They're coming along fine."

"It's for my hair," I say, lying fast.

"Your hair is fine, too," Pop says. "Here, I brought you something. One of the New York City dames left it outside my door. The sweetheart-you-shouldn't-have just about killed me. I had to come up and get some sap."

"What is it?" I ask, taking the plant and sniffing.

"Pineapple," Pop says. "It's a fruit. Not from around here. This one isn't quite ready, you need to leave it in the sun for a day or two – and cut off the spikes before you eat it. Now, go wash that crap out of your hair. I gotta get to the pool."

Getting the resin out of my hair is misery. The honey isn't enough. I have to wash it two more times with soapwort and even so, some hair sticks to my horns. It also seems to have made my scalp itchy. And where did all that get me? Diane is still with Jeffrey.

I'm bummed, I need something sweet. There's a stand of raspberry bushes at the base of Belleayre Mountain, near where Thor lives, that's particularly thick. I'm making my way there, wondering if there's some other way to hide my horns and what Diane could see in an idiot like Jeffrey, when I smell humans making love. The woman's scent is not as strong as the girl at the tennis court but there's no mistaking it. I also smell satyr.

Thor appears, grabs me and pulls me down.

"Ssshhh," he says. "There's two of them."

He points through the branches of a tree to a pair of naked humans. I can't believe, at this distance, I didn't smell them sooner.

"I only just picked them up," I whisper.

"It's the guy's aftershave," Thor says. "Spruce. He must put it on with a pail. I almost tripped over him."

I look through the bushes.

A young woman, plump and fragrant as a rising loaf of bread, is in a naked embrace with a man. Nymphs are voluptuous, but one never finds the abundance of flesh of this beautiful girl. Her belly is a pillowy mound, her thighs, delectable. Her pinkening skin reminds me of the blush rose, *Cuisse de Nymphe*, Nymph's Thigh. I also find her scent, which reminds me of egg challah, delicious.

The man has a narrow waist and wide shoulders. His back, I am pleased to see, for I have taken an instant dislike to him, has a spray of pimples, an unsightly human disease which thank the gods satyrs are immune to.

Human males have a limited understanding of sensuality, but this guy is so primitive and selfish, it's disturbing. I've seen more consideration of the female from barnyard bulls.

"This is painful," I whisper to Thor.

"Yeah," Thor says. "But it'll be over in a few minutes."

It's more like one.

The man's ass humps one, two, three times, then he lets his full weight collapse on the girl. He doesn't even support his upper body with his elbows; he just falls. I poke Thor with my elbow. He shrugs like he's seen it before. The man lies there, inert. I wouldn't believe it if I weren't seeing it with my own eyes – this low-life has actually fallen asleep on a lady. The woman nudges him.

"Can't breathe," she manages to say.

The guy rolls over on his back and says nothing.

The stupidest satyr knows that tenderness after satisfaction is even more important than tenderness before. A satyr never leaves a nymph until she is glowing in his words.

Holding you is like swimming in silk. You have made this the most wonderful day of my life. Swear to me you will come to me tonight in my dreams.

I can see, as the woman pulls her pink panties over the sweet mound of her belly, that although she is trying to behave as if everything is fine, she is hungering for the words. She's lingering, waiting.

The man reaches for his cigarettes, lights up, and finally speaks.

"You know, Rochelle," he says, "If you lost ten pounds, you'd be perfect."

The woman looks as if someone had slapped her. Then, instead of lobbing a rock at the creep, she pretends she is not hurt.

"I've got to get back, Tom, my mother will be waiting," she says and hurries off, down the mountain in the direction of the little town of Pine Hill.

The creep finishes his cigarette, gets dressed, and leaves.

Thor and I are both upset.

"Did you hear what that guy said?" I say, as we head up the mountain.

"Un-fuckin'-believable," Thor says. "I've seen this guy around. He's a lifeguard at the lake, down in Pine Hill. She's in the bungalow colony next door to the butcher."

Thor may be a daredevil, walking the chair lift cable, doing pull-ups at the deserted fire station on top of Belleayre, but when it comes to humans he's the most cautious satyr in the colony.

"You go into town?" I say, surprised.

"I don't, like, stroll through Main Street in the middle of the day," Thor says. " I sneak in through the woods. The butcher's wife is a fantastic baker. She makes these German chocolate cakes with pears and leaves them on the windowsill to cool. I've swiped them so often I don't know why she keeps doing it. That girl – what's her name, Rochelle? – is in the bungalow colony next door. She seems pretty down. I think she's hung up on this guy and it's bumming her out."

This story is really upsetting me.

"She needs somebody who appreciates her," I say. "Who'll make love to her and make her feel golden."

Thor laughs.

"Well, don't look at this goat," Thor says. "One of my brothers made it with a human, they took him out of a motel on a stretcher."

"That's a true story?" I say. "I didn't even know you had a brother."

"Rolf," Thor says. "He's a lot older. He runs with the Bovina colony. I think what got him in trouble was staying inside a building with her for three days. It was, like, concrete or something. Plus he jumped into her head."

"That's it!" I say. "We get into that girl's head!"

"Huh?" Thor says. "That's the most dangerous part."

"No, I don't mean really get into her head," I say. "We wait till the middle of the night when she's asleep and we stand outside her window and sing her songs about how great she is. Once she knows that, she won't bother with this guy. And if she wakes up when we're singing to her, she'll think she's dreaming."

"And when her mother wakes up and sees us, is she supposed to think she's dreaming, too?" Thor says.

"I don't know," I say. "I guess it's a dumb idea."

We're now safely back in our own turf, on the far side of Belleayre Mountain. The raspberry thickets are so dense that a deer could get stuck in them. Thor and I push in, dropping to our knees for the berries that are hidden from the birds. I snap them high on the stem, so I have the taste of bitter green leaves playing off sweet berries. This is one of my favorite things, looking out at the world through the greens and pinks of a raspberry bush. I am lost in the smell and taste of it.

Raspberries – summer in my mouth.

The scent of raspberry is suddenly more concentrated. I look up and see Thalia, her lavender hair mounded on her head. Thor sees her too and grins. I flash on what Thor said about Thalia's middle finger. What was the word Ben used? *Awkward.* Although Thor, who's got a handful of berries, doesn't seem to think so.

He and I stand.

"Ethereal Creature, good morning," Thor says, kissing Thalia's hand.

I do the same.

"Yeah, yeah, yeah," Thalia says, pretending such courtesies are not necessary, though every satyr knows they are. "Danny, something's stuck on your horns. It looks kinda like spider legs."

Damn.

"It's nothing," I say. "Have some berries."

"You mean there are some left?" Thalia teases. "You guys didn't take them all?"

"Close your eyes and open your mouth," Thor says.

He steps close to Thalia and puts the berries in her mouth, one at a time, slowly. Very suave, the Playboy Advisor would say. I'd love to try that with Diane some day. Then, because we have eaten a lot of berries, and one must always leave some for the birds, we find a patch of soft grass.

"So, what's happening?" Thor asks. "What brings you to Belleayre?"

"My sister is coming," Thalia says. "I'm meeting her."

"You've got a sister?" Thor says and I know what he's thinking: *Does she look like you? Does traveling make her horny? Does she like blue-eyed goats?"*

"Yeah, Eloise," Thalia says. "You don't want her. She's like 100 years old."

"My mother is over 100 years old," Thor says, insulted because one thing satyrs are very sensitive to is any slight to their mothers.

No nymph wants to be caught bad-mouthing a mother, either.

"I meant no disrespect to your mother," Thalia says, quickly and formally. "She is an exceptional beauty, celebrated on two continents. Eloise is just an exceptional bitch."

"Where's your sister coming from?" I ask, trying to get this away from mothers.

"Woodstock," Thalia says. "She was posing for an artist who is probably right now drinking turpentine."

I scan the sky, where a young bald eagle who's yet to attain his white head and tail feathers has been circling lazily, and see a nymph in billowing pale pink sailing towards us. Bald eagles are rare; I ate that once in a National Geographic. The young eagle, who's probably never seen such a large creature aloft, sees the nymph too. He swings over to get a closer look, hovering directly in her path.

I see Eloise's fist dart out and come down hard on the eagle's head. There's a loud squawk. The stunned bird plummets for several feet, then recovers and manages to fly away.

Eloise, her red hair fluttering, floats down to earth.

"Someone should outlaw those fucking birds," she says.

"They're endangered," I say.

"That's a beginning," Eloise says.

Thalia makes the introductions; Thor and I kiss Eloise's hand. I have never kissed the hand of a woman who's slugged a bald eagle. It's surprisingly delicate, small and very soft, with celestine crystal nails. Eloise, with her dark red hair and pale skin, is a stunning nymph, though she scares me.

Thor is having the opposite reaction. His goat is rising. I can smell it.

"Eloise, you must be beat after your trip," he says. "Would you two ladies like to hang out? I have a great German cake back at my place, made with pears and brandy. I guarantee you've never tasted anything like it."

"Oh, that would have been great," says Thalia, with what I know is genuine regret, since we're talking about pastry. "But that theater group in Dry Brook is holding auditions."

"The Ridge Players?" I ask, impressed, because while there are a lot of troupes in the mountains – satyrs have a theater tradition going back to the ancient Greeks – the Ridge Players are the most prestigious in the Catskills.

"Yeah," says Eloise. "I've had it with painters. That jerk in Woodstock painted me with three boobs. I wanted to jam his nuts up his throat."

If my balls could speak, they'd be whimpering like terrorized fox kits. I make a mental note never to provoke Eloise.

We make our goodbyes. Thor and I kneel before the ladies, give them a leg up into the breeze, and watch as they're carried away.

"Man oh man," Thor says. "What a nymph!"

Ben steps out of the woods.

"What nymph?" he says. "What did I miss?"

"Thalia's sister," I said. "Really scary."

"No," Thor says. "Really cool. Did you see the way she slugged that eagle? That is one hot chick. So, anybody want to help me out with that cake?"

We head to Thor's cave. The cake has pieces of Bartlett pear and veins of dark chocolate and is so good that even Ben, who finds food secondary to sex, is impressed.

"Poire Williams, that's the brandy," Ben says. "Where'd you get this again?"

"The butcher's wife, down in Pine Hill," Thor says.

That reminds me of the girl who looked so miserable.

"Ben," I say. "There's a human girl we have to help."

"Oh no," Ben says. "Not that again."

"No, not Diane," I say. "A girl in Pine Hill. She's in love with a man who made love to her and then told her she was fat."

Ben is disgusted.

"Humans," he says. "Just when you think you've heard everything."

"It was pretty bad," Thor says, taking another hunk of cake. "He didn't even kiss her hand when he left. He just split."

Ben nods.

"It's too bad she's not staying at your hotel, Danny," he says. "Your father could cheer her up."

This is not a picture I want to think about.

"He's way too old for her," I say.

"She's at a bungalow colony," Thor says. "It's too small for its own goat. She'd need somebody to notice her when she's in town. And I've only seen her at the lake, waiting for that creep to pay a little attention to her. Danny has this idea, we go sing to her when she's asleep. Convince her how gorgeous she is, and when she wakes up, she dumps the jerk."

"And we wake up the entire bungalow colony," Ben says. "Great idea."

"We could disguise ourselves as humans and sing under

her window," I say. "They sometimes do that. I've read about them. They're called . . . uh, troubaderos."

Ben doesn't believe me.

"Yeah," he says, "I see them all the time in Fleischmanns. They're the ones in the fur hats and the black coats, right?"

I hit him with the one thing he cannot resist.

"Oh, c'mon Ben," I say. "It's a great caper."

CHAPTER FOURTEEN

It's weird that Pop is so uptight about me being in human territory because swiping their pears, seducing their women, stealing their first barrel of May wine — just generally making mischief — is part of the satyr tradition dating back to Europe. These days it's stealing wine from a liquor store, but the idea is the same. Ben, as the best thief in our gang, is respected even by the old goats who consider him a smart ass.

Daring with women is particularly admired.

Pop has a friend named Lucian who ran off with a human the morning of her wedding. Afterward, the lady refused to go back and get married. She agreed only when Lucian promised to meet her every summer in the same spot and though the lady's hair is now white and she leans on a cane, this has gone on for fifty years.

Naturally, this caper is sung.

On the morning of her wedding day
A satyr dallied with a lady,
When he gave her all his love,
She didn't want to go back,
Go back, go back, she said she'd never go back.

The Challah Girl Caper, in my mind, is more glorious: a selfless undertaking in the name of love.

Thor, Ben, and I meet after dark in the woods on Highmount.

We're carrying ropes of fragrant flowers and we're dressed full human: jeans, T-shirts, and hats, for which I'm grateful. I've finally been able to scrub off the hair that was stuck to my horns but my scalp is still itchy. My Yankees cap is a much easier disguise.

We move quickly, behind the Grand Hotel.

Suddenly, a girl's voice, sweet but surprisingly powerful, comes booming through the trees.

"Do you think the British will give in?" she asks.

Thor, Ben, and I drop quickly to the ground.

"We'll give in first," a young man says, angrily.

The three of us exchange confused looks, then crawl on our bellies to the edge of the woods towards the voices. A beautiful blond female giant is talking to a curly haired male giant in a leather jacket. They're both tall as maples.

"Holy moly!" Thor says. "Look at the size of those guys!"

They're like the giants in the stories Pop told me when I was little, big enough to swallow us. But looking up through the trees, I see that these giants are not real. They are moving images, projected on the back of the hotel. Dozens of humans are sitting in the grass, watching them.

I've read about these things.

"It's a movie," I whisper to Thor and Ben. "A moving picture, pictures that move. They show them in a theater in Fleischmanns. I didn't know they could show them outside, too."

We look up at the images. The blond girl has such perfect hair and skin she could be a nymph, though she seems much nicer. The curly-haired guy, on the other hand, could be a real pain in the ass.

"You know," Ben says to me. "That guy looks like you. Only he's obviously about to score."

Thor is hooked.

"This is really cool," he says. "Whadaya say we stick around and watch it?"

"No way," Ben says. "I spent all afternoon getting these fucking flowers. You guys talked me into this, and we're going to do it."

We walk quickly around the hotel. I spot a delicious-looking piece of pale pink paper on the ground and read it before popping it in my mouth.

"Hey guys," I say. "They show these things every week."

"Yeah?" says Thor. "What were we watching?"

I have to wait a moment for the paper to go down.

"'Exodus,'" I say. "Produced and directed by Otto Preminger. Starring: Paul Newman, Eva Marie Saint, Jill Haworth, Sal Mineo. Photographed in Super Panavision 70. Technicolor."

We sneak through the woods around Pine Hill. It's a small village but it's rowdy. We hear carousing in Claudy's bar, where the locals drink, and German beer songs from the Pine Hill Arms Hotel. And of course, as is the case when you get close to all these towns late night in summer, we have to watch out for waiters and college girls, humping in the woods like rabbits.

"Keep your nose peeled for spruce," I tell Ben. "That lifeguard douses himself with it."

We're in town now, staying three trees back from backyards and lawns. We pass an abandoned hotel with broken windows, the sharp-peaked volunteer fire department building where a few guys are sitting out front drinking beer, and the butcher's house. I catch a sickening smell of murdered cow. There is no chocolate cake cooling on the sill. I suppose it's too late.

We arrive at the bungalow colony. There's a lot of open ground. The bungalows are identical: White buildings with peeling paint and small porches, open windows with screens.

"So which one is hers?" Ben whispers.

"I can't remember," Thor says. "They all look alike."

"Okay," Ben says, "Let's just stay low to the ground and sniff her out. What's her scent?"

"Egg challah," I say. "Seedless. With a lemony scent I've smelled on them before."

"Jean Naté," Ben says. "It's a perfume. They all use it."

We drop to our knees and creep along the grass, sniffing.

"Dachshund," I say. "Sour cream, herring, Lipton's tea."

"Boiled potatoes, pea soup, eeewww, rank," Thor says, screwing up his nose. "These people should not eat cabbage."

"Dead mouse," I say. "Two days, I'd guess."

"Can you guys shut up?" Ben says.

"I've got it!" I say, so excited I jump up and look through a kitchen window.

Then I squat down.

"No," I say, embarrassed, "That actually *was* challah."

Ben, meanwhile, is paused under another window.

"Hey, you clowns, here," he says.

We crawl over and squat, inhaling: warm, sweet, egg challah. The girl is even more delicious asleep than awake.

"Yeah," I say. "That's her."

"Okay," Ben says. "Game on."

We stand and peek in. Rochelle is asleep on her side on a narrow bed, the sheet kicked to her feet. She's wearing a sleeveless white cotton nightgown that is gathered above her breasts and is dotted with pink rosebuds. The cotton is so fine it's almost transparent. She's so beautiful that we take a moment and bow our heads.

"Thank you, great goddess Venus," we murmur.

Then Ben removes the screen.

"Can you manage her?" he asks Thor.

"Please," Thor says, insulted.

He jumps through the window into the bedroom, light as a cat. Then he scoops up the girl and passes her through the window to Ben. The girl stirs a little as Ben holds her.

"Sssh," Ben murmurs, and rubs his face very gently across hers.

"Mmm," she says, as if sampling something new and delicious, and continues sleeping.

Ben carries Rochelle into a grassy clearing in the woods and lies her down. We arrange the flowers on her shoulders and around her head so she is afloat in scent. Thor and I take out our pipes and begin to play, very softly, the Lorenz Hart song I love, "The Shortest Day of the Year."

Ben sits by Rochelle's side, stroking her fingers. Rochelle, in the first stirrings of arousal, rubs one thigh against the other. Flowers and songs of love and the adoration of satyrs on a summer night – this will work. She will wake up a goddess.

I smell goat.

Not an old goat like Pop but a goat who's older than us and who's slipped up beside me. I turn my head. The satyr beside me is an older, more muscular version of Thor, with the same sky-blue eyes, except that his horns are longer and darker. He's also the best-looking satyr I have ever seen, a satyr absolutely at the top of his game.

"Oh boys," he says. "You are so out of your league."

We stop playing.

"Rolf?" Thor whispers. "What are you doing here?"

"It's summer," Rolf says, keeping his voice low, too. "What the fuck do you think I'm doing here?"

"You're still doing humans?" Thor asks.

Rochelle stirs.

Rolf bends down next to her.

"You're dreaming, in a field of flowers," Rolf says, "And four satyrs surround you, drinking in your beauty."

I thought Ben was good, but this guy's voice is so cognac-velvet smooth, I'm almost ready to change teams.

"A human almost killed you," Thor whispers to Rolf, pissed. "Now you're bird-dogging on *our* turf?"

Ben is still stroking Rochelle's fingers.

"Guys," he whispers, "Can you take it the fuck somewhere else?"

Thor and Rolf step back into the woods. I resume playing, though I can still hear most of what they're saying.

" . . . so, I guess it built up my resistance," Rolf is saying. " . . . there are so many more hotels here. And now I got this thing going with the butcher's wife. When she's in the mood, she leaves a cake on the windowsill. But I think she's losing interest because lately, they're not around . . . "

Thor says nothing. I know he's toying with the idea of letting his older brother think he's lost his touch.

"I was eating them," Thor says, finally.

There's another pause as Rolf thinks about it.

"Well," Rolf says. "They are great cakes."

"It's that pear brandy," Thor says.

Ben is now stroking the back of Rochelle's hand. I've moved on to another song, "I'll Buy You A Star," by the esteemed Dorothy Fields and Arthur Schwartz. You can't do right by a love song without giving it your full attention, and this one is one of my favorites. I'm playing to heal Rochelle, to help her move through summer with the confidence of someone who knows she is deserving of love, but I'm also hoping a night breeze will lift the song up the mountain to Diane.

Ben sings:

I'll buy you a star, not just a star,
But the best one in the sky.
You'll have a cloud to sleep on.
A cloud as light as an angel's sigh . . .

Thor and Rolf, who seem to have reached some kind of agreement, walk out of the woods. Rolf leans down and picks up Rochelle, who stirs in her sleep. I may never have heard the voice of a woman in love, but I recognize it now.

"Tom," she murmurs.

Damn. That lifeguard. This was not the result we expected.

Rolf carries Rochelle back to her cottage. Thor jumps into her bedroom. I lift Rochelle's hand and kiss her fingertips.

Ben sighs and does the same. Rolf gently passes Rochelle through the window to his brother, who puts her back in bed, covers her, bows his head respectfully, and leaves.

We quietly pad away.

"You get it, guys?" Rolf says. "She's in love with that jerk. You can sing her songs and try to convince her she deserves better till your horns droop – she's so hung up on that guy she's locked anybody else out. Breaking that spell is *not* gonna be easy. You guys better go back to your little flutes. You're nowhere near ready for humans."

We hang our heads and say nothing because when a senior goat is chewing you out, there's nothing to do but take it.

A new, wonderful smell floats by: freshly baked cake, warm pears, and chocolate.

We turn to the house next door. A window is open and a cake is cooling on the sill.

Rolf grins.

"Gentlemen, that's my cue," he says. "You can have the cake."

He disappears.

I grab the warm cake and we head back into the woods, dispatching it before it even has time to cool and washing it down with sparkling spring water.

"That really is one fine cake," Ben says. "Now where do you think we can find this Eloise?"

CHAPTER FIFTEEN

I guess I should talk about orgies. There are a lot of stories about satyrs that are nonsense, like we can't read or that we have horse's ears or the lower bodies of goats. But taking part in what humans call orgies is a cornerstone of our culture.

We would never, of course, use the word "orgy," which suggests indiscriminate debauchery. We call it "Celebration" and though I hate to get all religious, it's a form of prayer, an appreciation of summer and the privilege of being a sentient creature who can choose what to do with his or her life.

It's not entirely sexual, either. Celebration starts with good company and food. It may follow an event, like the theater, or it may be the event itself. Unlike Venerable Mother's Day, it does not require a showy spread. The food can be simple, though it must be of quality: cheese and fruit and nuts and of course, wine. Wine is a sacrament. You gather in a beautiful glade, you drink and talk, taking care to truly appreciate the pleasure of fellowship and savor the food and feel the music. And to exult in the body, of course. Celebrations are a place where Displaying and preening are expected. Then the caressing begins. That, to tell you the truth, is as far as I have ever gotten.

In my second summer, when a satyr is first permitted to attend Celebrations, I lay beside a nymph named Galatea. She was a pastel nymph, with blue-gray eyes and pink crystal fingernails, so delicate she was practically a breeze. I offered her a purple fig and was charmed by the graceful way she peeled it apart, exposing its pink flesh.

I lay with her a long time, stroking her arm with my finger tips, finally getting up the nerve to kiss her mouth, which tasted of figs and spicy Canadice grapes. She was fragrant and sweet, and her crystal fingernails scattered lights about us, like pink fireflies. I was not surprised when Mario came over and bowed to her, then me, and asked if he might join us. Galatea purred and stretched, kissing me first, then turning to Mario and kissing him.

I thought of Gatsby and Daisy. Would Gatsby have lain in the grass with Daisy and her husband, waiting his turn? Would he have invited them both to his bedroom to show them his shirts?

It's true that group love is not required in Celebrations. Couples often content themselves with one another, but if a second or third satyr asks to join and a nymph is interested, it's wrong to refuse. And community worship binds a colony together.

Still, after Mario joined us, my interest faded. When Galatea moved my hand to her belly, I stroked her only for the half an hour courtesy required, then kissed her hand and face, and withdrew.

Galatea, after that evening, moved on to another colony, as nymphs will. I never saw her again, but I dreamed often of her through the winter sleep. In the dream, my fingers had drifted below her belly and were caressing her. Then I forgot all about her pleasure and was lost in my own, humping like a beast. I will certainly not act that way when my time with a nymph finally comes.

Now, the first Celebration of the season is coming up. It will take place right after the Ridge Players' new show. I'm not sure what to do.

It feels like it would be wrong to make love to anyone else when the only woman I want to make love to is Diane, but when I see a woman like Rochelle, it's as if my dick has a mind of its own. Like my dick is saying, "Yeah, yeah, but what about *me*, Danny? A dick has needs too."

My motives were pure the night we went to Rochelle, I only wanted to give her confidence, but when I saw the outline of her body in that see-through nightgown, all sense of decency evaporated: I wanted to jump on top of her and hump her like a bear.

The arguments with Ben may be wearing me down, too.

"It is *not* disrespectful to make love to a woman when you are hung up on another woman," Ben says. "It's only disrespectful if you don't give that woman your full attention. Or shout out the other woman's name."

I'm horrified.

"That happens?" I ask.

"No, of course not," Ben says. "It's rural legend. Nobody would ever do that. But I'll tell you what is true: if you don't start fucking, you're going against everything it means to be a satyr. We've got health and mountains and food and sun and nymphs — *nymphs*, Danny, the most beautiful women in the world. You're pissing on that. It doesn't take away your feelings for Diane if you make love to a nymph. You've got to get started, already."

The decision's got me going in circles. I head up to Crump's Castle to think about it and spot Thalia, half a field away. I have a feeling she nests near here, but nymphs usually veil their lairs, rendering them invisible, and it is presumptuous to ask. Thalia is sitting against a stone fence with a book of some sort, so absorbed in what she is doing she doesn't notice me. It looks like she is sketching, but when I get closer, I see I'm mistaken. I'm so surprised, I forget to even greet her properly.

"Thalia," I say. "You can write!"

Thalia flips her book closed, offended, and sticks out her hand for me to kiss like it's a command.

"Of course I can write," Thalia says. "We're not all air-heads."

"No, no, of course not," I say. "I just didn't know. May I sit with you?"

Thalia, still peeved, nods.

"So what were you writing?" I ask.

"I was just playing around with something," Thalia says.

"Oh, c'mon, show me," I say. "I write too, you know."

"No, no," Thalia says. "It's not finished. I don't like people seeing things till they're finished."

"Well tell me what you're working on, at least," I say.

"It's the Greek chorus, for the new show," Thalia says. "I wasn't sure whether to write it for a split chorus of men and women like in "Lysistrata," where it makes sense, because there it's men versus women, or do a single chorus like in "Oedipus the King." I re-read "Lysistrata" in the original Greek, to see how it played. Then, halfway through I decided the hell with it, who cares what they did in 400 B.C., this is my take. What's the point of writing if you can't do your own thing?"

I'm so flabbergasted I don't know what to say. I've never known a nymph who reads, let alone in another language. Literacy, for most nymphs, is looking at a magazine cover.

Thalia mistakes my silence.

"Sorry," she says. "I get obsessed. I haven't even told you what the show is about."

The whole mountain knows what the show is about. Ridge Player productions are a highlight of summer.

"The Goddess Marilyn and the human warrior king, J.F.K.," I say. "He was dipped into a tub of money at birth, making him impervious to poverty."

Thalia is pleased.

"You know the legend," she says.

I laugh. Even though it is rare for satyrs to read newspapers, J.F.K. and the Goddess Marilyn are so fabled their deeds were carried on the wind.

"Well, sure I know the legend," I say. "J.F.K. was an arrogant king, the Goddess Marilyn took on human form to humble him."

"This piece goes even further," Thalia says. "I don't want to ruin it for you, but it goes into J.F.K.'s treachery. It's shocking, really."

I'm remembering Thalia's beautiful voice.

"And you'll be in it," I say. "You'll be singing. Who do you play?"

Thalia looks annoyed. I've said the wrong thing again.

"I'm playing that frumpy cow, Jackie, the comic relief," Thalia says. "And I won't be singing. The director said my voice was too big for the part – too, get this, *operatic*. Three guesses who planted that idea."

I flash on Eloise slamming the eagle on the head.

"Your sister," I say.

Thalia nods.

"The humans consider Jackie beautiful," I say, trying to make Thalia feel better.

"Exactly, the humans!" Thalia says. "Their women are grotesque. You know their toenails are body waste? That's why they paint them, to cover them up. Why the Goddess Marilyn took human form, I don't know. I guess it was her idea of a joke. And naturally, Eloise, who hasn't acted in decades, gets to play her."

That really surprises me.

"Eloise?" I say. "But the Goddess Marilyn was a blond."

"You ever hear of peroxide?" Thalia says.

"No," I say.

A few days later, in early evening, I head to the performance with Thor, Ben, and Glynnis, whose jewelry collection has expanded to include diamond earrings, several rings, and an emerald pin in her wild red hair. It makes me glad I like a nymph whose indulgence is pastry.

The theater is in the Dry Brook Ridge Wild Forest, which has an altitude of 3,500 feet. Humans, who never come here at night, have to take an old logging road up Pakatakan Mountain, then follow several miles of trail to the summit. We just take the direct path southwest through the woods, which takes us to the hill overlooking the amphitheater.

The word of mouth on this show has been great. I see a lot of familiar faces, including George, which surprises me – I've never thought of him as a theater-lover. The audience is excited and well prepared, with baskets of ripe, red tomatoes. There is no lumpen human clothing or disguise tonight. Satyrs take care to look their best for the theater, bathing in minted ponds, oiling our hooves and horns, wearing our most artfully woven flowers. I spent the afternoon weaving myself a yellow crown: buttercup, yellow hawkweed, the delicate cream and yellow blossom, butter-and-eggs, and black-eyed susan.

Seating is by rank, which means the younger you are, the further away you are. Still, we manage to find a good spot two-thirds of the way up the hill. That's where we're sitting when I see Melena and Pop, heading to a section near the stage. They are wearing identical crowns of blood-red roses, which is about as obvious as you can get. I'm stunned. I had no idea anything was going on between them.

I nudge Ben.

"Yeah, I know," he says. "Who do you think your father told to snag a bottle of Rémy for him this morning?"

"You're not bothered?" I whisper.

Ben laughs.

"Oh, Danny," he says. "Sometimes I wonder if you're a satyr or an over-grown cupid."

Okay, so I do find it awkward that my father and best friend are making it with the same nymph. What makes it even weirder is that Pop and Melena are one of those couples who radiate such sexuality, you can't *not* picture them doing it. And it's obvious, from the way they act with one another, they do it every chance they get. Melena casually adjusts Pop's crown; when they sit down, he settles her silks about her and gives her a little nip on her bare shoulder. It's embarrassing. It's also odd to me that Melena is still here while the other mothers have moved on.

I don't have time to think about it, though, because the play begins. Drums pound and the Greek chorus takes the stage, with a wry warning I'm sure was written by Thalia.

Dreary 'tis, to be a human,
Clouds of death forever looming.
Still, if doomed to such you be,
Try to be a Kennedy.

J.F.K., played by Rolf, enters, wearing a huge fake phallus over a dark suit.

"I have just increased the American presence in Vietnam and I have a terrible headache, no doubt because I have not had sex today," Rolf says. "What? Is it 10 a.m. already?"

There's a lot of raucous cheering and foot-stomping for the dazzling nymphs who play the film stars, secretaries, and friends' wives with whom J.F.K. has sex. And though Thalia was disappointed to be playing the flat-chested killjoy Jackie, you can't tell it from her performance. She's terrific. Her curves have been hidden in boxy suits, she wears absurd, round little hats which perch precariously on her head, but I can't take my eyes off her. She's adorable. And she's funny. She hectors J.F.K., often in the *double entendres* popular in classic theater.

"My husband, it is said you visit hotels and leave by little-used passages – and enter that way too," Jackie says. "I tremble to ask, but — are you bedding other women?"

"Beloved wife, how could you entertain such thoughts?" asks J.F.K., as a naked secretary, hidden from Jackie's sight, pops out from behind his desk and waves at the audience, who roar and cheer. I am probably the only one who feels bad for Jackie but I laugh with the others.

The Greek chorus chants a warning:

History, alas, doth show.
Wives are always last to know.
If there is a next time, honey,
Forfeit love and go for money.

The star of the show is Eloise as the Goddess Marilyn. When she steps on stage in a skin-tight, sequined dress to sing Happy Birthday to J.F.K., her body is so magnificent the crowd gasps. Eloise takes a deep bow. There is a loud rip. Eloise puts a hand to her mouth, feigns surprise, and turns around, looking over her shoulder. Her dress is ripped open, exposing her bare ass. This audience is no stranger to fantastic butts, but Eloise's ass is so gloriously pneumatic she should be aloft. Eloise, who knows exactly what she's bringing to the party, wiggles playfully.

"Oh, no," she says. "This is *so* embarrassing. Are we too late for the 11 o'clock news?"

Dante, playing a costume assistant, rushes on stage and sews the gown closed. Eloise turns back to the audience, where J.F.K. is now seated, and does a breathy version of "Happy Birthday." She isn't much of a singer, but, at the risk of being sacrilegious, neither, it is said, was the Goddess Marilyn. When Eloise sings, "Thanks, Mr. President," J.F.K.'s fake dick pops straight up and the audience roars again.

The chemistry between Eloise and Rolf, who's got to be the hottest satyr on the mountain, is tremendous. Eloise, though I hate to admit it, is an excellent actress. At the close of the show, the Goddess Marilyn is found dead in her bedroom, poisoned by the dark sorcerer Nembutal, who may be in alliance with the ambitious Kennedys. As J.F.K. and his younger brother R.F.K. stand over her body, even tough old goats are moved as J.F.K., who still loves the Goddess, makes his goodbye:

Oh, those knockers, oh, that butt,
N'er will I forget this spot.
Did we get all the evidence, Bobby?

The cast takes three bows before ceding the stage to Eloise, who deftly catches the tomatoes that are tossed at her, and at her last bow, takes a big bite and grins. The satyrs yell and stamp their hooves, the nymphs are cheering.

The Champagne is opened. There is a crowd around Eloise and Rolf, but I am happy to leave the stars to others. I feel awkward saying hello to Pop when he's here with Melena, but it would be ridiculous to pretend not to see them. I find them, bow my head respectfully to Pop as we're out among the colony and kiss Melena's hand. Then I move on.

I congratulate Dante, then Thalia. She has changed back into a short gown but is still wearing the funny little hat. She's enchanting.

"You were wonderful," I tell her. "You have a gift for comedy. And the stuff you wrote for the chorus was really funny."

"Thank you, Danny," she says and kisses me. On the cheek, but it's a start.

It's a mid-summer night. The radiant moon emerges. The older goats and nymphs go off to their celebrations and the younger crowd begins ours, opening our packs of cheese and wine and sweets, sitting about the fire.

I've brought a special treat which I'm betting Thalia will love. It has to be prepared properly, but I'm confident I know how.

I tell everyone to grab a sharp stick, then bring out a box of graham crackers and stacks of Hershey's candy bars and pass them around. Then I break up the chocolate and stack it on the crackers. I'm usually comfortable as the center of attention only when I'm playing my flute, but I find I'm enjoying this. Maybe my gift is dessert.

"Now here's the secret ingredient," I say, bringing out two big bags and passing them around. "Marshmallows. You skewer the marshmallow on a stick. Okay, everybody got one? You put it in the fire, you can even let it catch fire. You wait for them to do this. . . . "

The marshmallow shapeshifts, melting, blackening, and bubbling.

There are appreciative murmurs from the crowd. Ben is smiling and giving me a 'Go get 'em' look.

"Then you do this," I say, putting the marshmallow between the chocolate and graham crackers and pressing it into a sandwich.

I present the gooey sandwich to Thalia. She takes a bite and grins.

"Oh my gods!" she says. "This is fantastic. The marsh stuff melts the chocolate and glops it all together. It's great!"

"It's a sacred Boy Scout food," I say. "They take it together as communion."

"Oh, Danny, you are so sophisticated!" Thalia says.

I sit together with my friends, eating sacred Scout food, happy, laughing. The fires are dying.

Ben moves close to Glynnis and whispers something. Then he slowly traces the outline of Glynnis' lips with his finger, an ancient homage, and kisses her cheeks and her forehead. They lie down together. Glynnis strokes one of his horns. Across the clearing, I see the auras of satyrs and nymphs embracing, halos of electric blues and pinks are rising from individual bodies and blending. The glen will soon be illuminated in the pink and violet fog of summer love. Later tonight, the glowing purple haze will rise over the mountain. Humans, if they spot it, will swear they have seen an unidentified flying object from outer space.

I turn to Thalia. She has a tiny piece of graham cracker in the corner of her mouth. I lean over and lick it off. Then I kiss her mouth. She tastes of chocolate and marshmallow. I lift her fingers to my mouth and kiss them.

"Ethereal Creature," I say. "It's an evening in summer. Make it perfect. Be with me."

Thalia smiles.

"Well," she says, "It *is* an evening in summer, made for our delight."

I know community is important, but I don't want to be quite so close to everyone my first time.

I stand and hold out my hand to Thalia and we look for a spot away from the crowd. There's a large spread of thick moss, so soft and inviting that the gods must have thrown it there just for us. We sit down. I can hear two pipes playing in the distance. The evening is just as I have dreamed.

"Take off your gown and let me look at you, Thalia," I say. "I've been aching to all night."

I can hear my voice tremble, but it's a pretty good imitation of confident.

Thalia smiles, gets up, and slowly pulls the gown over her head. She stands in the moonlight, naked. There are so many beautiful curves, I don't know what to exult in first: her plump thighs. The little space between the top of her legs and her flower. The breasts which bow slightly, then rise. The wonderful raspberry nipples I tasted in what seems a lifetime ago.

"Oh, Thalia, you're so beautiful, I don't know where to start," I say.

Thalia smiles and turns around.

There are two diagonal ridges beneath her shoulder blades, the vestigial fragments of wings, and two dimples above her ass.

I don't think I've ever been this hard. I know this is supposed to be a time of praise, but Thalia's beauty has made me stupid.

"Oh, Thalia," I say.

The lust is so thick in me, I would love to throw her on her back and just fuck her. It's taking all of my strength to remember I am not a beast but a satyr and this is a holy night. I kneel and kiss one dimple, then another. Thalia trembles. I lightly run my fingers down the outside of her hips. Thalia turns. I kiss her belly and stroke her hips, then pull her down beside me, adoring, stroking.

How long this goes on I do not know. I've slipped into another world, where everything is silk and fragrance. I brush my fingers across her breasts. Thalia sighs and moves my hand lower. I caress her, taking my cues from her response.

Thalia lifts her face to me and kisses me.

There's a sound like thunder and a flash of white light and suddenly, everything changes.

It's like in times past, when a lady kissed a frog and he changed into a prince. Only now what's changed is that the light is noon bright, it's daytime, and I'm on the hill at Crump's Castle. And the woman kissing me is Diane.

It's an apparition, frozen like a mirror over my head. Thalia sees it also. We both stare. The vision hangs over us a few seconds, then, tinkling like glass, breaks into little pieces and disappears. I'm too shocked to say anything and so is Thalia.

"Oh gods," Thalia says, finally. "I've never seen one of those. And that girl with you— she was *human*. Her nose was enormous."

It would be stupid to deny it. I have insulted a nymph in a way I didn't even know was possible. All feelings of love and glorification are gone. I'm lying next to Thalia at a Celebration, totally limp. I can see from her expression that I've hurt her horribly. I feel like such a creep I can't even speak.

"First I have to play that cow Jackie and I don't get to sing, then a satyr lays with me and dreams of a human," Thalia says. "This isn't my night."

She looks around.

"You think anyone else saw?" she asks. "If anyone else saw, I'll never live this down."

I look around the clearing. The halos of purples and pinks are so fog-thick I can't even make out the outlines of bodies.

"I don't think so," I say. "The purples are really dense. I'm sorry, Thalia, I can't tell you how sorry I am. You're so beautiful. And I really like you —"

Thalia gets up, furious, and pulls on her gown.

"Yeah, right," she says. "You liked me so much you wanted to make it with that ugly cow."

I get up.

"Thalia," I say. "You're the coolest nymph I've ever met. You saw how much I wanted you. Please don't go. Please."

Thalia is still mad, but she sits down, crossing her arms, glaring at me.

"Thalia, you're the most beautiful, intelligent, interesting nymph I've ever met," I say. "You read, you write, you sing, you're funny. Nobody comes near you."

Thalia looks away from me, into the distance.

"Please, Thalia, say something," I say.

"Ok," Thalia says, finally. "Let's say I believe you wanted me. I still want to know what's going on. Satyrs fuck humans, the lure of the mud, that's known, you all do it. But to think about one woman when you're making love to another, when you're making love to *me* . . . that's just fucked up."

I don't know why, but I feel I can tell Thalia the truth. I owe her that, anyway.

"The beginning of this summer, a human girl – the one you just saw – fell down my mountain and I haven't been able to get her out of my head," I say.

Thalia is stunned.

"That cow?" she says. "You're hung up on *that*? And you're seeing her even when you're with other girls?"

There's no going back now. Thalia's probably heard the rumors anyway.

"I haven't actually been with any others," I say. "You're the first."

Thalia is quiet for a few moments.

"You know, I heard that, but I didn't believe it," Thalia says. "It sure didn't seem like that before. Now it makes sense. She's a witch. She only wants you to lay with her."

"I haven't actually been with her either," I say.

"*What?*" Thalia says.

"Oh, gods, Thalia," I say. "Do I have to keep saying it? I've never done it with anyone. No nymphs, no humans. Nobody."

"She put a spell on you," Thalia says, firmly.

I need to get this conversation over with.

"Not in the way you mean, but yes," I say. "Listen, Thalia, can you do me a favor and not tell anyone about this? Any of it?"

Thalia puts her arms around me.

"Sure, Danny," she says. "It will be our secret. Don't be too upset about the spell. There's got to be some way to break it."

CHAPTER SIXTEEN

It's a nice idea, that I'm going to pull off this trick and take my place among the community as a lover who can turn the night sky pink. But I sense, pretty early, this ruse hasn't worked. Thalia and I lay together among the others through the night, taking care not to leave too soon so no one suspects anything. But when the sun starts streaking the sky and the party breaks up, I can sense something is off.

Mario, from the Di Benedetto farm, who has been making his farewell to the two nymphs he has spent the night with, glances at me, looks embarrassed, then turns quickly away. One of the nymphs he's been with whispers something to her friend, who smirks, then nods, as if she is not surprised.

When I get back to the cave and finally fall asleep, I have a horrible dream: I'm at the Celebration, holding my hand out to Thalia, who smiles at me. But then Thalia turns into Eloise, who steps forward in a nasty, aggressive way and forces her tongue into my mouth and when she does, my horns fall off. I snatch them up off the ground and try to stick them back on my head, but there's dirt on the bottom and they won't stick and the whole colony has seen it and they're looking at me and whispering.

Midday, after I've finally fallen asleep, Ben bursts in.

"Let me see it!" he hollers. "There's a story going around that you couldn't get it up. One goat told me somebody put a curse on you and your dick shrank to the size of a rabbit's."

I yank my blanket up to my neck.

"Go away!" I yell.

Ben walks over and grabs the blanket. I give him a strong kick in the hip which knocks him onto his ass, which is terrifically satisfying. Then I stand up, throw off the blanket and, with as much dignity as a satyr who's been humiliated from Greene County to Delaware can muster, manage to Display.

Ben, rubbing his hip, checks me out.

"Looks fine to me," Ben says. "So, what happened?"

"What half the colony saw happen, apparently," I say, sitting back on the bed. "I was making it with Thalia –I mean, I was starting to make it with Thalia. Everything was good, great, actually. Then this apparition of Diane pops up. That's it. Party over. Done."

The reality of this –that everybody's heard I couldn't make love at a Celebration – is sinking in.

"Does everybody know?" I ask.

"Truth?" Ben says. "Eloise and Thor were maybe ten feet away from you. And you know how she talks. So yeah, it's out there. The nymphs are saying you just couldn't get it up, the guys are saying you were cursed by a human. Cursed is better. Makes you more interesting."

Something awful occurs to me.

"Do you think Pop knows?" I ask.

"No, of course not," Ben says. "Nobody tells the old goats anything. But otherwise – it's pretty much all over."

I've been humiliated before in my life. I was pummeled by Nico and George when I was little, I was the last one chosen for running and discus as a kid, I was the only goat without someone to tell me how beautiful I was on Venerable Mother's Day – that was the worst, until now. Now I am a satyr who was unable to make love. And everybody knows.

"This just sucks, Ben," I say. "I can't go out there with everybody talking about me."

"Yup," Ben says, "That's exactly what you *are* going to do. You're going to get out there and strut around like being cursed is the best thing that could happen – you've gotta be a pretty great catch to make a human so jealous she puts a curse on you, right? Then you're going to fix it. The problem is this Diane. She's got power I didn't know they had. You've got to go back to Thalia and try it again. She likes you, if you get into trouble, she'll help. Nymphs know all kinds of tricks."

"No," I say. "I'm not going to do that. I'm not going to use Thalia that way. Diane didn't curse me. That vision came out of *my* head. It happened because I was with the wrong girl. I'm going after Diane."

I scrub myself raw and smear some of the revolting pine sap gunk into my hair. I put on my nicest polo shirt and chinos and cover my hooves with two pairs of socks and stuff them into my sneakers. Then I cut over the mountain to Highmount, taking a route the guys avoid because there's a crazy human in a trailer up there with an even crazier dog.

There's also, I have forgotten, an excellent black huckleberry patch, which is where I run into Thor. He takes it all in:

my human clothes, my emasculating, gunked-up, horn-covering hair. He even sneaks a quick look at my crotch. I know exactly what he's thinking.

The poor sap is going over to see that human. With what's left of his dick.

We stand there awkwardly.

"Look, Thor," I say. "I know there's some weird stories going around, but none of it is true."

"They're not the size of a rat's?" Thor says.

"Now it's a rat?" I say. "This story gets worse and worse. Listen: *nothing* happened to my dick."

"I heard it was your balls," Thor says.

"Nothing happened to my dick, nothing happened to my balls," I say. "You want me to show you?"

"No, man, of course not," Thor says, which even I can tell means, "Absolutely. Because right now your credibility is shit."

I unzip the stupid chinos, whip it out and Display.

"There," I say. "You satisfied?"

Thor nods, embarrassed. I quickly tuck the goods away.

"So she just put the other kind of curse on you, where you can't get it up?" he asks.

There's nothing to do but go with it.

"Yeah," I say. "And now I'm going over to her place and make her take it back."

Thor punches me in the shoulder, which must be another dumb thing he picked up from skiers. How, when he's in a cave halfway down the mountain, I have no idea. Maybe shoulder-whacking reverberates through the earth the same way as words.

"Good for you, man," Thor says.

Right, I'm Ulysses on the hero's journey. Just toss in a six-headed serpent. And keep it away from my crotch.

I don't know exactly what I'm going to say when I get to Diane's, but according to Playboy, success with human women has more to do with action than words. You have to project strength and confidence. But weirdly, when I get to Diane's, I find her sitting on her porch, so relieved to see me she jumps to her feet.

"Danny, thank God!" she says.

Huh? What?

"You have *got* to give me a phone number so I can reach you," Diane says. "Listen to this: Rico Valdez and Yvonne Rio are coming to the Takanassee. One night only. I can't believe it. Jeffrey is working that night, and I really want to go. No funny business. We do this as *friends*, okay?"

An evening with Diane and *she's* the one asking? But cool, gotta be cool . . .

"Well, I have to make sure I'm not working that night," I say. "But sure. I'd love to help you out."

I'm also surprised that Diane is interested in Rico Valdez. Valdez is nothing like Bob Dylan. He's a Latin musician. The Maplewood House plays a lot of his stuff, mambo and cha-cha, which, for some reason, is very big with the Jews.

I also read a Life magazine story about Valdez and Yvonne Rio, who is his wife. Valdez is a fat, old guy who conducts his band while holding a chihuahua – this might be a mambo thing. Yvonne Rio, who was wearing a low-cut gown in the pictures and looked much younger than her husband, is the singer in his band. I was going to eat the magazine – if you get them fresh, glossy magazines are very crunchy – but Yvonne Rio was so beautiful, I decided to save it. She had a body that was more dramatic than any nymph's: her breasts were very large, but jutted so straight out it was like two invisible elves were holding them up. Her ass stuck out the same way. If you were with Yvonne Rio, I don't know how you'd decide what to go for first. It would be like deciding between cheesecake and ice cream. I'd love to see her in the flesh.

But for Diane, Rico Valdez seems wrong.

"You're talking about the mambo guy with the dog, right?" I say.

"Oh, he's an idiot," Diane says. "But it's a chance to get dressed up. And I love dancing to that stuff. My father taught me to cha-cha when I was a kid. You dance Latin, right?"

Dancing is a feminine grace. No satyr would emasculate himself by waggling his ass around.

"Latin?" I say. "Are you kidding? I grew up with it."

Nymphs dance, satyrs admire their dancing and when a satyr takes a woman in his arms it is to make love to her.

For humans, as Pop has explained to me, dancing is an extension of their copulation; they dance and later that evening, they make love. Since human men are unable to sustain the act for any period of time, sometimes finishing in as little as fifteen minutes, this faux copulation is necessary. Otherwise, you would have dissatisfied women saying, "Is that all there is?" all over the mountains. Dancing brings women to a state of high arousal; it is foreplay. And if I brought Diane to that state, well, it's obvious – she would have to have me.

I need dance lessons and I need them fast. The place to get them is The Mambo Shack, down at the hotel. I just have to make sure Pop isn't around.

I check out the pool. There's no sign of Pop, but I see Noah, dozing in the sun, talking to himself.

"Sweetheart, please, let an old man sleep," he's muttering.

"Noah!" I say. "It's me, Danny."

Noah sits up and looks around, then comes over.

"If you're looking for your father, I haven't seen him for two days," he says. "I think Lucille Mandelbaum has him chained to her bed."

I can never keep Pop's women straight.

"Is she the one who's married to a rabbi?" I ask.

"No, she's the one whose husband mysteriously disappeared on a cruise when she shoved him off their balcony," Noah says. "I guess you don't read *The Daily News* up here."

I think I know who he's talking about: Scary Makeup. I've read about women who murder their husbands in detective books.

"The one with the green eye shadow?" I ask. "She really killed her husband? What's she doing up here?"

"She had a smart press agent who told her to go where nobody would find her," Noah says. "And you don't say 'killed' when somebody beats the rap."

"What do you say?" I ask.

"Nothing," Noah says.

I sneak through the woods to The Mambo Shack and look through the window. No guests are inside, they're probably too bloated from lunch to move. Ricardo, the fake Cuban instructor, isn't there either. He's probably off somewhere making love to a guest or, as I once heard him refer to it, doing her "the big favor." But his partner Lucia is there, reading The New York Herald Tribune. We don't see that newspaper much up here, but I ate one once and it was much tastier than The New York Times.

I've never gotten a close look at Lucia. I've never seen a real Cuban either, but I know from Life Magazine they are good-looking and dark-haired. And if they don't like their President, they pick up rifles and chase him out of the palace. Then they dance in the street. They are a very passionate people.

Based strictly on looks, Lucia seems to be an excellent fake. Her hair is short and black and curly, her lipstick is bright red, and she is wearing tight pedal pushers and a top that leaves her middle bare. Women dance instructors don't mess around with the guests like the male instructors, but I can see how Lucia could sell a lot of lessons. I'm also wondering if her flower is as dark as the hair on her head. While I'm thinking about this, Lucia spots me and walks over to the window.

"C'mon in," she says.

I'm suddenly afraid this is a terrible idea. But if I can pass with Diane, I guess I can pass with Lucia.

"Are you related to Jake?" Lucia asks. "You look just like him."

That throws me.

"Yeah," I say. "But could you not tell him?"

"He thinks dancing is for sissies, huh?" Lucia says.

She walks to the window and pulls down the shade.

"My lips are sealed," Lucia says. "Just one thing you should know about dancing."

"Yes?" I ask.

"You're going to have to stand close enough to touch me."

Lucia smells like the gardenias Ben swiped at the beginning of summer. My hooves might be stuck to the floor, but the moment Lucia puts my hand on her waist, my dick returns to life. Great timing there, pal. I force myself to concentrate on what Lucia is saying: the man leads, take small steps, wait a few beats before you start and feel the music. I thought I was part of the music when I played my flute, but dancing, I feel it from my horns to my hooves. And I have a lady in my arms.

Lucia takes me through breaks and side steps.

"Now, one thing, very important," Lucia says. "You're leading, but you're also showing your partner off. You're letting her know how important she is to you by making her shine. You see a guy who's doing steps his partner can't follow, that guy's a jerk. Now, spin me out . . ."

I spin her out and bring her back, lost in mambo. Suddenly my sneaker is half-off. We both stop and look down. My hoof is covered by a sock, but it's obvious that whatever is underneath that sock is not a foot. Or is horribly deformed.

My face is burning. I am too humiliated to speak.

Lucia says nothing. She just kneels down and eases my sneaker back on my hoof.

"Don't worry about it," she says. "A boy in my neighborhood was born with a club foot and he's the best dancer on the block. You might want to think about leather shoes, though. They would give you more protection and support."

I suddenly want to tell her the truth.

"It's not . . ."

She cuts me off.

"Don't get hung up about your foot," she says. "You're a natural. I'll see you tomorrow, same time. We'll work on some other stuff, too. There's more to life than mambo."

I head up the mountain, shaken. I have never come close to telling a human what I am. I have no idea why I almost just did. Maybe Diane did put a spell on me.

A mambo tune drifts up the mountains, over the hotel's P.A. system. Lucia must have done that. My worries are overtaken by the beat. When I reach my place, I close my eyes and practice the steps, pretending I'm holding Diane.

"Forward, step, back. Back, step, forward."

I smell goat. Then I feel a hand on my shoulder and someone grasps my hand and starts dancing with me.

"Oh, Danny, you're so handsome," Ben says, in a high-pitched, girly voice. "But I think you just stepped on – oh, my goodness, is that a *hoof*? "

I push him away and go inside.

"My dance teacher says I'm a natural," I say, annoyed.

"A natural idiot," Ben says, following me in. "You've got a forest full of nymphs and you're wasting your time with a human who's making your dick go limp."

"It's not 'a human,' it's Diane," I say. "And she just asked me to take her to a fancy dance at the Takanassee. To see Rico Valdez and Yvonne Rio."

I gesture to the Life magazine with Rico Valdez and Yvonne Rio near my bed.

"*Them.*"

"Whoa!" Ben says, zooming in on Yvonne Rio. "Now this is a human I can see risking your health for. This is one beautiful woman. Can you believe the body? I've been around and I have never, I mean never, seen breasts like that."

Reading is not Ben's strong point, but he manages the headline.

"'Yvonne Rio – The Swingingest Sexpot in Show Business.' And she's married to this fat, old guy who leads the band carrying a dog? You think he takes it to bed with him? I guarantee you, this is a man and woman who have not fucked since the '50s. A satyr comes along who knows how to treat a woman right, that would be a night to remember."

"Wait a minute," I say. "All I've been hearing from you all summer is how dangerous it is to sleep with a human and now you're saying you want to do it?"

"It's dangerous if you're inexperienced," Ben says. "While you've been up on Highmount, having heart-to-hearts with the human about how she's never gonna fuck you, I've been a busy goat. I'd say, love wise . . . I'd give me eight seasons. Believe me, it would take more than one human to shrink this zucchini."

"Oh, please," I say.

"And it's not like I'd do a mind drop," Ben says. "I'd do it the old-fashioned way: flesh on flesh. It would probably be very exciting for Yvonne Rio to be pressed up against a man without a dog between them."

He's off into fantasies.

"I'm thinking up against a tree, with that gown hoisted up to her waist," Ben says. "Then I'll turn her around and make a meal of that ass. I don't suppose you'd let me borrow this magazine? For research purposes."

"Out!" I say.

"Two bottles of your best red says I'll make it with her on the first pass," Ben says.

We are two seriously motivated goats. Ben gets me money for my dance lessons, although I suspect Lucia is giving me a very reduced rate. He also steals rolls of cash for the big night and special night-club clothing – Rat Pack, which is worn by Sinatra and his friends in the far territory of Las Vegas.

Dante, who collects magazines, says the Rat Pack men, who all the women desire, do sometimes wear hats in nightclub bars. That's a good thing for Ben, who's said he'd never cover his horns with some disgusting gunk, even for Yvonne Rio.

On the big day, Dante, who is going to the show too, comes to Bungalow D with a magazine picture of dress-up shoes called 'wingtips.' He resins my hair, brushing off my complaint that it's making my scalp itch.

"For love, you suffer," he says.

Then he paints our hooves, creating heels and shoe-laces and tiny decorative holes called eyelets.

"Tromp l'oeil," Dante says. "It means tricking the eye."

He stands back, checking out his work.

"Now remember for half an hour, you do not move," he tells us. "You do not want grass sticking to a Johnston & Murphy shoe. And when you get to the club, whenever you want a human to do something for you, give them a ten-dollar bill. You know which one that is?"

"Dante," Ben says, annoyed. "I ripped off the waiters' crap game last week."

"I was talking to Danny," Dante says. "You go to the club, a guy at the entrance will ask you if you have a reservation. You say no, but maybe he could find something and slip him a ten. You do it very discreetly: fold it up in your hand and keep your hand low. Then you pretend nothing happened."

"Like farting," Ben says.

"Classy," Dante says. "I can see why the nymphs can't keep their hands off you."

When I go to Diane's place, her grandmother spits three times as usual. But Diane looks so good, I wouldn't budge if the old lady was coming at me with a pitchfork. Diane is wearing a tight green dress flecked with gold, with a short matching jacket and gold high heels. There's even gold paint on her eyelids. She shimmers like Venus.

At the nightclub, I give the maître d' two tens — I want to make sure this evening is perfect. He smiles at me like we're going to be great friends. Then he leads me and Diane to our table.

There's excitement in the room; you can smell it. And there's something else I can smell: goat. There are at least three satyrs here. They're all Pop's age and they are seated at tables with human women, all of whom, from their scents, have had sex that afternoon – or in the case of a smiling woman in silver lamé, an hour ago. I wonder if this hotel owner is one of the humans who can spot satyrs and is encouraging them to be here.

I also see Ben at the bar, standing next to Dante, with their hats pushed back on their heads. They may be the best-dressed, best-looking guys here. There's a buzz around them: women near them are pinking up, picking up something erotic and possibly dangerous. They're pulled in, the way they are with Pop.

The maître d' brings Diane and me to our table. It's so close to the stage I can see Rico Valdez sweating. He's wearing a white dinner jacket and, just like in the magazine, he's conducting the band holding a chihuahua, which wears a tiny straw hat.

Diane and I exchange a look and she giggles, but I can see she's impressed by the table. I slip the maître d' another ten.

Valdez launches into a goofy song:

If you're ignored by the sweet senoritas.
There's one sure way that you can meet-ah.
Get a cute little dog and bring it along,
Just try not to step on its feet-ah. . . .

That, happily, is all we see of the dog. Valdez passes him to a busboy and cues the orchestra into a rhumba with a fast, syncopated beat. I'm about to ask Diane to dance when a waiter comes over with a bottle of Champagne and two tall, skinny glasses. I glance over at the bar. Ben, who's positioned himself at the end, winks at me.

"Special occasion?" Diane asks.

This is the moment all my Playboy Advisor studies pay off.

"Special *girl*," I say.

The announcer's voice breaks in.

"And now, Havana's hottest export, the one, the only – Yvonne Rio."

At the table behind us, an older woman in a honey-colored mink stole is sneering.

"Havana my ass," she says. "She was born in Brooklyn."

The band moves into a cha-cha. Yvonne Rio steps out in in a tight, yellow dress. She's so charged, she's lightning. For a moment, even I forget I'm here with a girl I'm crazy about.

"My beautiful wife, Yvonne Rio, in the cha-cha-cha, Malagueña Salerosa," Valdez says. "Look all you like, *campaneros*. She comes home to my bed at night."

That's so disrespectful. Are all human males jerks? Yvonne Rio shoots an annoyed look at her husband. Then she starts singing in Spanish. I don't understand the words, but the message is obvious. If sex is heat, the temperature in the room just went up twenty degrees. I'd like to take Diane's hand, but I'm officially in friend territory. And the night is just beginning.

Yvonne Rio moves into "Hernando's Hideaway," a sexy, playful song, and steps off the bandstand into the crowd. Her fragrance is a mix of jasmine and roses, which is not a scent that can be ignored. She pauses at one or two tables, flirting, then moves on to the bar, stopping in front of Ben. Her back is turned to us so I can't see what's happening, but a few minutes later, when Yvonne is back on the bandstand, her face is flushed.

"Cha-cha!" she shouts. "Everybody!"

From what I've seen at the Maplewood House, there are two things that make Jews go wild: Viennese dessert tables and cha-cha. There's a stampede to the floor.

"Okay," I say to Diane. "Let's do it."

Diane grins. I offer her my hand and lead her onto the floor. She's a good dancer, she follows me easily, but it's more than that: This music — this rhythm — seems to have turned Diane into a different person. I've never seen her this flirtatious and sexy. When I spin her out, she takes her time, forcing me to pull her back, smiling at me over her shoulder. It's a smile that's almost a challenge. I'd love to pull her closer, but I don't want to blow it. And I remember what Lucia told me: Show the lady off. Diane wanted to dress up and be glamorous. I'm going to make her shine.

Yvonne Rio moves into a love song, this one slower.

I lead Diane through a complicated series of steps, our bodies brushing. Am I imagining it or is Diane dancing closer? Her breasts are now pressing up against me. She looks at me and smiles. It's not a friend smile; it's the smile a woman gives a man when she realizes she wants him.

She kisses me on the mouth, a slow, lingering kiss.

Okay, that's it: we're not just friends anymore.

I hold Diane close. I have never been happier in my life. I am exactly where I want to be with exactly who I want to be with. One song melts into another. I don't want to stop and, I can tell, neither does Diane. We are going to dance until dawn. Then I'm going to take Diane into the most beautiful glen in the woods and make love to her. Though she is human and it will be my first time, the forest will give me strength. It will be the first time for Diane, too, but it will be so passionate we will be illuminated in a lavender pink glow. I picture Diane naked, smiling up at me afterwards, overwhelmed by all the new sensations I have given her.

Somebody taps me on the shoulder.

"Mind if I cut in?" a man says.

I stop dancing, confused.

"Jeffrey!" Diane says. "What are you doing here?"

"Found a guy to swap with," Jeffrey says. And to me, "Danny, right? Thanks for taking care of my girl."

I look back at Diane.

"Yes, thank you Danny," Diane says, as if that kiss never happened and we're just pals. "It was really sweet of you. You're going to stick around, right?"

"Uh –" I begin, but before I can finish, Jeffrey has swept her away and I'm standing in a crowd of dancers like a jerk. The last glimpse I have of Diane, she's smiling.

I go to the bar embarrassed, hoping desperately Ben is still there so I can talk to him. He's gone, but I spot Dante. He's not having any trouble with his love life. The bartender, a blond guy who's built like Adonis, is bringing Dante a glass of Champagne.

"On me," the bartender says, before being waved away by a customer.

Dante is glowing.

"I'm in love," Dante whispers to me.

"He looks very nice," I say, too miserable to want to hear that somebody else's evening is going well. "Have you seen Ben?"

"Off in the direction of Yvonne Rio," Dante says. "He says you should meet him at his place, at noon. With the wine you owe him."

"Well, I'm heading out," I say. "Diane's boyfriend showed up."

"No!" Dante says. "And she didn't even invite you to join them? That's very poor manners, even for an extremely insensitive race."

"She sort of did," I say. "But she didn't sound very enthusiastic. Anyway, what am I supposed to do? Sit there and watch them dance?"

"No," Dante says. "You're supposed to find someone else to dance with and make her eat her heart out. This minute. Look across the bar. A very pretty girl is giving you the eye."

I look over. A girl with white-blond hair, delicate and flirtatious enough to be a nymph, smiles at me. I smile back politely though to me she might as well be a toad.

"Why don't you go over?," Dante says.

"I don't really feel like it," I say.

"Danny," Dante says. "A word of advice? Someone who makes you feel bad after you've gone all-out for them. That's someone to forget."

I don't want to talk about it. I head up the mountain to my cave, hurt and pissed. I took dance lessons for this. I smeared my horns with gunk that will have me scratching my head all night. One minute Diane is acting like she's in love with me, the next minute she's blowing me off. Maybe she had to pretend to be glad to see Jeffrey since he's supposed to be her boyfriend. She can't very well break up with him in the middle of a dance floor, but when I left them, she sure looked happy. She was fucking *glowing*. She was *clinging* to that jerk. Satyrs don't cry, but maybe it would be better if we could – maybe it washes the bad feelings away.

Back at my place, I can't sleep. The scene keeps playing in my mind over and over, like a loop. Diane made the first move; she kissed *me*. You don't kiss somebody like that if you don't mean it. Or was the kiss just brought on by the music? What's going on here?

At noon the next day, sick of trying to figure it out, I head over to Ben's cave, to hear what happened with Yvonne Rio.

He's not there, which is odd – he's usually very good about keeping appointments. There's no sign that he's been back here, either, his dress-up clothes are nowhere around. It might be only older, experienced goats who have sex with humans, but everyone knows that after you do, you need to restore yourself on mountain soil, absorbing strength from the earth. Of course, Ben could have done that anywhere.

I check out our usual haunts: the corn fields; the Kelder garden; the hotels where Ben pilfers the food delivery trucks. I can't find him anywhere.

He's not in the woods outside the Takanassee either, though I do find Dante. He's outside his cave, dozing in the afternoon sun. He has a ginseng root next to his dick, which is suggested after relations with those not of the loving species. I have the feeling Dante has been messing around with a human, too. Probably that bartender who was giving him the eye.

"Dante," I say. "You see Ben? He hasn't been back at his place all day."

"No," Dante says, not bothering to stand up. "But I heard them. That woman is a screamer. It went on forever. She was supposed to do a midnight show, but she didn't show. Valdez was left singing to the dog. Ben is probably in the woods sleeping it off."

"I couldn't find him," I say. "We were supposed to get together at noon, remember? And he hasn't shown up."

"Maybe Valdez hasn't left yet and Ben's with Yvonne," Dante says. "We can check it out. I'll get the gear."

Twenty minutes later we're inside a V.I.P. cottage, wearing the bus boys' short red jackets and hats with the Takanassee insignia. A chambermaid is stripping the sheets off a pullout couch. Dante asks if she can give us a few minutes; the guest who checked out thinks he may have left something behind.

"Call me sentimental, but it makes me sad to see a Latin lover sleeping on the couch," Dante says, examining the sheets after the chambermaid leaves. "He had let himself go, though. Let that be a lesson, Danny: never get fat."

There is no scent or sign of Ben.

We move to the bedroom. The sheets are rumpled and the scent is strong: Yvonne Rio's jasmine and rose. There's also a powerful smell of sex, but only female.

Dante spots the pillowcase with the spots of dried blood first. He sniffs it, then he passes it to me.

I inhale.

"Ben," I say. "No question. Could he have had a nosebleed?"

"It's possible," Dante says. "But what I think is, he did a mind drop. And he got stuck."

I am so stunned I need to sit down.

"No," I say. "He'd never do that. This was his first human. It was just going to be flesh on flesh. He told me."

"Uh-huh," says Dante, not convinced.

"You said you heard screaming," I said. "You couldn't have heard screaming if he was in her mind."

"I said I heard *her* screaming, not him," Dante says. "Let's say he started out flesh on flesh. Maybe outside on the grass, where he'd have max potency. Maybe here, while Valdez is on the bandstand if she doesn't want to get grass stains on her dress. Then, let's say, Valdez comes to the room and Ben has to hide. He panics and leaps inside her head."

"Doesn't a woman have to be unconscious for you to do that?" I ask.

"You're asking me?" Dante says. "I've never been near a woman.

"But that bartender last night — "

"A professional flirt – part of the job," Dante says. "Though it took me a while to figure that out. I probably didn't want to. Strictly between us, Danny, I've never made it with anyone."

"But the ginseng . . . " I say.

"It's a big weekend," Dante says. "I just want to be ready."

"Well this is great," I say. "Two virgins and Ben is stuck in some human's head."

Dante sits down on the bed with me. I have a thought that scares me.

"They couldn't have gone to New York City, could they?" I ask.

"They're headed for the Concord," Dante says. "They announced it from the bandstand. It's the hotel where the rich Jews go, the other side of the mountain."

"How far is it?" I ask.

"Too far to trot," Dante says. "Then they go to New York."

"We've got to go there," I say. "We've got to get him before they head back to the city. That could kill him."

"Good thinking," Dante says. "Any idea how?"

"We might have enough money to hire a car," I say. "I've seen ads for that around the hotels."

"How much you got?" Dante asks.

I check.

"Seven dollars," I say.

"Is there somebody at your hotel?" Dante asks. "Who has a car and can keep a secret?"

CHAPTER SEVENTEEN

"So your friend – Ben – is stranded at the Concord and needs a ride back tonight?" Lucia says, when Dante and I find her in the dance studio half an hour later, reading a newspaper and having a cup of very strong coffee. "It can't wait until tomorrow?"

"No," I say. "He could lose his job."

Lucia is looking Dante over, checking out his shoes.

"Uuuhuuh," she says. "Anything else that might be a problem?"

I say nothing.

"We think he took off with a woman," Dante says, finally. "Yvonne Rio. The singer. And she might not want to let him go."

"We're pretty sure she kidnapped him," I say.

Lucia bursts out laughing.

"I don't know which I like better: a satyr with a job or Yvonne Rio having to kidnap a guy," she says. "But let's cut the bull. Are we looking at a mind drop here? And if so, exactly how much experience has your friend had with humans? And please, don't tell me he's a beginner."

Dante and I stand there, busted and stupefied.

"What?" I say.

"Answers and pronto," Lucia says. "Time counts."

I'm still trying to figure out how Lucia can spot satyrs.

"It would have been his first time," I say. "He wasn't going to do a mind drop. But when we went over to the Takanassee to look for him we found a drop of his blood on her pillow. None of his clothes, just the blood."

"Madre de dios," Lucia says. "She's got him all right. How long do you think he's been in there?"

Dante is as confused by Lucia as I am.

"We think he made it with her after the first show last night," Dante says. "That would have been around 10:30 or 11:00. I heard them outside. Then sometime, they went back to her room."

"Under 24 hours," Lucia says. "That's something, anyway. Okay, do you guys have any sap?"

"Pop has a barrel at his place," I say. "If he's not around, I might be able to sneak some."

"No 'mights,'" Lucia says. "We need it. Ginseng?"

Dante pulls his shiny clean ginseng root out of his pants pocket.

"Fresh would be better," Lucia says, "But we don't have time. Can we say we meet just down the road from the hotel in half an hour?"

"Lucia," I say. "How do you know all this stuff?"

"My car's a red Olds," Lucia says. "We gotta move. And Dante, your hoof is chipping."

Half an hour later, we're in Lucia's Oldsmobile, rattling down the mountain to Flesichmanns, picking up Route 28 and going east. Lucia is dolled up in a dress with a low neck, tight waist, and a big skirt; Dante and I are in our fancy club outfits. I've got a half-gallon jug of sap I've swiped from Pop's cave. I don't know how fast is too fast, but I have a feeling Lucia is doing it. I'm also worried about the car. I seem to have some immunity, but Diane's car is open and in this one, you're enclosed in metal. I doubt that Dante has ever been in a car.

"Lucia, this car . . . machines aren't healthy for us," I say, still not certain how much she knows.

"I wouldn't worry about it," Lucia says. "It's only an hour and I'm taking a route that will take us straight over the mountain. It's mostly state park. Just roll down the windows. If you get sick, we'll pull over and you can put some moss down your shirt."

This is too weird.

"Lucia," I say. "You've gotta tell me. How do you know about all this?"

"*Santeria*," she says. "It's like a religion. I'm an *osainista*. I work with herbs. I studied it in Cuba."

"But you're not really Cuban," I say. "You're a fake."

"C'mon, you think anybody would hire me if I said I was really from Cuba?" Lucia says. "They'd figure I was lying. The only way to get the job was to pretend I was fake."

"You're a fake fake?" Dante says.

"Yup," Lucia says.

"And Ricardo?" I ask.

"Richard?" Lucia says. "He's 100 percent authentic asshole. But to answer your question, no, he's Italian. He's not my cousin either, thank Christ."

We come to Big Indian, with the 10-foot totem pole of the Indian who was murdered for love. Lucia takes such a hard right, it throws me against the door. We start climbing Route 47, a narrow dirt road. There's an occasional house, a small hotel, a YMCA camp, but increasingly, it's what humans think of as wilderness.

"I used to teach at the Concord," Lucia says. "They have something like ten dance teams. This is also the fastest way to the ponies."

Dante and I look at her blankly.

"Monticello Raceway," she says. "You kids really *are* sheltered."

There are no other cars on the road, it's completely dark. I smell needle pine and mountain laurel and wild rose, and lots of animals: deer, squirrel, black bear. At one scary turn, the headlights illuminate the startled eyes of a bobcat. The air is so fresh that even though I am in a closed car, I feel invigorated.

"The air up here is fantastic," I say.

"There's a hemlock forest up here that's untouched, like, primeval," Lucia says. "When they were setting up tanning operations in the Catskills, maybe 150 years ago, they'd tear the bark off the hemlock to make the tannic acid. Tan from the word tannic, get it? It destroyed a lot of the trees. But for some reason, they didn't bother with this stretch. Maybe it was too hard for them to haul it out. The Dutch settlers thought hemlock forests were cursed. Maybe they were right. You can see how a forest god wouldn't be too happy with people ripping the bark off trees."

Dante, however, is not doing well. He looks like he is about to throw up.

"Lucia," he manages to say. "Can we pull over?"

Lucia stops. Dante jumps out of the car and runs to a white birch and wraps his arms around its trunk. It gently encircles him with its branches.

"Interesting," Lucia says. "I've never seen one do that. He must have a very good heart."

We thank the tree for its kindness and get back into the car. Soon we're descending the mountain. The road improves as we see signs for Fallsburg and Kiamesha Lake.

"So boys," Lucia says. "What's the plan?"

There's a moment of silence as I realize Dante and I haven't really figured this part out.

"We'll run in, sniff Ben out, and grab him," I say. "You'll wait in the car. We take off."

Lucia takes another whiplash turn.

"The Concord is 2,000 acres with 1500 guest rooms," she says. "On weekends, they get people like Tony Bennett and Barbra Streisand – those are huge stars. They've got three nightclubs. The main one has 3,000 seats. Do you know which club Yvonne's playing? Do you know how to get backstage? Do you even know how to do an extraction?"

"I guess you'd better come with us," I say.

"Good idea," Lucia says.

We've come to the entrance of the hotel. There's a big green Concord Resort Hotel sign at a long roadway, flanked by stiff, manicured gardens. Beyond that, there are tall buildings, made of concrete, steel and glass. This place is nothing like the wooden hotels with the deep porches on our side of the mountain. I might have a little more immunity to steel than most satyrs, but I don't want to test it.

"Lucia," I whisper, as she turns into the entrance. "This hotel could make us sick."

"I know," she says. "That's why we're going to make this fast."

We walk into the lobby.

It's enormous and open, maybe three stories high, with a blue-tiled fountain in the center of the room and a wide, blue-carpeted open staircase that soars up and around two walls.

Dante stops in his tracks.

"It's a floating staircase," he whispers. "Morris Lapidus – he's been in Architectural Digest. See the way it hangs in the air. Lapidus said a staircase isn't a staircase unless it's curved. And those slabs of walnut on the walls intersecting the blue tile – that's modernist."

"Dante!" I say. "*Ben.*"

"Oh right, sorry," Dante says.

Men in tuxedos and sharp suits and women in gowns and cocktail dresses are all around us. I smell no satyrs. If something goes wrong, we are without allies.

Lucia is reading a lobby sign.

"Fucking A," she says. "They're opening for Tony Bennett."

"That's bad?" Dante asks.

"That's in twenty minutes," Lucia says. "It's unlikely Yvonne is going to be napping. She might be throwing up . . . did she strike either of you as the nervous type?"

Dante and I shake our heads.

"I never got that feeling, either," Lucia says. "We need her distracted or out. Wait here a minute."

She goes off.

"You know, it's possible Ben isn't in her head," I say to Dante. "He could be just hanging out with her."

"In front of the husband?" Dante asks.

"Yeah," I say. "I see your point."

Lucia comes back, tucking an envelope into her purse.

"Okay," she says. "They're in the Imperial Room. That's up the stairs. The dressing rooms are in back of the theater – if Yvonne's got Ben, that's where he's going to be. You've got to get into that room and get him out. Then you go to the back of the building. You'll see doors to a loading dock, then a service road that leads to the highway. You'll wait for me there. Got it?"

Dante and I nod nervously. At the second floor, Lucia leads us through a side door to a backstage area, crowded with speakers and electrical cables, then to a row of dressing room doors, with names on the doors: 'Mr. Tony Bennett.' 'Mr. Rico Valdez.' 'Miss Yvonne Rio.'

"You picking up anything?" Lucia asks, stopping in front of Yvonne's door.

Dante and I sniff. I'm getting a whiff of Ben and a lot of jasmine and rose and the powerful scent of a very aroused woman.

"I've got him," I say.

"And. . . . ?"

"I think they're doing it," I say.

"So she's asleep?" Lucia says and before I can answer, she yanks the door open and shoves me in.

Yvonne Rio is stretched out on a large chaise. She's in a flowered robe with very wide sleeves, her eyes are closed, and – the critical sign – her breasts are definitely heaving. I stumble and knock over a huge vase of flowers. It crashes to the floor.

Yvonne bolts awake.

"What the fuck?" she sputters.

Lucia slams the door shut behind me, leaving me alone.

I go blank.

"Uh, ethereal creature . . . " I begin.

It's amazing how fast Yvonne Rio goes from arousal to fury. There's none of the post-sexual stupor I've seen in Pop's women. I guess the trick is to let them finish.

Yvonne stands up, picks up a large ashtray on a stand beside her, and flings it at me. She's got a good arm. It shatters inches from my head.

"How'd you get in here, you little creep?" Yvonne screams. "I'm going to have you fucking arrested! You're going away for life!

Ben's smell is as strong now as if he's standing in front of me. Which in a way, he is.

"Ben!!" I yell. "We're here for you! Come out!"

Nothing happens. Maybe the woman has to be unconscious for this to work. I know from Mickey Spillane I can make Yvonne Rio unconscious if I whack her hard enough on the head, but I am not sure I can whack a woman. And what would I whack her with? I look around the room, frantically. There's a tray with the remains of dinner: fork, knife . . .

Yvonne sees me looking at the tray. She grabs the knife and kicks a leg out from under me. Then she's on top of me, with one hand on my shoulder and the knife at my throat. I never knew a woman could be this scary. I stare into her eyes, hoping for a glimpse of Ben.

"Don't you have to do a show?" I manage to croak.

Someone pounds at the door. I hear a woman speaking with an exaggerated Spanish accent.

"Mees Rio, Mees Yvonne Rio?"

"Call the police!" Yvonne yells. "There's a rapist in my room!"

"Mees Rio," the woman says. "I have a message for you. From Meester Dean Martin. He says I must to give it to you in your hand. "

Yvonne's voice changes.

"Dean Martin?" she asks. "He's *here*?"

"Weel you hopen the door, Mees Rio?" the woman asks. Yvonne gets off me like I'm a rug she's tripped over and goes to the door. Lucia is standing there with an envelope. Dante is beside her.

"Meester Martin, he tells me to wait for your answer," Lucia says.

Yvonne tears open the envelope.

"Oh my God," Yvonne says.

In the dressing room, Ben materializes on the floor in his suit, damp and pale. He looks around, confused, then annoyed.

"I had a hat!" he yells.

A hat plops on the floor next to Ben.

Ben grins and puts it on his head.

"Slick," Ben says.

Then he passes out.

Yvonne is paying no attention to us.

"Yes!" Yvonne is saying to Lucia. "Tell Mr. Martin, yes!"

I pull Ben upright, dragging him out the door. Dante grabs him on the other side. We drag Ben, barely conscious, towards the exit. Yvonne doesn't notice; she's down the hall at Valdez's dressing room, pounding on the door.

Five minutes later, Lucia pulls up at the meeting place. Dante and I load Ben in the back seat, and I get in beside him.

Dante climbs in front with Lucia, who passes me a bottle of sap.

"We need to get a lot of sap down him before we let him sleep," Lucia says.

It's a struggle. Ben is so weak he can't lift his head and he keeps dozing off. It's not until we're halfway up the mountain that I think to ask Lucia what was in the note.

"Dean Martin, saying he was there to see Yvonne; he thought she'd be perfect for his next movie," Lucia says.

"I get it," I say. "It distracted her so completely, there was no room in her mind for Ben."

"*Exactamente*," Lucia says.

CHAPTER EIGHTEEN

We're halfway home, not far from the hemlock forests, when Ben starts wheezing. It's such a strange, rasping sound that at first I think it's the car. Then I look at Ben. His eyes are open, but he's staring, not seeing, and his chest is working too hard. He's panting.

Lucia, who's been concentrating on the road, hears it too. "Shit," she says.

She pulls off the road, rushes to the back seat, and puts her hand on Ben's forehead.

"Get him out," Lucia tells me and Dante. "We need to find a stream."

Dante and I manage to get Ben out of the car and hoist him onto his feet, supporting him between us. He's not really walking, we're carrying him.

Lucia rushes to the trunk of the car and takes out a satchel and a blanket. Then she points east into the woods.

"That way," she says.

I haven't heard any rushing water, but Lucia is right: after a five-minute walk through the woods, we come to a narrow, fast-moving stream. We lay Ben on the grass. Lucia opens the satchel, spreads a white cloth on the ground, and places a bottle of rum, three cigars, and a beaded necklace on it. She stands, raises her arms, and chants in a language I've never heard.

Then she turns to me and Dante.

"Strip him," she tells us, "And throw him in."

"That water's got to be freezing," I say.

"Now!"

Dante and I take off Ben's clothes. His eyes are now closed and his breathing is more labored. Even moving quickly, we can't miss the scratches on his back and what looks like a bite mark on his ass. I grab Ben under his shoulders, Dante picks up his hooves, and we take him to the stream. The water is frigid. Just walking in, my hooves go numb. Watching out for sharp rocks, Dante and I carefully lie Ben down in the water.

Ben's eyes bolt open.

"Mother *fuck*!" Ben yells.

Lucia is squatting next to him on the ground.

"Inhale and hold," she tells Ben, then she shoves his head under and chants something in the strange language.

Ben comes up sputtering.

"Okay," Lucia says. "Haul him out."

Ben is awake now and shivering. We sit him next to the stream. Lucia wraps the blanket around his shoulders and starts rubbing his body vigorously. Then she holds the bottle of sap to Ben's mouth.

"Slow," she tells him.

Ben nods, drinking.

"Dante," Lucia says, "Can you find me some yarrow, for the cuts?"

I am suddenly engulfed by forest rot. Not the sweet mulch of disintegrating leaves and branches and fallen flowers: something sharper and meaner, like the body of a rotting skunk. I look up at Dante, standing across from me. He is frozen, staring in terror at whatever is behind me. I look up over my shoulder and see a creature so terrifying, I think for a moment it must be a bad dream.

The thing that's standing behind me looks like a human man who's lost half his body. He has one leg, one arm and – worst of all – one eye in the center of his head, like a cyclops. One ear is enormous, the other is tiny. His clothing is tattered and he's balanced on a twisted tree branch, which he's using as a crutch. He's staring at Ben's crotch.

"Nice pair," he says. "I'll take the left one."

If this is a nightmare, the detail is excellent. The half-man has a knife at his belt, engraved with leaves and berries.

Ben sits on the ground, the blanket around his shoulders, staring at the thing. It wouldn't be a bad time to close his legs, but I understand being too petrified to move.

Lucia, however, is perfectly calm. She addresses the monster like he's a special guest she's been expecting.

"All respect to Osain, great orisha of the forest and the healing plants, and deepest thanks for the use of the stream and herbs," Lucia says.

The god, if that's what it is, ignores her greeting.

"The dick looks good, too," he says. "Give me two inches, I'm not greedy. It looks like he's got plenty."

Lucia looks him straight in his one eye.

"The boy is a satyr, a creature of the woods," she says. "He is as sacred in these mountains as the hemlock. His parts are not for harvest."

"What do I care for the pagan religions?" Osain says, taking out his knife.

Lucia steps between the god and Ben.

"We bring gifts," she says. "Cigars and rum from the motherland. If they displease you, take his cock."

Ben is finally spurred to action. He covers his dick with his hands.

"*Noooooo!*" he wails.

Neither Lucia or the god pay any attention to him.

"It *is* hard to get a good cigar up here," Osain says to Lucia. He walks to the offerings.

"Cohiba Lanceros," Osain says, impressed.

"Deal?" Lucia says.

Osain takes another look at Ben's package, thinking it over. Then he picks up the cigars and rum.

"This time," he says and walks into the woods.

I am so shaken, I'm not sure I can walk. Somehow, Dante and I manage to get Ben to the car where he passes out again.

When we get back to our mountain, Ben is barely conscious. Dante and I have to carry him to his cave. We put more yarrow paste on his cuts, as Lucia has instructed, pack him in grass, and get Dante's ginseng to tuck into Ben's crotch.

I remember the story of the two-season satyr who, after making love to a human, found himself with a dick shrunk to the size of an infant's. I take a few moments to discreetly assess Ben's equipment, then realize Dante is doing the same. It's clear Ben is in no way diminished.

Dante and I exchange a satisfied look and cover Ben with his army blanket, which, I realize, he's swiped from The Maplewood House.

Ben manages to open his eyes.

"Mwaaaah!!" he says, blowing us a kiss.

Then he falls asleep again.

Dante and I spend the night beside Ben. At sunrise, we gather grass wet with dew and pack it on him. I wake Ben up and get some more sap down him before he conks out again. Dante picks watercress, I get a gallon jar of maple syrup from the hotel pantry. Pop's sap is purer, but I don't want to risk swiping another batch so soon.

Dante goes off to find fresh ginseng. It grows wild in the Catskills and some of the locals sell it because it can bring a lot of money, but even with its bright green leaves and shiny red berries, it can be hard to find. A few hours later, Dante comes back with two large roots, one of which is shaped like a man and has special powers.

"Don't you want to keep one?" I ask him.

"No, it might as well go to someone who needs it," Dante says.

I stay with Ben. A few hours later, though he is still dead to the world, his color has returned to normal. Lucia comes over and gives Ben a sponge bath, which I know he will be very sorry to have missed, particularly the part where she crushes horse chestnut seeds to a lather and makes sure any Yvonne Rio residue is gone. I excuse myself for that part.

I get food, straighten up the cave, bring in fresh flowers and herbs for Ben's bed and fold his clothes. Ben is a terrible housekeeper; the only thing he cares about are his wines, stored on a rack he built in the rear of his cave.

By noon the next day, Ben is able to sit and is starting to sound like himself.

"What is this shit?" he says, after I've forced him to swallow two big spoons of syrup. "It isn't even fermented. Weren't you supposed to show up here with two bottles of wine?"

"Weren't you supposed to show up?" I say.

"Good point," he says. "I had some bad nightmares. How long have I been out?"

"Since we got you home?" I say. "A day and a half. Don't you remember?"

"It's sort of coming back," Ben says.

"So, c'mon," I say. "What was it like in there?"

"Surprisingly spacious," Ben says, yawning. "But you know, I'm still kind of sleepy. Think you could get me something to eat?"

Three hours later, I'm back with peanut butter, apples, a sack of spinach, and a few Catskill Mountain cauliflowers, which are the size of soccer balls. Ben eats a cauliflower, an apple, and half the jar of peanut butter. Then he tells me his story.

"First of all," he begins, "What a woman! I don't know if all human women are like her, but she is like, I don't know, man, she is peaches and cream! And insatiable. Can peaches and cream be insatiable? It's like the cream is screaming for your mouth."

"Can we start at the beginning?" I ask. "You're ranting."

"So it's a balmy, summer night in the Catskills," Ben says. "The moon is full, the grasshoppers are chirping . . . "

I whack his arm.

"So I'm at the bar," Ben says. "I saw you and your beloved on the dance floor, by the way. You were looking smooth. Dare I assume that Danny has finally dipped his wick?"

"The boyfriend showed up," I say. "Can we get to this damn story?"

"Yvonne Rio is mesmerizing," Ben says. "I was going to play it cool, but it was tough. All the time I'm watching her I feel like my tongue is hanging to my knees. I manage to catch her eye during her second song. You know, she does this bit where she comes off the stage and makes eyes with the people at the front tables? She stops at the bar in front of me, I look into her eyes, take her hand, lift it almost to my lips – it's the 'almost' that gets them. Try to remember that."

"Yeah, yeah," I say, "Moving right along."

"This woman's scent is something you don't forget," Ben says. "Jasmine and rose and powerful, like somebody used 10,000 jasmine flowers and dozens of roses. Makes it very easy for me to find her when her set is over. I go to her dressing room, knock on the door. She opens it, looks at me like she's expecting me and says, 'Tell me you hate dogs.' I say, 'More than you could possibly know.'"

I laugh.

"So I don't know how human courtship goes," Ben says, "But I figure nobody does it like a satyr, so I go by the book. 'Ethereal Creature,' I say, 'I've been dreaming of you ever since I saw your picture . . . .' She stops me and says, 'Could this dream – which I'm sure involved reading Emily Dickinson aloud to one another – be packed into fifty minutes? Because that's how much time I got before the next show.'"

"Who's Emily Dickinson?" I ask.

"I don't know," Ben says. "Some filthy human writer, I guess. Anyway, I've been planning the full goat: an hour of drinking wine and telling her how gorgeous she is, an hour of kissing her fingers and maybe, *maybe* stroking her hair. But she's this fantastic woman married to a guy who's paying more attention to his dog than to her. I tell her, 'We're in the mountains. Let's go natural. Let's do it outside.' I pick her up, which almost breaks my back – these humans are much heavier than nymphs – and take her in the woods behind the casino. I push her up against a tree – she's said she wants it raw – pull up her gown and go for the gold. And she's ready. She's wet, she's warm, she's so sweet I never want to pull out. I nibble her neck and trace her lips with my finger; next thing I know, she's got my finger in her mouth and she's sucking it, *pulling* on it. This woman is on fire. This woman has *power*. She comes in maybe four, five minutes. I didn't even know women could do that. So I find a good patch of soft grass, lie her down and go down on her because I don't want this to be a fast roll in the hay; I want to bliss her out. I want her to remember this when she's *ninety*. But she stops me and says, 'Let's go to my room. The insects are eating me alive.'"

"I do not want to go back to her room. I know if you're making it with a human you stay close to the earth to keep up your strength. I'm also afraid of the husband walking in. But she says she and Valdez haven't shared a bedroom for years and he never comes back between sets. And I'm love drunk. I mean, if she said, 'Take off your hat and show the world your horns and fuck me in the middle of Main Street,' I would have done it. She's feeling the same way. That late show? She could care less."

"We go back to the room. She strips down, totally naked but tells me to keep my clothes on – she has some kind of fantasy about that. We get on her bed, which is another trip, it's got layers of this silky fabric and I start fucking her again. I'm, like, on another planet. Then I smell someone in the other room. 'My husband!' she says, 'Hide!' The next thing I know, I'm in her head."

"Just like that?" I ask. "But how did you do it?"

"That's the weird thing," Ben says, "I don't know. I was just there."

"Was it scary?"

"No," Ben says, "It was just like being in her room. Valdez has seen the lights in the room, he comes in. I can tell Yvonne's confused about where I've gone – when you're inside them, you can pick up what they're thinking. She gives Valdez some bullshit story about needing an aspirin for a headache and he leaves. She looks around, sees an open window, figures that's how I got out, and goes to sleep."

"That's when you're supposed to be able to get out," I say. "I mean, I think that's when Pop does it."

"That's what I thought, too," Ben says. "I should just be able to will my way out, right? But before I could try it, she's in the room with me."

"She's dreaming!" I say.

"Right!" Ben says. "She's on her knees. It's discourteous to interfere with a woman's pleasure . . . "

"You're such a gentleman," I say.

"Yeah," Ben says. "I pride myself on that. Then she's dozing and I decide to make my break. I figure I'll just will myself outside, onto the grass. But as I'm trying to do that, she wakes up, grabs me and won't let me go. I would never hit a woman of course, but it gets pretty rough-and-tumble. She bites me and draws blood."

"The blood on the pillow," I say.

"Probably," Ben says. "I got to admit, though, it turned me on. So I fuck her again. Then I'm so exhausted, I guess

I fall asleep. Next thing I know, I wake up in another room, with mirrors. Yvonne's sitting on my lap, wearing this weird robe with big floppy sleeves that keep getting in my face. She's just so beautiful and sexy, before I know it, we're doing it again. It's fantastic, the best ever, I can't keep my hands off this woman. Then all of a sudden, she has no thoughts of me at all. Bam! I was out."

This isn't quite adding up.

"You were in her head for almost a day," I say. "There must have been some moments when she was sleeping, when you could have gotten out."

"I guess I might have been a little torn," Ben says. "You're in a woman's head, you start to know her. Yvonne got married at seventeen, her father basically sells her to Valdez; he demands a hunk of her salary, Valdez takes the rest. Valdez controls every part of her life: what to wear, what to sing, where they're going to live. He slaps her around. This is a smart, funny, talented woman. I hope she dumps him. I told her she should. Did you hear anything about them doing another show up here? I've got to have that woman again."

"Whoa! Stop right there!" I say. "She almost just killed you."

"It almost killed me because I went too fast," Ben says. "The old goats are right when they say you have to take it in stages. Before I did the mind drop I felt great. It was being in her head so long that made me sick. That concrete and steel hotel didn't help either. And these human women want it so bad. I see how your father could get addicted to it."

The next day when I bring Ben sweet noodle kugel from the hotel, he doesn't even look sick – although he is definitely enjoying room service. He's just finished the kugel when the scent of honey and Japanese wisteria fills his cave. Melena, in a hunter-green toga, with a twist of bright green ginseng leaves in her hair, is standing at the entrance. She's carrying a small package wrapped in wax paper, festooned with tiny, pink sweet peas. I'm stunned. I have never known a nymph, let alone a senior nymph, to come to a satyr.

I rise and bow over the hand she offers. Melena smiles at me, then turns to Ben. From the look in his eye, I would say he's made a full recovery.

"I understand you've been ill," Melena says to Ben. "I brought you baklava in new honey. To restore your strength."

"I'm better," Ben says.

Melena smiles wickedly.

"You don't want it? The hell with it," she says and tosses it to me.

"I think I owe you one," she says.

I make my thanks and take off and head home but for once, I have no appetite for sweets. Ben's been taking all my attention the last few days, keeping me from getting hung up on what happened with Diane at the Takanassee, but now I can't stop thinking about it. Ben has the woman he's crazy about – she even came to him, with a gift. Mine dumped me.

That evening, spur of the moment, I put on some clothes and return to the Takanassee, and stand on a hill overlooking the hotel, hidden in the trees. There's a party on a large deck around the pool. A bar has been set up under brightly colored Chinese paper lanterns and guys and girls, who look around Diane's age, are slow dancing. One girl even looks like Diane.

I hear grass rustling and see Dante beside me. He's got a bottle of cognac.

"I swiped it when they were setting up the bar," he says. "Want some?"

"Oh, yeah," I say.

I take a swig and pass it back. We sit down on the hill, watching the dancers. Some move around the floor, mirroring one another's steps; others are barely moving, just swaying. The lanterns are bathing them in pink light.

"So, what's it like, dancing?" Dante asks.

I think about it.

"It's taking the two most powerful things there are, music and love, and putting them together," I say. "And when you do it with someone you really like, it takes you to another place. It's a way of making love, I think."

Dante nods.

"You're thinking about that human – the one who left you standing there the night we all got dressed up?"

"Yeah," I say. "It's stupid. She has a boyfriend. But I still can't stop thinking about her."

"I get it," Dante says. "I've been there."

"You have?" I say, surprised.

"Story of my life," Dante says. "But even if a guy did like me, he wouldn't admit it."

"Why?" I say, feeling a little awkward talking about it, but curious.

"Danny," Dante says, "Do you know any satyrs who are making it with other satyrs? That might happen on Greek pottery, but I assure you, it is not happening in New York State in 1963. Not openly, anyway. There is not a satyr in the Catskills who would admit to being with another guy."

"What about humans?" I ask. "This is such a big hotel. New people are coming and going all the time."

"Tricky business," Dante says. "You put the moves on the wrong guy . . . well, just take a look at my nose."

I look at the little bump. I always thought it made Dante's face interesting. Now, I realize, it makes me stupid. Satyrs don't fall out of trees any more than squirrels.

"You didn't really fall out of a tree," I say.

"I tried to kiss the golf pro," Dante says. "He said I was disgusting – a 'disgusting little faggot.' I'd never even heard that word, but I knew by the way he said it, it was bad. I hid in my cave for a week, till I knew he was gone."

"I'm sorry," I say.

"Yeah," says Dante.

Down at the party, the music changes to a teenage love song I know, by a singer called Frankie Avalon. It is, incredibly, about a human imploring the goddess Venus to help him find love. It's sappy, but secretly, I've always liked it.

"Listen to that," Dante says. "I wonder if those jerks have any idea who Venus is. They're such idiots. But there they are, every night, with somebody to hold . . . "

I stand up and hold out my hand.

"Dante, get up and dance with me," I say.

"What?" Dante says. "We can't do that. I don't know even how."

"There's nothing to it," I say. "I'll lead you. Just close your eyes and pretend."

And hidden in the trees, we dance.

CHAPTER NINETEEN

Diane's kiss at the Takanassee Hotel has left me in limbo. I'm desperate to know if it was a signal that she's ready to get romantic. I know I have to be the one to contact her because she has no way of getting in touch with me, but I don't want to be humiliated the way I was at the dance. Instead, I get in the habit of going to the woods outside her house to see what's going on. When Diane is by herself, reading on the porch or listening to music, I'm happy; when Jeffrey comes over, which I've seen him do twice, I'm depressed. I tell no one I'm doing this, of course – it's my secret.

Meanwhile, to make things even crazier, out in the colony, Ben is a hero, a three-season satyr who made it with a human. One evening, when Ben, Dante and I are at Slippery Rock waiting to meet up with the gang, the guys jump out of the woods with flutes and tambourines and a crown of flowers and burst into a raunchy song.

Once was a lady so bounteous fair
That people paid to see her.
When Bold Ben lay her on the grass
She said, I'm gonna keep him.
I'll steal him! I'll steal him!
Because sweet Gods – and here the guys grab their dicks – *I feel him.*

Ben and I crack up.

And Danny, Yeah! the guys sing, grabbing their dicks again.
And Dante, Yeah! Oh, Venus, how I feel him!!

All the guys now want to make love to a human girl. The fact that I was one of the guys who rescued Ben has wiped out any stories about my failure at the Celebration. And I took a human dancing in an enclosed building – that makes me an expert on infiltrating their habitat.

Mario asks me if I'll teach him to dance. I have him swipe a transistor radio so I can get the right music and next thing you know I'm teaching the whole colony. The guys are especially interested in slow dancing, which, from their observations, seems to be the most direct route to sex.

Dante has stumbled across a bit of information that's gotten the satyrs even more excited. Human women are going wild this summer because there is a potion – a pill – that prevents them from becoming pregnant. It's making them like nymphs, who only get pregnant when they want to. When Pop said humans were behaving like somebody put something in the water, he was right. They're taking free love pills.

One morning, heading up Belleayre Mountain to the berry patch, I pick up the delicious scent of Rochelle, the Pine Hill girl. But the voice I hear when I duck for cover is not a human's. It's Thor's.

"No, Rochelle, don't get dressed, let me look at you," I hear him say. "You can't go. You're killin' me here. Just let me take one more bite of that gorgeous ass."

Rochelle giggles.

I often don't understand the words Thor picks up from wintering under a ski slope, but now it's no problem.

"Man, oh man, that is one bodacious bod," Thor says. "You are, without a doubt, the hottest chick I have ever seen in my life. . . . brains *and* beauty, how did I get so lucky? . . . one more kiss. . . . I was lyin,' two more . . . no, that doesn't count, a real kiss . . . look what you've done, you're gonna leave me this way?"

Prolonged farewells are a common courtesy after love, but if this goes on much longer it's going to be winter. When I finally hear Rochelle walking away, I come out. Thor is lying on his back, the picture of a satiated satyr – although this one has a pair of pink panties on his face, which he is inhaling like a rose.

"So, I guess you got over your fear of humans," I say.

Thor sits up with his love token.

"You better believe it, man," he says. "You know that love pill Dante heard about? It's for real. Rochelle told me, dig this, 'The pill gives a woman dominion over her body.'"

"What does that mean?" I ask.

"They feel it's okay to get on top," Thor says. "And who isn't into that? Lay back, look up at that incredible rack. It was just like you said. All Rochelle needed was a guy to let her know how great she is. And get this – she also wants to satisfy *me*. When did a nymph ever ask you if something felt good?"

I wonder if this is the gods' idea of a joke: send every satyr but me a human who wants to make love to them day and night.

"So you've been seeing a lot of her?" I ask.

"For sure," Thor says. "We're going to that moving picture thing at the Grand Hotel on Highmount tonight."

This was a satyr who didn't even like being around abandoned hotels.

"You're kidding," I said.

"Nope," Thor said. "Ben was right — with clothes we fit right in. And it will be dark. You should come."

Diane lives just down the mountain from that hotel. Maybe she'll be there.

"Okay," I say.

Shortly after sunset, Ben and I arrive in the woods behind the Grand Hotel. Everyone's heard about the talking giants; the woods are loaded with nymphs and satyrs, several of whom have found good seats in the trees. I see Thor, hiding his horns under a floppy canvas hat, with Rochelle, on the lawn where the young humans are crowded together. Thor is holding a box of popcorn loaded with so much butter that I can smell it across the lawn. I get it – if I had a girl with thighs that wide and welcoming, I'd want to keep her plump, too. I scan the crowd for Diane but don't see her.

In the woods, I see Thalia, arriving with Eloise. Eloise is wearing a gown that mimics a morning glory, velvet maroons darkening to midnight blues; Thalia is in a washed out dress the color of straw. It also looks like Eloise is chewing Thalia out. I have a feeling I shouldn't intrude, but then Eloise spots

Ben or, more likely, the 1955 Chateau Latour he's brought and makes a beeline for him. I go to Thalia.

"My sister is such a bitch," Thalia says. "I spend all day looking for silks for her, I practically prostrate myself to a Japanese morning glory, and when I come back with this fucking fantastic gown, what does she say? 'This purple is too bright. It's vulgar.' So, tonight I put it on and when she sees it on me, she decides she wants to wear it after all. Then I put on a yellow dress that I got in May from this sunflower that happens to like me, and just as we're almost here, she glares at it and fades out the color. Because, get this, the yellow is so bright it hurts her eyes. She's making my life hell. I have no time at all to write. Are there extenuating circumstances for murdering an older sister?"

"Not that I know of," I say.

"The Greeks were always killing their relatives," Thalia says. "They got away with it."

"One, they were gods," I say. "Two, not always. Zeus wasn't exactly forgiving."

"Good point," Thalia says. "I could find myself pushing a boulder up a hill for the rest of my life. With Eloise sitting on it complaining. 'Faster. There's nothing to see here. Why did you have to choose *this* hill?' "

I laugh. Thalia always makes me laugh.

"So what are we going to see?" Thalia asks.

"'Bye Bye Birdie,'" I say. "An animal movie, I'd guess."

"I've never seen a moving picture," Thalia says. "But I've read about them. I know how they work."

"You do?" I say.

"Yeah," Thalia says. "They move a skinny strip of pictures past a light, very fast. Not pictures, exactly; they're bright

THE SATYR IN BUNGALOW D   203

where it's usually dark and dark where it's usually light but it creates a picture when you shine light through it. It's called a negative."

"Thalia, how do you know all this stuff?" I ask.

"There's a guy named Britannica," Thalia says. "He's written a book about everything that begins with an *F*: fascism, film, France. A little bit about the *E* words and *G* words too, but they're obviously not as important. I found it in the Fleischmanns dump."

An image of a slender goddess, holding a torch, appears on the screen. There are gasps from the nymphs and satyrs. Thalia and I squeeze in next to Ben and Eloise on a wide boulder.

"Danny," Thalia whispers, "Do you notice how all the human guys have an arm around their girls?"

I scan the crowd.

"You're right," I say. "It must be the movie etiquette. A thousand pardons, Thalia."

I put my arm around Thalia's shoulders. I think of Thumper, my baby rabbit. Thalia is a soft, sweet little bundle. She snuggles into me.

"I like this etiquette," she says.

On the screen there's a burst of happy music and a newspaper with a front-page story about a singer called Conrad Birdie. A voluptuous, red-haired woman explodes onto the screen against a sky-blue background, singing. She's wearing a yellow, low-cut dress that shows off her tiny waist and beautiful breasts; she's so glorious and full of summer joy I want to make her an honorary member of the tribe.

Men and goats roar their approval. Even the nymphs, who always make fun of human women, are dazzled.

"Oh, gods," Eloise says. "Look at her. She's not human. Is she?"

"She's a special human," Thalia says, "She's a movie star. They know her everywhere in the world."

"I can't stop looking at her," Eloise says.

As love stories go I would not say "Bye Bye Birdie" is as deep as "Gatsby." The red-haired girl's boyfriend does not have to wait five years to get her back, either. He just punches Birdie in the face and that's that. The lyrics aren't at the level of Lorenz Hart, either. But there is one song the redhead, Ann-Margret, sings, that gets to me. It's about needing just one special boy to be happy, not two or three.

When the picture ends, everybody has someone to love and Eloise has found her new calling.

"Did you see the size of her face?" Eloise says, as we head back up the mountain. "This is way bigger than the theater. I've got to be in one of those."

"Can't be done," Thalia says. "They don't make movies here."

"Oh, please, like you know anything about it," Eloise says.

I jump in.

"No it's true," I tell Eloise. "They make movies in the far territories on a mountain called Hollywood. It has a big sign. Women climb it and jump to their deaths when nobody will hire them or they reach the age of thirty-six. But the people who are in a lot of movies – the stars – become royalty. Like the Goddess Marilyn. They put down red carpets for them so their feet don't touch the ground. They have followers who worship them and beg them to write their names on a piece of paper, which they cherish forever. Anything they want, they get."

Eloise is rapt.

"*Anything?*" she asks.

"Anything," I say. "They put it in writing."

"How do you know all this stuff?" Eloise asks.

"Movie magazines," I say. "I haven't eaten a lot, but they all had stories you couldn't find anywhere else. Real inside stuff."

Eloise turns to Thalia.

"I want those magazines," she says.

Ben, who hadn't seemed to be paying attention, jumps in.

"Eloise, it would be my honor to bring you movie magazines. How about tomorrow morning? I'll bring breakfast, say blueberries and cream puffs? You won't even have to leave your nest, you can read in bed."

Ben has Eloise by the arm now and is leading her away.

"By the way, where is your nest?" I hear him say.

Thalia watches Eloise disappear with relief.

"Eloise reads?" I ask.

"Ever see a chicken try to fly?" Thalia asks. "It's like that. She doesn't get very far. And it's painful to watch."

I like hanging out with Thalia.

A few days later I call out to her on my pipes – "Musetta's Waltz" is my tag — and we meet at Crump's Castle. Thalia has great news.

"Get this: Eloise has decided she's going to Hollywood," she says. "She's making me read her movie magazines, so she can plan her grand arrival. They're idiotic but I don't care. If I can finally get rid of Eloise, it will be worth it. Want to go to the dump and see if we can find some books?"

It's a sticky, humid day. The dump is a bust and the sun beating down is making it particularly smelly.

"Nothing," Thalia says, disappointed, "Not even a pencil."

Inviting a nymph to your cave is not done. Melena did Ben a great honor by coming to his den when she heard he was ill, but that was unusual − for a nymph, such surroundings are considered too coarse. But Thalia is a free thinker. She told me once the other nymphs thought she was weird because she wrote songs, which is of course a masculine calling. Thalia reminded them that Sappho wrote. Then she explained Sappho to me. This being the case, I decide to be open-minded, too.

"I have some books at my place," I say. "There's one about women at a temple of higher learning you might like. It's called, 'The Group.'"

"Are they celibate, like Vestal Virgins?" Thalia asks. "I can't stand those women. They're such pills."

"They do it all the time," I say.

"Let's go," Thalia says.

It's actually very comfortable, having Thalia is my cave. We have wine and sun-dried asparagus and Thalia admires my library − I have seven books. I even show her my drawing of the satyr and his family that I've never shown anyone.

Thalia picks it up and reads the signature.

"Fragonard," she says. "He's in my *F* book. He was French, he lived around 200 years ago. It's sweet. Is the idea that they live together all the time? What do they do in winter, when she takes her sleep in the trees?"

"Well you've got to remember a human drew it," I say. "He wouldn't know about that."

"Mmmm," Thalia says, taking a drink of wine. "And speaking of those, what's going on with the one with the big nose?"

I could tell Thalia a lot about Diane: a week ago, her boy-friend Jeffrey picked her up. A few days ago, a girlfriend from the city visited. Last night, she stayed in her room listening to Bob Dylan. I saw this from my hideout in the woods. But some things you don't want anyone to know.

"I guess I'm still stuck on her," I say.

"But no fucking?" Thalia asks.

"Uh . . . ," I begin.

"Yeah," says Thalia, "That's what I figured. But I've been thinking about it and I have a new theory. See, origi-nally, I thought the human put a spell on you just for the fun of it. She makes you want her, but she won't let you have her; the kind of thing my sister likes to do. But what I think now is, she has human brain conflict. There is this doctor, Freud, he's in the *F* book too. Freud says the human brain is split into two parts, the conscious part on top and the unconscious part on the bottom. The top part can want one thing while the bottom part wants the opposite. It sounds to me like her bottom brain was ready to do it with you the night of the dance, but the boyfriend arrived. Why not try again?"

"I don't think I could take getting rejected again," I say.

"Your call," Thalia says. "But no sex – it's not good for your dick. It shrinks it."

"Thalia!" I say.

Thalia shrugs.

"It's a muscle, you don't use it, it withers," she says. "That's just science."

I'd like to believe Thalia's theory about human-brain conflict, but I just can't get up my courage to talk to Diane. Checking up on her is a habit I still can't break – and it's getting worse. I'm now doing it twice a day. I'm lying in the brush one morning, looking up at Diane's window, hoping to get a glimpse, when somebody grabs my shoulder.

"Hey, jerk-off, you know this is stalking, right?" Ben says. "It's also, as a satyr, pathetic."

"I'm not stalking," I say. "I just want to know what's going on."

"C'mon," Ben says, "We're getting out of here."

We go to a field near Crump's and sit down against a stone wall.

"So let's get this straight," Ben says. "You're still hung up on this human idiot, but you're also not making a move. You're just hiding in the grass like a scared little mouse making yourself miserable. That about sum it up?"

"I guess," I say. "I'm not crazy about the mouse part."

"We're more than halfway through summer," Ben says. "There are beautiful nymphs all over the place. Are you going to waste your life like this?"

"Ben," I say. "She's all I can think about. What do you want me to do?"

"I want you to start acting like a satyr," Ben says. "Come with me this afternoon and squeeze some new peaches onto naked nymphs and lick them clean. Peaches, naked girls, summer – this is *it*, Danny, we are living the life. But if you're not going to do that, do something. Ask the damn human out. Squeeze her butt. Kiss her."

"Wait," I say. "All summer you're telling me to keep away from humans. Now you think it's a good idea?"

"I'm not telling you to fuck her," Ben says. "I just want you to spend some time with her, see that she's just a girl, and come back to earth. You're hung up on her because you can't have her. It's this unattainable thing; it's giving you these feelings which, being so intense, you confuse with love. And being dumped by your mother didn't help. You expect women to walk out."

"*You* came up with this?" I say.

"I was talking about it with Melena."

I'm pissed.

"What the hell, Ben," I say. "You shouldn't be telling her this stuff. I don't want everyone in the damn colony to know."

"I talked to Melena because I'm worried about you," Ben says. "Just get off your ass. Behave like a goddamn goat. *Do* something."

He's right, but I don't want to get myself in another situation like the one at the dance. I need to go over to Diane's and tell her I'm not interested in seeing her as a friend anymore. Short and sweet. I won't let the spitting, grunting grandmother throw me off either.

I pull out my jeans and T-shirts, smear the disgusting gunk, which I swore I would never use again, back in my hair and go over to Diane's.

The grandmother is sitting on the porch with the Yiddish newspaper. I am so used to her spitting three times when she sees me, I'm starting to think it would only be polite for me to spit three times in return. But mothers, particularly mothers of mothers, require extra courtesies.

"Good afternoon, Mrs. LeVine," I begin in Yiddish. "You are looking well today."

The grandmother grunts – I'd call it a "spare me the bullshit, sonny" grunt — then goes to the front door and hollers upstairs. It doesn't matter that I'm not wearing my Yankees cap. She's given me a name and she's sticking to it.

"Diane," she hollers. "It's The One With The Hat. Come down."

Diane, when she comes down, is cranky. She's wearing a shirt that looks like she slept in it and her jeans are stained. The grandmother shoots me a final nasty look and goes inside. Diane sits down on one of the big wooden chairs.

"I broke up with Jeffrey," she says.

WHOA!! THAT IS FUCKING GREAT! Quick, put on a cool face.

"Oh?" I say.

"We were never on the same track," Diane says. "He doesn't read, he's not that bright. . . . he was fucking Betty Weinstein. One of his little tennis friends. You don't have to pretend to be sympathetic. I remember that kiss on the mountain."

"I remember that kiss at the dance," I could say.

Instead, I gather every bit of courage I have, walk over to Diane, pull her to her feet and kiss her on the mouth.

"Want to take a drive to Woodstock?" I ask.

CHAPTER TWENTY

I don't know why nymphs think human women are coarse. Diane is more beautiful than the moon when I meet her at her house the next night. She's streaked her eyelids with black liner; her lashes are lush as ferns. She's dressed all in black, just like the beatnik girls I've seen in magazines: black turtleneck, black short skirt and black tights. Her legs look fantastic.

She puts down the top of the T-Bird and we get on Route 28 and head east, picking up Route 212 just outside Phoenicia. It's an area that's new to me. We drive along a twisting, narrow two-lane road, where I see no towns, only signs for towns: "Lake Hill," "Shady." On our right, craggy hills descend towards a rushing stream. It's beautiful. I would be amazed if there is not a satyr colony here.

Woodstock doesn't seem much bigger than Fleischmanns, but it's very different, like the pictures of New England small towns that I've eaten in The Saturday Evening Post. A village green is dominated by a church. The wooden buildings are smaller and seem older. I spot the Café Espresso, in a two-story building next to a stream.

Most of the traffic stays on Tinker Street, so that's where I direct Diane. Down a hill, I see a crowd hanging outside a restaurant called Deanie's.

"You're gonna love this place," I tell Diane.

I'm still not crazy about being around strange humans and the restaurant, when we go inside, is heavy with the smell of murdered cow and pig. But the guys, like me, are wearing jeans and pale blue work shirts. I fit right in.

Diane has a burger, I have a salad. It's kind of funny, the human eating with her hands while the satyr is eating with a knife and fork. I handle them well, too. All that practice in The Maplewood House kitchen is paying off.

We walk back through town to the Espresso. It's small, I doubt it could hold over fifty people. It doesn't strike me as the kind of place where you give the human $10 to give you a table, it's more a place that could use a paint job. The small round tables are covered in checkered red-and-white table-cloths and topped with chianti bottles with candles stuck in them and wax dripping down the side.

I look around for big-shot musicians. I've seen enough of Diane's record album covers to believe I could spot one. All I see are people in work shirts and jeans and black skirts and tights. Woodstock has a very strict dress code.

"You see anybody?" Diane whispers.

"No," I say. "Not yet."

The waitress brings coffee. It's hard to have a conversation when the other person is completely distracted.

"So there was a book you were telling me about . . . " I say.

"Holy shit!" Diane says.

I look to where she is staring. Bob Dylan, wearing a beat-up leather jacket and a corduroy hat, has just walked in with a dark-haired woman who looks familiar. For a famous guy, he's surprisingly short. Two men, carrying guitar cases, are with them.

"That's Bob Dylan and Joan Baez," Diane whispers, "They just played the Newport Folk Festival. Do you think they're going out? She is *not* the woman on his album cover. And that tall guy next to him, with the mustache and goatee, that's Peter Yarrow."

From Peter, Paul and Mary, right. The beatnik folk singers.

"The other guy is John Sebastian, I think," Diane says. "Aren't you going to go over and say hello?"

Oh, crap, that's right. I told her I knew the guy. But planting my flag in boyfriend country has given me confidence.

"No," I say, firmly. "Everybody wants a piece of him these days. Let him have a night off."

Dylan is looking over at us. Staring, actually. Then he breaks into a grin, nods at me, and turns back to his friends.

"Well, he certainly seems glad to see you," Diane says, impressed.

She moves her chair closer. If she's ever taken more of an interest in me, I can't remember it.

"Do you think he's going to play?" Diane asks. "If Bob Dylan plays ten feet away from me, I am going to flip."

If she knows as little about Bob Dylan as I do, I might as well make things up.

"I think he's just here to relax," I say. "After playing for a lot of people, you just want to kick back."

"Is he very intense when he plays?" Diane asks.

"Like you wouldn't believe," I say. "When he's playing, he's in another world. Music to him is like breathing. Some songwriters can't write when they're depressed. They just sit there all day and stare at the mountains waiting for a muse –"

"A *muse?*" Diane asks.

Ooops.

"But that's other writers," I say, quickly. "Not Dylan. No matter what's going on in his life, he can write."

Diane is hanging on every word. I could use a muse at this point myself.

"If you study his songs, some of them are really depressing," I say, wishing the little runt would play something already.

Diane wants more.

"And some of them are not," I say. "I prefer the not depressed myself."

"Oh, my God," Diane says, "Peter Yarrow just took out his guitar."

Yarrow tunes his guitar, smiles, and starts picking out a song. The room goes quiet. The dark-haired woman starts singing about a woman in a long black veil, visiting the grave of her secret lover. I may not have recognized Joan Baez but I remember Diane playing her music. Baez has the purest, most beautiful voice I have ever heard. No amount of practice gives you a voice like this; it's a gift from the gods.

Dylan takes a harmonica out of his pocket and joins in. He's not competing with Baez; he's complementing. It's like dancing. Dylan wants to make the woman look good.

When they finish, there's silence in the room. Nobody is sure whether it's cool to applaud or not. Then people nod and murmur.

"Nice." "Yeah."

Yarrow passes Dylan his guitar. Dylan slips a strap over his shoulder and begins the song I've heard so many times at Diane's, "Blowin' in the Wind." At the second verse, Baez joins in. When they finish, nobody cares about cool.

"Yeah, man!" people are yelling. "Wild!"

Diane leans in and squeezes my hand.

"Thank you, Danny," she says. "This was amazing."

Baez smiles and whispers to Dylan. Dylan nods. A few minutes later they get up to leave. At the door Dylan turns back, looks at me, grins, and tips his hat. Then they leave.

Diane is speechless.

"I can't believe it," she says, finally. "Bob Dylan tipped his hat to you. Why would he do that?"

I can finally be completely honest with her.

"I have no idea," I say.

We leave. Diane is clinging to me the way the girl on Bob Dylan's record album clings to him. As we head home she can't stop talking.

"This was the best night of my life, Danny," she says. "Sitting ten feet away from Bob Dylan and Joan Baez. Nobody will believe it. Bob *fucking* Dylan!! I don't know why it had to happen the night before I have to go back to Great Neck, but it's okay. I won't be away that long and when I'm back, we can hang out. Even if you're working. You can pick me up after and we'll hang out all night. We'll watch the sun come up. It will be fantastic."

"Yeah," I say, like of course we'll be doing that because *I* am the boyfriend.

We speed home. Heading up the mountain at Highmount, I expect Diane to take a right on Barley Road to her house, but she passes it and makes a sharp left, heading up the mountain to the Belleayre ski center. She pulls into the deserted parking lot.

"C'mon," she says, getting out.

Diane wants to make love; I can smell it. All these weeks I've been dreaming about it and now it's going to come true. I would prefer to make love to her on the grass, but Ben and I know, from seeing it so many times, that young humans like doing it in cars. Diane takes my jacket, tosses it in front, and pushes me in the back seat. Then she gets in. It's cramped, but I don't care. I'm so turned on, I'd do it on the hood. This is, however, going much too fast. I must make a declaration.

"Ethereal Creature," I begin, but Diane pushes me flat on the seat, shoves her tongue in my mouth, then moves down to my neck, nuzzling that hollow which makes it difficult for me to remember how to form words. My brain is useless. We're now flying on automatic dick.

Diane moves to my chest, unbuttoning my shirt.

"Oooh," she says. "You are *so* hairy."

"That's bad?" I manage to say.

Diane bends to a nipple, licking and nibbling.

"No," she says, emphasizing her words with little bites. "It's like a big –" chomp! – "wild"– chomp! – "animal. I *love* it."

She clamps on my nipple, sucking. She's got one leg between my legs and the other on the floor, and she's rubbing her crotch against my leg. Her skirt has scrunched up above her ass. My dick is so hard I can feel the metal zipper of my jeans cutting into it. I feel I am going to explode. A satyr must never allow himself satisfaction before he gives it to a woman.

Delay! The list, recite the freaking list.

Anise root,
Aster,
Bee balm,
Bergamot,
Bishop's cap,
Bladder campion,
Blackberry –

"Do you have protection?" Diane asks.

Celandine,
Chicory,
Chickweed –

"Huh, what?" I ask.

"Protection," Diane says. "A rubber?"

I think I know what she's talking about. Those slimy little hoses that reek of male fluid that I've seen at deserted lookouts.

"Sorry," I say. "No."

"I gotta get on the pill," Diane says, more to herself than me.

She unzips my jeans and yanks them down.

"My God!" she says. "You *are* an animal."

I try to get my hand under her tights, but she pushes it away. She puts her fingers in her mouth and wets them, then cups my balls.

Chickweed,
Honeysuckle,
Chickweed,
Honeysuckle –

Her fingers move to my dick. She's pulling up, stroking down. There's an ache at the base of my balls that's growing. I feel a spasm so intense that I am nothing but spasm, from my hooves, through my balls, through my eyes.

I am in another world. One spasm, then another. I am above the earth, riding waves of joy. It seems like a very long time before I open my eyes and feel the leather upholstery sticking to my ass and remember I am in the back seat of a car. I have a terrible feeling I have disgraced the loving species by achieving ecstasy before the lady, but Diane does not look unhappy. She is sitting back, wiping her hands with a tissue.

"Next time," she says. "You have to introduce me."

CHAPTER TWENTY-ONE

Ben is not an early riser, but I do not care. I am so eager to tell him about Diane, I burst into his cave at sunrise.

"We did it!" I say. "Diane loves me! She gave herself to me in the back of her car."

"Wait a minute," Ben says, sitting up. "Are you saying you aren't a virgin anymore? This is fantastic! And with a human! You aren't sick?"

I sit down.

"Well," I say, "I can't say I'm *technically* not a virgin. We didn't do it, do it. But she did, you know, do it to me."

Ben is looking at me, waiting.

"With her hand," I say. "That still counts, right?"

Ben does a maybe-yes, maybe-no thing with his hand.

"She was willing to do it," I say, "but I didn't have a rubber."

Ben laughs.

"Actually, you probably did. Humans carry them in their back pockets. You probably had one in the jeans I got you."

He gets up, goes to the pile of clothes in his cave, finds a pair of chinos and pulls out a small, aluminum packet. Inside, there is a small circle of rubber.

"*That*?" I say.

"You roll it out," he says, showing me on his finger.

"It's, like, miniscule," I say.

"You got that right," Ben says. "But it's what men wear so they don't get women pregnant. It's like that pill."

"Wait – are you saying a satyr can make a human pregnant?" I ask.

"Naaah," Ben says. "Of course not. It would be like a cat making a dog pregnant. Impossible. But Diane didn't know you're a satyr."

I have an idea.

"But you know," I say, "These rubbers are a barrier, right? So they might work to make sure I don't get sick. Diane's got this wedding on Long Island, she won't be back for two weeks, but then – "

"*No*," Ben says. "No, no, no! You had a date with her, she liked you, you messed around. A woman gave you pleasure and you gave her pleasure –"

With your best friend, you have to be honest.

" – That part, not so much," I interrupt. "I wanted to."

"It was still very goat," Ben says. "It should give you confidence. Human, nymph, the equipment is pretty much the same, the humans just have more bulk. Now it's time to spread the love around. It's August; nymphs are buzzing around the mountains like bees. "

"I don't want to spread it around," I say, annoyed. "I keep telling you. I found my girl."

Ben hits his head with his hand and shakes his head, exasperated.

"It was a *hand job*," he says. "I know you're hung up on this girl, I congratulate you on getting a hand job, but that doesn't mean you're the only guy she wants to be with for the rest of her life. It just means she had a nice night and wanted to make sure you did, too."

I get up, annoyed.

"It means way more that," I say. "I should have known you wouldn't get it."

I walk out, pissed. Last night was a turning point. Diane *wanted* to give herself to me completely and that's the important thing. Next time I'm going to be ready; I will have a pocket full of rubbers. Screw Ben.

I go back to Bungalow D, put on some clothes and my Yankees hat and head down to the hotel to get some French toast, which I could really use. There are still guests coming out of the dining room, so I go to a patch of woods not far from the pool to wait.

The poker players are tucking maple leaves under the nosepieces of their sunglasses to keep their noses from burning and are setting up their card table. The women are slathering on Coppertone.

Lucille, the husband-killer with the heavy makeup, looks like she's mad at the world this morning. But the rabbi's wife, who had been dozing, is in the brightest suit I've seen her in, geometric yellows and reds, and she is glowing. At the beginning of the summer when she came to the pool, she'd hitch down the skirt of her bathing suit to cover her legs. Now she glances down, notices a slice of butt, smears some oil on it and smiles.

The husband-killer is studying the rabbi's wife, too. She gets up, gathers her things, and walks over.

"Hello," she says. "I'm Lucille. I've seen you here all season. I thought we should finally get acquainted. Two women on our own."

"Sure, come sit," the rabbi's wife says. "I'm Mamie. I'm not really on my own. I have a husband in the city. And you're The Merry Widow."

The husband-killer looks surprised.

"A joke," the rabbi's wife says. "I know you didn't do it. Anyway, who hasn't wanted to give a husband a shove? At least you'd get his attention. The only thing that gets my husband excited these days is pot roast."

The husband-killer laughs and sits down.

"You're a good-looking woman," she says. "I'm sure that's not the only thing that gets him excited."

The rabbi's wife shrugs.

"After thirty years, it happens," she says. "I come up here, I have the sun, the mountain air, I sleep like a baby.

"Yes," the husband-killer says, "I see you out here napping. You look so happy. I sometimes wonder: what's she dreaming about? Some old flame?"

It hits me, suddenly, the husband-killer didn't come over to make friends with the rabbi's wife. She must have seen Pop when he was with the rabbi's wife in the woods or going into his bungalow. The husband-killer is jealous.

"An old flame?" the rabbi's wife says. "My husband was the first man I was ever on a date with. Two more and we were standing under the canopy. I was seventeen. That was it; end of story. But you, you're a free woman. And there are some nice-looking men up here. That Noah Yablonsky. He's got a big business in the city. Music. And the one with the hairy chest who sits next to him. What's his name? Jake?"

Uh-oh. The rabbi's wife could be jealous, too. This is just like a Mickey Spillane novel: two jealous dames, although I don't think Spillane ever had a dame who was married to a rabbi. And the one to worry about is obviously the one who pushed her husband off the ship. I wonder if I should tell Pop that the women are onto him but then he'd be mad at me for hanging out near the pool. And these women aren't going to do anything, they're just a little jealous.

It's late enough, now, that I can go to the kitchen and get myself a snack. Mrs. Belinsky is absorbed in The Forward, Artie is fixing himself pancakes. They smell fantastic.

I go give Mrs. Belinsky a squeeze.

"Danny, my darling, you're hungry?" she asks and without waiting for an answer hollers across the room, "Artie, cook something for the boy!"

Artie, for a reason probably having to do with college girls, is in a good mood today. He nods at me and actually smiles. Mrs. Belinsky puts down her newspaper to get some fruit, so I won't have to go for five minutes without eating: grapes, cantaloupe and of course, prunes, which no breakfast in the Catskills can be without.

Artie makes a stack of pancakes, then brings them over to the table and sits down. I find myself thinking of my drawing of the satyr's family. It's nice to sit together. Artie and I load our pancakes with butter and maple syrup from Streeter's farm up the road and pour ourselves milk from The Maplewood cows.

Mrs. Belinsky, scandalized by what she's been reading, gives us the story.

"Listen to this," she says in her Yiddish-English mix. "Elizabeth Taylor, the one who converted to marry Eddie Fisher, is running around with another man. An actor, this Richard Burton. Who is also married. I never trusted that one. She runs around with the *tzitzkelas* hanging out like she's the only woman on earth who's got them. You know the wife I liked? The last one, Debbie Reynolds."

"Another shiksa," Artie teases in Yiddish.

"Eddie Fisher took her to Grossinger's to get married," Mrs. Belinsky says. "Jennie Grossinger loves him like a son, she makes him a wedding. Then Eddie Fisher goes back to Grossinger's with this Elizabeth."

"They even go to the other side of the mountain to fuck around," Artie says.

"Artie!" Mrs. Belinsky says. "Watch the mouth!"

Artie laughs and leans over and gives his mother a kiss. She swats him away, but I notice, when she does it, she's laughing also.

We're finishing our breakfast when the rabbi's wife, who's changed into a flowery dress, walks in.

"Mr. Belinsky, I hate to bother you, but the mice are making a nice house for themselves in my bungalow," she says. "Do you have something I could use to get rid of them? Not a trap, I hate those things. Some kind of powder I could scatter around, maybe?"

"Sure," Artie says. "Bungalow C, right? I'll be right over."

"No, no," the rabbi's wife says. "Why should I put you to that trouble? Put a little in some foil; I'll take care of it myself."

I can't believe what I'm hearing. This woman really is planning something and it's not about mice. She's going to bump off the husband-killer by putting poison in her drink. She could slip it into the prune juice they all drink in the morning, that would cover the taste of anything.

And what if the rabbi's wife isn't planning on bumping off the husband-killer? What if she wants to bump off Pop? Pop's sense of smell is great, but when Artie gets the poison for the rabbi's wife, double wrapping it in aluminum foil, it's odorless. I'll just have to handle this myself. Tail the rabbi's wife like Mickey Spillane, and see what she's up to.

I thank Artie and Mrs. Belinsky for breakfast and leave the back way, through the yard with the chickens, to the woods behind the rabbi's wife's cottage. A few minutes later she comes out, stuffing a wadded-up handkerchief into a pocket. She looks extremely pissed. She is definitely up to no good.

The rabbi's wife grabs a walking stick next to the door. But she doesn't go to Elk Creek Road, which guests take when they feel obligated to get off a lounge chair and get some exercise. She heads through the woods up the mountain. She's not in bad shape for an older human. She walks fast, whacking bushes out of her way with her stick. I'm not the only one who senses she's in a nasty mood. A timber rattler, hanging out in the sun, beats it under a rock. She walks to The Acropolis but when she gets there, she doesn't go into the hotel. She walks in the direction of the waterfall.

I race through the woods to beat her there. Pop is sitting beside the falls with Melena. He's wearing the outfit he wears around the pool: porkpie hat, shorts, shirt, and sandals with socks. Melena is in her hunter-green toga. Her skin seems paler than the last time I saw her, which makes the contrast with her dark hair more striking. She and Pop are facing each other, holding hands, and talking.

I run over.

"The rabbi's wife," I say to Pop. "She's headed here. I think she wants to kill you."

Melena laughs.

"Oh, Jake!" she says. "You never learn."

Pop looks towards The Acropolis. There's nothing to see but we can hear a stick whacking through the brush. A coyote runs out, terrified.

"Well," Melena says. "Somebody is not in a good mood."

Pop turns to me.

"Get Melena out of here," Pop says.

I feel shy around Melena and from what I've seen she can move pretty fast on her own. But I grab her hand and we run into the woods. In moments, she's breathing hard.

"Wait!" she says.

"Are you okay?" I say, surprised.

"Yeah," she says. "I just want to see what happens."

From the way she's breathing, I doubt that's the reason she stopped, but we squat down. The rabbi's wife has cut out of the woods and is making a furious path towards Pop.

"Where is she?" she yells. "Don't lie to me, Jake. I know that tramp is here."

Pop smiles at the rabbi's wife as if he is delighted to see her.

"Mamie," he says. "The very woman I have been thinking of all morning."

"The hell you were," the rabbi's wife says. "You leave me and two minutes later, you're with somebody else. Don't deny it. I can smell her on you."

I exchange a look with Melena.

"That's actually pretty good," Melena whispers.

Pop takes the woman's hand.

"If you're smelling anything, it's an old goat in rut," Pop says. "I see you and I have to admit, I go crazy. I want to do things I couldn't say out loud. Especially to a devout rabbi's wife."

The woman glowers, but it's obvious she's softening. I can feel the woods sigh in relief.

"So, what are you doing here?" she asks.

"I came to get you a treat," Pop says. "Some Greek pastry, pistachios with honey. I was going to take you into a field of flowers and feed it to you, piece by piece, in your delicious little mouth."

Pop traces the woman's mouth with his finger.

"I *am* going to put it into your mouth. And do you know what I'm going to do to you then?"

The rabbi's wife is looking at Pop like he's put her in a trance.

Pop whispers something into her ear.

"Oy!" she says loudly.

Then her knees give out and she sinks to the grass.

Pop follows her down.

"In fact," Pop says. "I think I'm going to tear down your panties and fuck you right now. Maybe I'll tie you to a tree and whip you a little first. Get that gorgeous, ripe tuchas nice and pink."

I'm shocked and embarrassed. This is not the gospel according to the loving species that I've ever heard. I'm also learning more about Pop than I want to know although Melena seems amused.

"Oh, your father," she says. "I could watch him work all day."

She turns her attention to me.

"With you, I think, it's different," she says. "You . . . "

She doesn't finish, she looks like she's dizzy. I think she is ill. I'm still intimidated by Melena, but she needs help.

"Ethereal Lady, may I assist you?" I ask.

"Perhaps an arm?" Melena says, but she looks so weak that I pick her up. She is remarkably light. I carry her where she directs me, deep into the woods, where a grove of maples are turning early, their leaves dappled an orange gold. I see a nest of royal blue and lavender silks under a rocky overhang and set Melena down gently.

"I should let you sleep," I say.

"No, no, sit with me a bit," Melena says. "Tell me how the music is coming along. Your father is such an old friend, and we've never had the chance to talk."

I sit down next to her, feeling awkward.

"You're a songwriter, yes?" Melena says.

I'm embarrassed.

"Not much of one," I say. "I'm trying, but nothing's very good."

"Oh, yes, your muse problem," Melena says. "You were very interested in finding one at the lunch."

"I didn't really learn anything," I say.

Melena laughs.

"They take an oath," she says. "But I'll tell you a secret: you don't really need them."

"What?" I say.

"They don't give you the ideas," Melena says. "They just give you the confidence that you can come up with the ideas. So naturally, artists get very hung up on them. The thing to remember is, you can be your own muse. And don't compare yourself to other composers. They don't matter. It's about you.

Just write from your heart. Go with your feelings, let them carry you."

"That's it?" I say.

"Always worked for me," Melena says.

"You're . . . a songwriter?" I ask.

"Painter," Melena says.

She gestures to the orange gold trees.

"I was working with the yellows," she says. "I thought I'd play with giving them more gold. It's early but, you know, poetic license . . . "

"They're beautiful," I say.

The tiredness seems to sweep over her again.

"I don't know what's wrong with me today," Melena says. "I'm forgetting things. I know there was something else I wanted to tell you about writing . . . Perfect, that's it. Forget perfect. Perfect is the enemy. That's important. Promise you'll remember?"

I don't know why she's so concerned about this when she obviously needs to rest.

"Sure," I say. "Okay."

Melena smiles.

"Good," she says. "Now, may I give you a mother's hug?"

I'm confused.

"But you're not . . . ," I start to say.

Melena cuts me off.

"It's okay. Mothers always have a little extra," she says.

She puts her arms around me and rests her head close to mine. A sweet wave of warmth washes over me, from my head to my hooves. I feel strangely, blissfully content. I could sit here forever, but Melena is not my mother and I know I should let her rest.

I make my goodbyes and head home, first making another stop at the bungalow of the rabbi's wife. Looking through the window, I see a saucer next to a small hole near the floor. In it, a piece of cheese has been sprinkled with white powder.

Case closed, as Mickey Spillane would say.

Chapter Twenty-Two

Dancing is having a big effect on the colony. Mario drops by to tell me he and Micah infiltrated an outdoor party at one of the hotels and he ended up making it with a college girl behind the children's dining room.

"That stuff about slow dancing being an aphrodisiac, it's true," Mario says. "They have a love god, Elvis, and he sings this song, "I Can't Help Falling in Love With You." The girls go crazy. They give you a signal they're ready; they put both arms around your neck and then the guy is supposed to put his hand on their ass, and they're like doing it, standing up, with their clothes on. Want me to show you?"

"Gods, no," I say.

"There's another thing the guys do," Mario says. "When the song is over, they put one arm behind a girl's back and dip her backwards. The lower they go, the more the women love it. But I'll tell you something, I think that's the only interesting thing they do. Because when you make love to these girls, they know nothing. They've never even heard of the Leda bite."

I hate hearing how successful everybody has been with human girls when I haven't yet gone all the way with Diane, but I can't stop myself from asking the question.

"How many humans have you been with?" I ask.

"Three," Mario says. "The last one made me nervous. She kept trying to take off my hat. I had to grab her wrists and hold her down – which made her go crazy. She ecstasied twice."

Meanwhile, it's full-tilt August. Fruit trees and vegetable patches are bursting; the grass is starting to yellow. The hotel guests, feeling the nights grow cooler and September in the air, are grabbing all the summer they can. They're insatiable. They follow lunch with poolside snacks, then dinner, then midnight Viennese tables, heavy on desserts with whipped cream.

Then they fuck.

I don't know how humans can make love after a day of non-stop eating, but they do. You hear the moaning through the window screens. One night, passing the apple orchard, I see Noah making it with the Austrian. I've seen her on cool evenings, wearing a barbarous dead animal pelt around her shoulders, a blond mink. Now Noah's got the mink under his shoulders and the Austrian on his face. I once ate a fashion magazine story about resort wear. I wonder how they'd feel about this look.

There's also something new at The Maplewood House. One morning when I go down for an early lunch, I see Artie outside, helping a farmer load shingles onto his truck. When

Artie comes inside, he takes out a roll of bills and shows them to his mother.

"Look at this," he says. "You know how much we made on that load of shingles from the city? Eighty dollars."

"That's going to be a big help when the rain comes through the roof," Mrs. Belinsky says.

Artie pours himself a glass of milk.

"'Belinsky Brothers Building Supplies,' Ma," he says. "Shingles, lumber, nails. They got no place to get that stuff up here. That's the business this family should get into."

This is an idea that is definitely bad for the goats. What happens to me and Pop if the Belinsky family shuts down the hotel? We may be creatures of the forest, but like Pop said, when was the last time I had to think about finding a decent piece of fruit? French toast doesn't grow on trees. And I like hanging out with the Belinsky family.

I need to talk about this with Thalia. She's not at Crump's, but heading further up Bushnellsville, to a blackberry stand, I spot Glynnis. She's brightening her lips with berry juice, checking her image with a copper compact that looks familiar.

I bow and kiss her fingers.

"Ethereal Creature, the berries should be begging color from your lips," I say.

Glynnis smiles and offers me some berries.

"You looking for Thalia?" she asks. "I heard your call. She's gone. She left for the far territories. The day before yesterday."

"No," I say. "That's impossible. She would have told me."

"Her sister told her they had to go and they went," Glynnis says. "She left something for you. If you wait, I'll go get it."

Twenty minutes later, Glynnis is back, carrying a large book with a wine-red cover. The title, "Encyclopedia Britannica," is in gold lettering.

Inside, on the first page, there is a note:

"Dear Danny, My sister has demanded I accompany her to Hollywood Mountain and I cannot refuse. It appears to be very distant. I don't know if I will ever see you again. Perhaps the winds and the gods will take pity. (Not my sister, that miserable bitch.) I just wanted you to know at the Celebration, when you kissed my mouth, the world glowed pink. And if you're still hung up on the ugly cow, I hope you get her. Your friend, Thalia."

I go back to the cave with the book, totally blindsided. It's my fault, I think. If I hadn't talked up Hollywood, Thalia would be hanging out with me right now. We'd be at the dump, looking for books. Thalia was so smart. There was no word beginning with "F" she couldn't explain. We'd started writing songs together. I'd never had a female friend and now she's gone. I feel abandoned.

I sit outside the cave watching the sun set, so lost in thought I don't smell Ben.

"Okay, listen to this, I just heard something wild," he says.

"Thalia left," I say.

"What do you mean?" Ben says. "It's only August."

"Eloise decided they had to go to Hollywood Mountain and they left," I say. "I'll probably never see her again. I didn't even get to say goodbye."

"Oh," Ben says, sitting down. "I'm sorry. Had you, like, started messing around with her again?"

"No," I say, "But we were getting to be good friends."

This is a concept, platonic satyr-nymph relations, that I know Ben does not get. But he's trying.

"That sucks," he says. "I'm sorry. I know you liked her a lot. But listen, I just heard something that's going to make you feel better. And get that hand-job human out of your head for once and for all."

"*Diane*," I say, annoyed. "She's got a name. I don't want to put her out of my head. She'll be back in a week. We have plans."

"Listen anyway, because it's wild," Ben says. "They're bringing mermaids to The Hotel Mathes."

I love Ben but sometimes he acts like he has rocks for brains.

"Mermaids?" I say. "That can't be right. They live in the ocean."

"Nope, it's them all right," Ben says. "Look at this poster. The week after next."

The mermaid on the poster is practically naked. She's wearing a tiny top that shows most of her breasts and she has a glittering green fishtail that starts just below her hips. If a tail with scales can be thrust out seductively, she's doing it.

"They've got to be fake," I say. "How would mermaids have gotten to the Catskills?"

"Kidnapped, obviously," Ben says. "What I'm thinking is, we go to The Mathes, rescue them, and love them ragged."

I may be the only virgin satyr in the Catskills, but no one can be this stupid.

"You can't make love to them," I say. "They've got tails. Where are you going to put it?"

"I don't know," Ben says. "I've put a lot of study into this picture and I can't figure it out. You got the top of a nymph, then you got fish. But it's gotta be somewhere. They make little mermaids, right?"

"But they're in the water, Ben," I say. "We don't swim, remember?"

"I scoped this out," Ben says. "The far end of the pool is really shallow. We don't need to swim. We wade in, the mermaids see us and swim over. We grab them, run across the road and toss them into Vly Creek, just past the dam. The current is really fast there. We meet them downstream. Believe me, I've thought of everything."

"Forget it," I say.

"I'm glad you're in," Ben says. "Tell no one. This caper is strictly me and you."

Naturally by the time the show rolls around, our whole crew is in the woods outside The Mathes. Thor, hearing about mermaids, insists on coming with us and Dante is here, too. The draw for him is the design of the bar, with the enormous portholes that let you look into the pool and see the swimmers.

It's a big night. The women are wearing tight wiggle dresses inspired by the Goddess Marilyn, with fur-collared sweaters or mink stoles and high-heeled shoes with pointy toes. The men are so slick they seem shellacked.

We four goats, decked out in our Rat Pack best, are looking pretty sharp too. Ben has procured some very cool gray fedoras, which we're wearing tilted to the side, like Sinatra. Some very pretty girls are checking us out. One is giving Thor the eye and goats being goats, he's flirting right back. Our troops may be diminished before this rescue is begun. I'm still a little nervous packed shoulder to shoulder with humans, but the buzz in this club is contagious. And Ben's time in Yvonne Rio's brain has paid off.

"Jack Daniels, rocks, four," he says, stepping up to the bar.

When the drinks come, the four of us click our glasses, a Rat Pack salute. I take a big drink. Jack Daniels tastes like kerosene smells. If we were in the woods, I'd spit it out.

"Sip!" Ben hisses.

I'd rather just use the revolting Jack Daniels as a prop. It is creating a nice warm feeling, though. I take a small sip, which tastes less awful this time and check out the crowd. The smells and music are intoxicating: flower and fruit blossoms on the women; spices and citrus on the men; Sinatra on the sound system, singing that the best is yet to come. I'm feeling much more relaxed. Then I see Noah across the room, with his hot Austrian, who's wearing a tight orange dress and her blond mink stole. I feel a flash of panic.

"Ben," I whisper, "One of Pop's friends is here. Noah, from the hotel."

"Shit," Ben says. "Did he see you?"

Noah is nuzzling the Austrian's neck.

"I don't think so," I say. "He's into this woman he's with. But —"

The lights dim. A voice comes over the PA system.

"Sailors dreamt them, poets sang them – and tonight, you'll see them. For the first time ever in the Catskills, The Hotel Mathes is proud to present . . . 'The Mermaids of the Mountains.'"

We crush close to the windows that look into the pool.

A mermaid with long blond hair, a glittering blue-green tail, and a tiny, blue sequined top swims to a porthole and blows a kiss. There are gasps in the room. The mermaid disappears for a moment, then returns with three gorgeous mermaid friends. They swim in and out of view, through hoops and garlands of water lilies. Their long hair streams in the water. Sinatra is now asking a lady to fly with him, to fly, come fly away. Jack Daniels, rocks, is an excellent drink. If satyrs could swim, I'd be in there with the mermaids. Maybe I should try it. Losing my virginity to a mermaid would be wild.

Ben nudges me.

"Back door, behind the bar," he says. "We're moving."

The bar is packed, but Dante and Ben and Thor and I get out as quickly as we can. Outside, we crouch at the wall, next to the garbage cans.

"Okay," Ben says, "Here's the plan. Those hoops and stuff they keep changing – I'm betting they keep them at the far end of the pool. That's the shallow end. We go down there and when the mermaids swim to that end, we grab 'em."

"We can't," I say. "They'll be in the middle of their act. Everybody will be watching."

"We got no choice," Ben says. "If we wait until they're done, the humans will take them away and lock them up. The audience won't see us long and when they do, they'll think we're just some crazy drunks. We jump in, grab the mermaids, then it's a short hop across the road and into the creek. These girls are going to be so grateful."

"*Love* grateful," Thor says.

"But there are so many people," I say.

"C'mon," Ben says. "And stay low till I give you the signal."

We crawl along the grass towards the far end of the pool. There's no one on the grounds. We crouch low, at the shallow end. I hear cheering and applause.

"Shit," Ben says. "I think it might be ending."

A mermaid swims towards the end of the pool.

"Now!" Ben says and jumps in.

The water is waist-high, which makes it hard for Ben to walk, but he reaches a mermaid and grabs her shoulder. She's startled. She breaks loose and starts to swim away. Ben catches her again. The mermaid turns and sinks her teeth into his arm.

"Y'know," Thor says. "She doesn't look grateful."

Thor and I jump in as the other two mermaids swim up.

"What the fuck are you doing, assholes?" one says, ripping off her tail.

Thor and I stare.

"Changelings!" Thor says.

The changeling with the legs shoves Thor into the water. I grab him, trying to pull him out, and slip. My hat slips off and floats away. Dante jumps in the pool to retrieve it. I'm sputtering, swallowing water, trying to get up. In the middle of the pool, three Sinatra hats – no, make that four – are floating away.

There is more shouting now, a growing crescendo, coming from the lawn near the deep end of pool. Humans are running up from the nightclub, hollering their heads off.

"Horns! They've got horns!"

"Is this part of the act?"

"Let go of them, you creeps!"

Thor manages to pull himself up out of the pool. He races into the woods and is gone.

Dante, struggling to move in the water, isn't so lucky. He's just made it to the side of the pool when a hotel guard grabs him by the shoulders, drags him out and belts him in the stomach. Dante collapses on the grass. I hear an enraged bellow that can only come from one of the Greeks.

"Leave him alone, you prick!" George hollers, running out of the woods.

If I ever doubted the story about George slugging a bear, I don't now. George hits the guard so hard, he goes flying. Then George picks up Dante, tosses him onto his shoulder, and takes off into the woods.

Ben, meanwhile, is in big trouble. His mermaid has gotten him by the arm and pulled him down. They're thrashing wildly. I stumble through the water and try to tear the mermaid off. The mermaid won't let go. A satyr never, ever strikes a lady, but if she keeps holding him under, Ben will be taken or drown. I make a fist and slug the mermaid in the jaw. The mermaid falls back into the water, releasing her grip on Ben.

A human girl hollers my name.

"Danny?" she screams. "You piece of shit!"

I freeze. It can't be Diane, she's not supposed to back in the mountains for days. But it is. Diane, in a cluster of girls; Diane, enraged; Diane, who just saw me slug a woman. I spent the summer trying to show her my best self. Now I've done the worst thing you can do and Diane saw me do it.

"It was you!" Diane yells. "You were the creep who felt me up on the mountains. I *knew* I'd seen your face before!"

I need to say something, but I can't. I just stand in the water, dumb. Ben, who's gotten himself upright, grabs my hand and drags me to the side of the pool, and shoves me up on land. We go sprinting across the lawn. A human makes a grab for me, but I brush him off. In water we may stumble, but on land, there's no way humans can keep up. Still, we run five miles, as fast as we can, into the woods, not stopping till we get to Ben's cave.

"Whoa!" Ben says. "That was fuckin' wild! Best caper ever!"

I can't believe what I'm hearing.

"Ben, you think this was a game?" I say. "Don't you realize how fucked we are? They saw our horns! Diane thinks I'm a creep who felt her up when she was unconscious. Pop is gonna exile us."

"It'll blow over," Ben says, grabbing a bottle of wine. "Men with horns? They'll think we were part of the show. Your father might be a little pissed but he's a satyr. He'll appreciate an epic prank."

I feel like I'm in a bad dream. Ben, high on the stunt, is sitting down, opening the wine and taking a long drink.

"I can't believe I let you talk me into this," I say. "What was I thinking? I'm an idiot."

"And let's not forget that you hit a woman," Ben says. "Too bad, did you see the way she was holding on to me? I could have got lucky."

"I hit her to free you, you jerk," I say. "And I feel like shit about it."

"I absolve you, brother goat," Ben says.

But I'm not really listening.

"And the thing is, I love her," I say. "I love Diane."

CHAPTER TWENTY-THREE

It's obvious to me, given the shit show we've started, we can't stay at Ben's place. We stuff two bottles of wine and some cheese in our packs and take off, looking for a place to hide out.

I'm not worried about the hotel people coming after us. I'm worried about the locals, like the one who shot Pop's friend Seth. I've seen them out nights with their flashlights and dogs, hunting raccoons or, though it's against their laws, deer in summer. Once they hear about horned men, they'll be out with their pitchforks and deer rifles.

Sure enough, we're barely up Halcott Mountain, when the Fleischmanns Volunteer Fire Department siren echoes through the hills.

"That's it," I say. "They're coming after us."

Ben just points down the mountain in the direction of The Roaring Brook Hotel. Flames are shooting out of the main building. Artie was right when he said the hotel would be burned down for the insurance money. Business was so bad, the owners didn't even wait till after Labor Day.

Ben and I keep running east over North Dome and West Kill Mountain. We're heading to the steep peaks overlooking Devil's Tombstone, between the towns of Phoenicia and Tannersville. I've never been, but Ben says it will be a perfect place to hide. It's named Devil's Tombstone because there's a boulder in a notch below the peaks where, human lore has it, the devil sometimes rests. Satyrs, of course, don't believe in that nonsense.

The hills are slippery with trickling mountain springs and loose, damp shale. It's especially treacherous as we head up the mountain at Devil's Tombstone. I can hear a rushing stream far below us. It's not a place from which you'd want to fall. But the brush and trees are thick, and there are a lot of rocky overhangs. We find a good one near the peak. It's not a cave, but it's deep, covered with a thick drape of vines and branches. We push the vines aside and have our wine and cheese, ravenous from the run. I'm bone tired. I stretch out beside Ben.

"Well, at least, we're in a place nobody will find us," I say.

Next thing I know, somebody kicks me hard in the ass. I open my eyes to daylight. There's a circle of old goats glaring down at us and one of them is Pop. His face is such a mask of rage, I'm scared.

I elbow Ben awake.

"Oh shit," he says.

Pop grabs us by our horns and yanks us out. He really is a scary strong goat.

"Do you idiots have any idea how much danger you could have put the colony in?" Pop says.

"Wait," Ben says, "*Could* have?"

An old goat, who I recognize as the one I saw walking with a woman in Fleischmanns, slaps Ben across the face so hard I see marks.

"Shut up," he says.

Ben rubs his face.

"A little harsh for the loving species, no?" he says.

The Fleischmanns goat slaps Ben again.

"Nope, you're right," Ben says. "Thoughtless."

Pop has never hit me, but he isn't the senior satyr here. That's got to be a sinewy, black- haired goat whose horns curl and whose legs are bent like a ram's. He looks, actually, like the scary satyrs in paintings who have flipped terrified sheep on their backs and are fucking them. I wouldn't be surprised if he brought out thorned ropes.

"March," the Fleischmanns satyr says.

Ben reaches down for our supplies.

An old goat kicks them out of his hands.

"Silly me," Ben says. "What was I thinking?"

The old goats march us west, through the woods, in the direction of Belleayre mountain. We come into a clearing and the ruins of a mountain house I never knew was here. Two wooden pillars are rotting on top of what's left of a green veranda, and there are remnants of a shingled roof. The house is overgrown with poison ivy, ferns and brambles. In the back of the house there are cement stairs leading down to a basement. I smell mold and wood-rot.

"Get in, assholes," Ram's Horn says.

I look over to Pop, but his face is still that angry mask.

Ben and I walk down the stairs. Tangled wiring hangs from the ceiling; there's a rusting furnace and broken furniture. Disintegrating mattresses are leaned up against the wall. A broken pipe drops out of the ceiling and drips into a large barrel; water seeps down a wall that's covered with green mold. The light coming through the cracks in the basement ceiling is only enough for me to see that the floor is wet too. The basement is enormous. Looking towards the back, I see the red eyes of a rat staring at me. I hate rats.

A few minutes later, three more old goats arrive with Thor. He's got a purple bruise under his eye and he is having trouble standing. The satyrs drag him down the stairs. Thor sits down heavily on the wet floor.

"What happened?" Ben asks. "What did they do to you?"

Thor doesn't answer.

Ben turns to the old goats who are now gathered at the top of the stairs.

"What is this?" he shouts. "Three of you gang up on a guy? That's great, you should be proud."

Ram's Horn ignores him.

"No food, no water," he says. "Don't bother trying to get out. You won't."

Ram's Horn and the other old goats form a line across the entrance.

"No!" Ben yells.

Ram's Horn gives Ben a nasty smile. He and the others, Pop included, chant something in the old language and piss across the entrance of the cave. Then they leave.

Old goat piss and an incantation create a force field that can throw you twenty feet. We're locked in. Ben and I throw some mattresses on the floor. There's a mouse nest in one, but I don't hear any squeaking and the mattress is dry. We sit with Thor in the gloom.

"So do you have any idea what they're going to do with us?" Ben asks. "Or where Dante is?"

"Nope," Thor says. "I was hiding on the other side of Slide Mountain when they grabbed me. I guess my mistake was throwing the first punch. Those old goats really know how to fight."

I remember something.

"Pop said we *could* have put everybody in danger," I say. "That sounds like nothing bad happened. Do you know what he was talking about?"

"No," says Thor. "They weren't looking to shoot the shit. I've never seen satyrs that mean."

He drags himself up, walks to the water barrel, takes a mouthful, then spits.

"Shit!" Thor says. "It tastes like something died in there."

He sticks his arm inside the barrel, feels around and pulls out the body of a mole. The smell makes me want to throw up.

"Fuck!" Ben says. "That's disgusting!"

Thor walks to the entrance of the basement and heaves the mole up the stairs. It hits the piss barrier and explodes, scattering bits of putrefying mole corpse across the basement. A tail lands on Ben's arm.

"I think that's the gods telling you to keep away from mermaids," I say.

Ben plucks off the tail.

"I think you're right," he says.

Satyrs can go for a long time without eating and drinking – we hibernate through the winter, after all – but it's different when you're awake. We spend our first day in the basement scrounging for food. We find a pile of acorns a squirrel has stashed, some mushrooms growing on the slimy basement floor, and a trickle of moderately clean water going down a far wall. It just makes us hungrier.

What's worse than going without food is knowing that summer is ending. The nymphs will only be here a few more weeks. The New York girls are heading back to the city. Rochelle may already be gone, Thor says. It's really bumming him out.

"Such a cool chick," Thor says, "She says I completely changed the way she thinks about guys. She's writing this thing she calls a manifesto, about how if a guy doesn't appreciate you, you tell him to get lost. She says she might even write a book."

What I'm miserable about is Diane. I'd been dreaming about the time we'd have together when she got back from her sister's wedding, when we would finally make love completely. Now Diane thinks I'm a horned pervert. I'll probably never see her again.

The basement we're locked up in is a few miles from Diane's house. If I could get close enough to the basement entrance, I might be able to look across the valley and see the lights of her house. But with that barrier, how close is safe? I don't want to get thrown across the room like a dead mole. And I sure don't want Ben and Thor to see me. I wait till late at night when I'm sure they're asleep and then I quietly climb part way up the stairs, trying to get a glimpse. I think I see the light on her green porch. I stand a long time and stare.

Our third day in the basement, late morning, I hear an incantation outside the entrance and the sound of water tossed on the ground. I rush to the stairs. Two of the satyrs who dragged us here have Dante. His suit is filthy and he looks frightened. George is next to him, holding a burlap sack.

"Move it," an old goat tells Dante.

George gives Dante the burlap bag and pats him on the shoulder – only it's more than a pat, it's a tender, lingering squeeze. George takes off.

I can't believe what I just saw.

"*What?*" I mouth to Dante.

Dante shakes his head at me, a sign to keep quiet, and walks down the stairs.

Ben and Thor run to the entrance.

"Hey, how much longer do you guys think you can keep us here?" Ben yells. "We've got rights, you know!"

The old goats just do their chant and piss routine and leave.

We surround Dante.

"Tell me there's food in that sack," Ben says.

"Corn and apples," Dante says. "Cheese and bread too, I think."

"Oh, thank you, great god Dionysus," Ben says. "You didn't forget your little goats after all."

He puts his hand into the sack, pulls out an ear of corn, and takes a big bite.

"Wet silk – I swear I can taste the dew – fantastic," Ben says.

We sit down and gorge ourselves.

"How did you talk them into letting you bring this?" Thor says. "We've been scraping mushrooms off the floor."

"Melena," Dante says. "I was hiding out with George in back of The Acropolis, and four old goats grabbed me. They were taking me away when Melena shows up. I think she must know the top guy whose name is Diego – you know, the scary one who looks like a ram. One smile from her and he's a different guy. She takes his arm and they walk away, but I can hear her telling him no damage was done, goats will be goats, she happens to know when he was young he was a wild kid himself. They're away for maybe an hour. When they come back Diego is actually *smiling*. Melena tells me not to worry and gives me the sack of food.

"*So* many reasons to love that nymph," Ben says, taking another ear of corn.

"Dante, wait – do you know what she meant by no damage?" I say.

"I know everything," Dante says proudly. "I even have the newspaper."

He reaches into his jacket pocket and brings out a wrinkled copy of *The Catskill Mountain News*, where the stories are usually about a new snowplow or a farmer's wife visiting her niece three villages away.

I grab the paper and read out loud:

Fraternity Prank Disrupts Swim Show

Guests at The Hotel Mathes in Fleischmanns, attending the synchronized swimming act, Mermaids of The Mountains, got an unexpected show Saturday night when several horned men attempted to kidnap the "mermaids."

"It was like something you'd see in one of those Old Masters paintings when the satyrs carry off the nymphs," said hotel guest Dr. Loren Fishman, of Manhattan.

"It was wild," Dr. Fishman's wife, Mrs. Carol Fishman added. "When the mermaids fought back and dragged the satyrs into the water, you thought they were really trying to drown them. They were really good."

Noah Yablonsky, the spokesman for The Hotel Mathes, insisted to this reporter that the horned men who tried to abduct the mermaids really were the famous creatures of myth.

"Of course, they were real satyrs," Mr. Yablonsky said. "Everybody knows the Catskills are loaded with them. They didn't mean anything disrespectful. In their world, you're supposed to carry beautiful women away. What are you going to do, let them be lonely?"

Pressed, however, Mr. Yablonsky said the satyrs "just might" have been college pranksters.

Their horns?

"There's a rumor you can pick them up for $1.99 at the Woolworth's in Kingston," he said. "But don't quote me.

"That guy Yablonsky is a friend of Pop's," I say, excited. "He stays at The Maplewood."

"No harm, no foul," Thor says.

"What does that even mean?" says Ben.

"It means the colony's safe," I say. "They tossed us in here to teach us a lesson, but nobody got hurt. They've got to let us go soon."

"Then it's time for a nap," Ben says. "Got to keep our strength up for our triumphant return to the ladies."

Ben and Thor go to the back of the basement and sack out. That gives me the chance to talk to Dante.

"Okay, you've gotta tell me," I say. "You and George. Something's going on."

Dante smiles. If it were brighter in here, I'd swear he was blushing.

"That night at the Takanassee," I say. "Was he the one you meant when you said there was somebody you loved?"

"You won't laugh?" Dante asks.

"No," I say.

"I think I was in love with George from the minute I saw him this summer, at The Arrival." Dante says. "I always felt out of place at those things. What was I going to do with a nymph if I caught her? I've never felt anything for girls. And when George and Nico showed up wearing those loincloths, I thought it was the silliest thing I'd ever seen. Then George snatches Thalia and all I could think was, 'I wish that was me.' I wasn't that far away from him and after he grabbed her, he saw me staring at him and winked. After that, I couldn't stop thinking about him, which I knew was ridiculous. He'd abducted a nymph, how much more hetero does it get?"

Something comes back to me from my reading.

"Don't some guys do it with, like, both?" I ask.

"Humans, for sure," Dante says. "There was once a honeymoon guest who tried to kiss me. That was too weird, I dodged him fast. But goats? I figured you picked a side and stayed on it. And George had to be straight – he was so macho. But when we're alone, he's a different guy. Before Mother's Day, I had found a trunk of brocades in the old carriage house on the Fleischmanns estate. You know how scary those buildings are with the trees fallen through the roof and the nails and the rotting floorboards. George went in and carried it out for me. He was always doing stuff like that. We'd sometimes work close salvaging things and when he brushed up against me, my skin tingled. That sounds stupid, right?"

I think about Diane and the thrill I felt when she took my arm when we were climbing.

"No, not at all," I say.

"Thank you," Dante says. "I'm still not sure who I can talk to about this. Anyway, I kept hoping all summer I would meet somebody. It doesn't happen. It's the end of August and I'm thinking, great, another winter in the cave looking at pictures of Cary Grant. Then we go to The Mathes and that guard slugs me. It knocked the wind out of me, I couldn't move. George comes running out of nowhere and picks me up, just like he grabbed Thalia. You know how you dream something and all of a sudden it comes true and you can't believe it's really happening?

"Oh yeah," I say.

"Anyway, we run like hell, up beyond the Pavlos property and collapse in his cave," Dante says. "And then he kisses me."

We sit silently for a while.

"I'm happy for you, Dante," I say.

"I never thought it would happen for me," Dante says. "I really didn't."

Two days later, late afternoon, two old goats come and get us: the Fleischmanns satyr who hit Ben, and a satyr with the torn ear of a tomcat. It's muggy when we step out of the basement, the kind of day that ends in a ferocious Catskills thunderstorm that rumbles over the mountains and upends the hemlock.

"Okay, so we're free?" Ben says to the Fleischmanns satyr.

The satyr glares at him.

"You're free to get in that stream and clean yourselves up," he says. "And move it. We need to be up at the Pavlos property fast."

"What about our clothes?" I say, because I've gotten to like my sports jacket.

The Fleischmanns satyr looks disgusted.

"Give them to me," he says. "All of you."

We strip off our clothes. The satyr strikes a fire, and tosses them in. Torn Ear hands us clusters of bay leaves and we get in the stream and scrub.

"You have any idea what's going on here?" Ben asks me.

"Not a clue," I say.

An hour later, as storm clouds are gathering, we're on Pavlos' mountain. Stepping out of the woods, into a clearing, I can see something big is about to happen. There are dozens of satyrs and nymphs from as far away as Andes and Downsville. They're forming a large circle, speaking in subdued voices, greeting one another somberly.

The two goats who've escorted us walk away and join a group of old goats across the field. I see Pop, who either doesn't see me or more likely, is pretending not to see me. Melena, in a white toga and a crown of white flowers, is talking with a group of older nymphs. George and Nico are behind her. Melena says something that makes one of the nymphs laugh. Then they embrace and Melena and her sons move down the line.

Ben, Thor, Dante and I huddle together, Dante not taking his eyes away from George.

"I've got a bad feeling here," I say.

"Me, too," Thor says. "I'm going to go find Rolf and get some intel."

A few minutes later, Thor is back. I can tell from his face the news is bad.

"It's Melena," Thor says. "That insect spray, DDT. It got her.

And to Ben, "I'm sorry, man."

Ben looks stricken.

"No, no," he says. "That can't be right. It's got to be something else."

"It's true," Thor says. "She picked it up in the tree she wintered in. That's why she was here all summer. She knew it was going to be her last one and this was the mountain she loved. And her sons were here."

I feel sick. DDT is poison.

"Can't she take something?" I say. "Aren't there herbs?"

"They would just drag it out and make her another kind of sick," Thor says. "She doesn't want that."

I know what's going to happen now. I've never seen it but I know.

"I'm sorry," I say to Ben.

"Yeah, yeah," he says and I know he's trying to keep it together. "I know."

Melena and her sons are coming towards us. She is walking tall, though slowly, and while she is pale she is still very beautiful and her wisteria scent is still strong. I can't believe she is mortally ill.

She stops in front of us.

"My bad boys," Melena says. "They didn't treat you too horribly, I hope."

"No, Ethereal Creature," I say.

Melena holds out her hand. I kiss it. Melena takes my hand.

"Remember what I told you about the muses . . . " she says.

"I don't need them," I say.

Melena smiles and gives my hand a little squeeze and moves down the line to Thor.

"Ethereal Creature," Thor says, kissing her hand.

I can see he wants to say something more but the words he needs aren't coming, so he says what he can.

"The corn and apples. That was so cool of you to do," Thor says.

"It was a great caper," Melena says. "Legend. It will be sung."

Melena walks to Dante. He bows over her hand and kisses it. Melena takes George's hand and places it on Dante's hand. She holds it there for a long moment, so the colony can see the union is blessed.

"Protect one another," Melena says.

Ben is next in line. He is trying to look confident and sure, the satyr who sauntered out of the tall grass in early summer, but he is struggling.

Melena holds out her hand. Ben kisses it, then looks into her eyes. If I didn't know what a true satyr Ben was, devout in the pursuit of all women, I could swear I was witnessing singular love.

"Ethereal Creature," Ben says, trying to keep his voice steady. "It was an afternoon in summer . . . "

Melena is having difficulty too.

"You made it perfect," she says. "You came to me."

Thunder is crackling.

Melena turns to go. Ben grabs her shoulder and pulls her to him and kisses her on the mouth. It's a shocking breach of protocol, there's a gasp from the crowd. But when Ben releases Melena she is smiling.

"My wild boy," she says.

Then she turns to Nico and George.

"It's time," Melena says.

Nico and George are having a difficult time also. But they nod and run with their mother to the center of the field. The wind is picking up, so strong that the trees are bending. I can see lightning crackling above the mountain.

Nico and George crouch at their mother's feet, linking their hands to give her a leg up. Melena puts her hands on her sons' shoulders, puts a foot on their hands and nods. They throw her, with all their strength, up into the wind.

Melena flies like a goddess towards the lightning, reaching out her hand to greet it as an equal. For a moment Melena is lightning herself, a glorious nymph sketched in fire. Then she explodes in thousands of wisteria blossoms which float down on the crowd.

We all stand silently for several minutes. Then nymphs and satyrs pick up a handful of blossoms and, without speaking, disappear back into the woods. Ben just stands, looking down at a cluster of blossoms which have drifted towards his hooves.

I put my arms around him.

"I'm sorry," I say. "I can sit with you."

Ben holds himself rigid like he's afraid he will break apart.

"Thanks," he says. "I just need to be by myself."

I squat down and pick up a handful of blossoms, open his hand, and press his fingers around them.

Then I go back to Bungalow D, heavy with sadness. I didn't know Melena well, but she was kind to me the way I imagined a mother would be kind and she treated me as if I were an artist too. She was so vital, so alive when I first saw her, not even three months ago. And now she is gone.

When morning comes, I don't want to leave the cave. I stay inside, lying in bed. All the women I cared for are gone. Melena is dead. Thalia has disappeared into the far territories. The pain of losing Diane, who will be back in New York by now, gets worse every day. There is nothing to distract me from thinking about her. I don't want to be distracted from thinking about her.

When my hunger becomes painful, I eat what's nearby: leaves, the last of the blackberries, dried twigs that have fallen to the forest floor. My skin is sickly and pale, even my nymph mark looks faded. I sleep all day and when I can't sleep I stare at the walls and relive summer with Diane: our dance at the Takanassee; the way she looked at me after Dylan tipped his hat to me in Woodstock; making love in the back of her car. I know I should be at Ben's place, comforting him, but my body is so heavy, it is difficult to move. After several days, Ben comes to me.

"I'm sorry," I say, when he walks in. "I should have been to see you."

"It's okay," he says, sitting down next to me. "I needed to be alone. I hung out at the waterfall for a few days."

"Did it help?" I ask, though the truth is I'm so bogged down in my own dark place, I don't much care.

"Honestly?" Ben says. "I think it might have made it worse. Being alone with your feelings when you feel like shit? Bad idea. But what about you? You don't look like you're doing too hot yourself. To tell you the truth, you're getting a little ripe."

I shrug.

"Listen," Ben says, "I know this thing about Melena is tough. Everybody's having a hard time with it. Last night I dreamed she walked into my cave. She said *that* was real and what happened with the lightning was a dream. She came into my bed and held down my shoulders like she used to do and kissed me all over my face. I could *feel* her, her belly was pressed against my belly, I was so happy. Then I woke up. But Melena had a good life, she went out the way she wanted. She wouldn't have wanted you to waste your life like this."

"Yeah, I know," I say, not moving.

"Look," Ben says. "I get it. You upset your father. Thalia's flown. The idiot human you liked went home. But it's a beautiful day, the grapes are ripe, you've got friends who miss you.

You'll feel much better if you get up and come out. *I'll* feel better. "

I say nothing.

"You want to at least talk to me about it?" Ben asks.

I would, but my throat is swelling. Water is coming out of my eyes, my nose is running. My breathing is ragged and gasping. It's impossible, satyrs cannot weep, but there it is.

"Danny," Ben says, "What the fuck? Is that . . . Are you *crying?*

"It's nothing," I manage to say.

"Bullshit," Ben says. "This is serious. I'm getting your father."

I wipe my eyes and find my voice.

"No," I say. "He's not the one I need to talk to."

CHAPTER TWENTY-FOUR

My first sight of the Galli-Curci estate makes me feel as if I have fallen forty years backwards, through a hole in time. All the other great houses are gone or in sagging disrepair, but Galli-Curci's, an imposing stone and timber mountain house, stands perfectly maintained: the paint pristine, the grounds groomed, as if waiting for the owner to walk through the door. It's a diva's home, commanding the mountain. I can see the upper Delaware River valley; the peaks of the Catskills, where the trees have started to turn; Plattekill Mountain, 26 miles away. Off to one side, down a sloping, meticulously clipped lawn, there's a pool and a stone patio. I imagine the world's most celebrated soprano swimming naked while my grandfather sits on the side of the pool, serenading her with his pipes. Then he wades into the shallow end and makes love to her up against the wall. I bet he was a spectacularly virile satyr.

I don't get too close to the house; there's said to be a caretaker who walks the grounds with a rifle. I stay in the woods. Somewhere on this immense property is my grandfather's cave. I just have to find it.

I walk north. The birds are full of song but not the one I need. Then I hear a mixed choir of yellow warblers and dark-eyed juncos and white-throated sparrows singing the opening bars of the aria I've been waiting for.

Quando m'en vo. . . .
When I go walking down the street,
People stop and look at me.

I listen respectfully until the verse ends. Then I take out my pipes and join in with the birds. We make an appreciative choir for one another. I sit down and wait. Even though the woods are thick, I can feel the warmth of the early September sun. I doze off. When I wake an old satyr is squatting next to me, gently shaking my shoulder. He looks like a weather-beaten version of Pop. His horns have age spots. One is missing a tip. A piece of an ear lobe is gone too. He's got a cane.

"Danny," he says. "I'm your grandfather, Maximillian."

I sit up and he hugs me to him. I breathe him in: old goat, grass, decaying leaves, musk. The lock of his embrace reminds me of Mrs. Belinsky, but Gramp is blood. I am warmed all over though I have only just met him.

Gramp sits back and looks me over.

"So the old man finally relented," Gramp says.

I don't want to hurt Gramp's feelings, but I don't want to lie to him, either.

"Not exactly," I say.

Gramp shrugs.

"Not important," he says. "Let's see what we got here. Very good-looking, of course. My nose, my eyes. Tall, for our line. And look at those shoulders. You're all grown up. You know the last time I saw you, you were a baby."

I've been so hung up on Diane, I hadn't even thought about this.

"You met my mother?" I say, excited.

Gramp waves his hand and I see that the tips of two fingers are missing.

"Accch," he says. "Let's not even get started with that drama."

"But you must have known who she was," I say.

"I was away," Gramp says. "By the time I got back she was gone and your father wouldn't say a word about her. Well, maybe a few words: 'Dead to me.' And you know how your father is when he makes up his mind. Whoever your mother was, she left him a beautiful baby. When I dipped you in the stream and thanked the gods, you had such sweet little hooves the trout rushed over to kiss them. You wailed all the time though."

"I don't remember," I say.

"No, of course not," Gramp says. "Let's go back to my place. Can you give me a hand?

I help him up. He walks slowly, with a limp.

"My legs aren't what they used to be," Gramp says. "Too much crazy living as your father undoubtedly told you."

I think it's best if I don't get into what Pop has told me.

"Are you sorry?" I ask.

Gramp laughs.

"Would you be here if you thought I was?" he says.

He leads us to his cave. It's unnaturally high and deep as if somebody carved it out with a bulldozer and brought in bluestone for the floor. The interior is more human than goat: there's a wide mahogany dresser topped with a tarnished silver tray and several etched wine glasses; a plump and faded red velvet armchair; and the most elaborate bed I have ever seen, human, with columns and a canopy and drapes. The bright fabric of birds and flowers could have been designed for a satyr.

"Keeps out the draft," Gramp says as he sees me looking at it. "And damn comfortable, too."

The cave has a pit for fire, which a healthy goat doesn't need. The walls are covered with framed photos of a dark-haired woman with strong features and in fancy dress: a kimono; a white gown with a fur trimmed robe; an off the shoulder dress with roses at the neck. There's also a yellowing poster for *Lucia di Lammermoor* at the Colon Theater in Buenos Aires. The date is June 17, 1915. The stars are Enrico Caruso and Amelita Galli-Curci.

"The opera singer," I say.

Gramps blows a kiss to the lady.

"The love of my life," he says.

I have, of course, brought gifts. Gramp grins when he sees them.

"Linzer tarts," Gramp says. "My favorite."

He picks up the bottle of wine and holds it close to his eyes to read the label. It's Italian; I chose it thinking it might bring back memories of his lover.

"Moscato D'Asti," Gramp says. "This does take me back. Grab those glasses and we'll sit in the sun. You reach a point when even on a warm day your bones are cold."

We go outside and settle ourselves on the grass. I open the bottle and pour.

"To the ladies and all their delights – like I have to tell a good-looking young goat," Gramp says.

I'm not going to shatter my grandfather's illusions and let him know what a loser his grandson is in that department.

"To the ladies," I say.

We sit, eating our Linzer tarts and drinking. The jam is warm, the wine is fizzy and light, with hints of orange blossom and honeysuckle. Suddenly I remember.

"I brought cheese and bread, too," I say. "I forgot. Maybe we should have started with that."

"Naah," Gramp says. "When you can start the day with jam, start the day with jam."

I feel a wave of contentment. It's good to be sitting here in the sun, with the grandfather I am finally meeting. But when it's September in the Catskills, even on a beautiful day you know the time for sitting in the sun is short. And directly across the mountain is Diane's house. I can't figure out how to tell my grandfather what's going on: your grandson fucked up so totally that the woman he loves told him he's shit. And, by the way, he's never even made love to her. Impressive satyr, huh? But Gramp has already figured out something is up.

"So, Danny," Gramp says. "It isn't that I'm not happy to see you. But I'm wondering: is everything okay?"

I blurt it right out.

"I'm in love with a girl," I say.

"Human," Gramp says and it's a statement, not a question.

"Yeah," I say. "She's gone back to New York. I can't stop thinking about her. She's not in love with me. Right now I think she kind of hates me. But she didn't always hate me;

before this thing happened she was getting to really like me. But she's human. And Pop always said . . . "

I stop, realizing there's no way to finish the sentence tactfully.

"Your father told you a human totally fucked up my life," Gramp says. "And you're hoping there was more to it than that."

"Yeah," I say. "Something like that."

Gramp pours himself some more wine.

"Not a story with a simple answer," he says.

"I don't care," I say. "I just want to know what happened."

"Not a short story, either," Gramp says.

"That's fine," I say. "I got time."

"Okay," Gramp says.

He sighs, like this is going to take a lot of energy.

"So where do I start? Our line is out of Europe. Your father told you that much at least?"

I nod.

"So I was born in Bavaria, which is in southern Germany, around 1901, 1902 on the human calendar," Gramp begins. "My colony lived on the Zugspitze, the highest mountain in Germany and in my opinion, the most beautiful. You had a lot of the same trees and flowers you have here, but these mountains, not even close. Belleayre Mountain is 2,000 feet. The Zugspitze is almost ten thousand."

This sounds a little like the stories Pop told me when I was small.

"Did you walk through clouds?" I ask.

"It seems like," Gramp says, "Though that just might be an old goat looking back."

I nod.

"There are refugees now in Fleischmanns who won't buy a German product, who spit when they hear the word 'Germany,'" Gramp says, "but it was a different country then. The Brownshirts, Hitler, that didn't exist. The air was sweet, the mountains were full of music: concert halls, little opera houses, everybody had a piano in the house. Richard Strauss, the composer, had a villa in Garmisch. And there were crafts-men in this other town, Mittenwald, who had made violins for maybe three hundred years. The music would come up the mountain and be absorbed into the trees, then the wood-cutters would chop down a tree for the violin – well, you can imagine the power of a Mittenwald violin."

"I belonged to a big colony and we were always up to some-thing," Gramp says. "Chasing the nymphs, playing cards with the goatherds, cheating the goatherds – I'll let you in on something: a family sends a son into the mountains to be a goatherd, he's generally not the sharpest card in the deck. Late August, you'd lie in the grass with your pals, debating an Anjou versus a Bosc versus a Comic for hours."

"We have the same arguments about apples," I say, pour-ing us more wine.

"Some things never change," Gramp says.

He pauses to take a sip of wine.

"And the sirens," Gramp says. "My gods. Is there anything better than a fuck on a riverbank? Those women get knocked for luring sailors to their deaths. What kind of jerk jumps off a boat when he can't swim?"

I feel a little awkward discussing sex with my grandfather, but there are things I need to know.

"Gramp," I say, "You were so close to the villages – did you ever do it with a human?"

"Why would I want to?" Gramp asks. "I'd see human women hiking; they couldn't compare to a German wood nymph. These nymphs had ropes of golden hair; they were so ripe all they had to do was touch a green pear and it was ready to eat. And of course I'd heard the stories about what happens if you mess around with a human. You get sick. They entrap you. You get stuck in her and the old goats have to call in the schweinebeschneider to chop off your dick."

"The *what*?"

"The pig castrator," Gramp says. "It's one of those stories they tell kids to scare them away from humans."

"I don't think they have pig castrators in Flesichmanns," I say, realizing as I'm speaking that I've squeezed my legs together.

"Consider yourself lucky," Gramp says. "Anyway it's the summer of 1912. I'm sitting in the sun in the hills around Garmisch when I hear a woman singing. I don't know what's more beautiful, the melody or the voice, I just know I've never heard anything like it. It's so sweet, so pure . . . this is going to sound crazy but the best I can describe it, it sounded like an invitation to another world. For the first time in my life I understood those sailors jumping off the ships. I follow the voice down the hill to a mountain house. I peek through the window and I see this dark-haired woman sitting at the piano, singing. She's not beautiful the way the nymphs are beautiful: She has a long face and a big nose and her hair is parted down the middle and slicked down, very severe. But she is a power-house. I live in nature, but it's benevolent nature; this woman is a force of nature who could take you someplace wild. It's like she's the master of two instruments, the piano and her voice. I didn't know the song she's singing but I know it now . . . "

Gramp starts singing.

"Quando m'en vo . . . "

"'Musetta's Waltz,'" I say.

"Yeah," Gramp said. "Then, it's just the most beautiful thing I have ever heard. I can't take my eyes off this woman. I know nothing about her but I know she is the one for me."

"Did she have a boyfriend?" I ask.

"She had a *husband*," Gramp says. "I realize that when I see her wedding ring – I was not totally ignorant of human custom. But I did not give a fuck. To me the husband was as inconsequential as a fly on a piece of fruit – flick him off. When you see the right one, nothing else matters. It's a body-to-body thing. You just *know*."

I love this story.

"I think so too," I say.

"The woman's name is Amelita Galli-Curci," Gramp says. "Curci is the husband's name. He's an aristocrat, a Marchese, which in Europe is more important than a count. You know what a count is, right? A big shot. That makes Amelita a Marchesa, a title she likes a lot. Luigi, the husband, is an architect and a set designer. They've only been married a few years, but there's already trouble. Luigi drinks too much, screws around, spends too much – well, Amelita likes to live large, too."

Gramp drifts off somewhere for a few moments. Then he comes back.

"Where was I?" he asks. "I lose track of things sometimes."

"You'd just seen Amelita for the first time," I say.

"Oh, yeah, right," Gramp says. "Amelita is not a kid when I see her, she's had 30 summers. She's not a star, she's been playing small concert houses in Europe, but she's made up her mind she's going to be a star. When La Scala, which is the big opera house in Europe, offers her a contract with only minor roles she tells them she will *never* sing there and tears it up. If I were giving advice about finding a passionate woman I'd say look for one who rips up contracts."

I want to get back to the romantic stuff.

"But when you meet Amelita the first time how do you know she likes you?" I ask.

"Yeah, right," Gramp says. "Well, Amelita's sitting at this piano and singing for at least an hour. I am crouching under the window, taking her in. Her scent is not like a nymph's with just the one flower, it's a combination of scents: bergamot, carnation, rose, violet, iris . . . "

"A perfume," I interrupt.

"Yup," Gramp says. "L'Heure Bleue from France. Not that I'd ever heard of captured scent at the time. Years later, when Amelita was away, I'd put a dab on my pillow to make sure I'd be with her in my dreams."

"Anyway, I don't know if she's visiting this house, if she lives there, but I know one thing: I don't want to let her get away. It's late afternoon when she comes out. She looks around like she thinks somebody is out there and turns up a trail. I stay in the woods, shadowing her, till I know we're a good distance from the house. Then I step into her path. Now here's where it gets wild. I'm dressed to pass: hat, clothes, shoes, the whole bit. But before I can say anything Amelita says, 'Good evening, goat.'"

"But how did she know?" I ask.

"She was one of those musicians that just could," Gramp says. "That can happen with the really good ones. I'm ready to court her, to tell her I've never heard a voice as beautiful as hers, to write her songs, to bring her a crown of flowers but none of it is necessary. She just takes my hand, she accepts me like we've been together for years. We just fit. I make love to her that night."

This is a story that's even better than Gatsby's.

"Weren't you worried about doing it with a human?" I ask.

"To tell you the truth, I wanted her so much I forgot all the stories," Gramp says. "After the first time I was a little nauseous and I couldn't move very fast. But I guess I built up a tolerance. And remember, there was no industry, we were in the mountains. Also, we didn't have long periods of time together. Amelita toured for months. If she was in a city close to a forest in warm weather, I'd meet her in the woods. I almost never spent time with her inside a building."

"Did you ever do a mind drop?" I ask.

"Once," Gramp says. "We were at her apartment in Milan and her husband walks in – that's probably how mind drops got started, husbands. I jump into her head, petrified, because in those days a husband could shoot a man he found making love to his wife and be considered a hero. The mind drop wasn't a big deal; when the husband left the apartment, I jumped out, no problem. The problem was that I hated being away from her.

"Spring, 1915, was especially bad. The war had begun in Europe, Amelita had been sick with typhus, in the opera house in Madrid she'd had to sing from a wheelchair. That really shook me. I guess it made me realize for the first time that I could lose her. Then that summer, she gets a big offer in South America. I can't travel with her across a large body of water, obviously. We get together in this port town called Huelva in the south-west of Spain, the night before she's sailing."

"Was the husband going too?" I ask.

"Yup," Gramp says. "Amelita finds a hotel where we can be alone for the afternoon, she books us the honeymoon suite. When I arrive she flings opens the door and she's naked except for a horned helmet she's swiped from *Die Walküre*. 'Now we both have horns,' she says. I don't think I ever laughed so hard in my life. It was also really, *really* sexy. I am not a kid at this point. I once made it with a nymph on the rocks overlooking the Partnachklamm gorge, which is a hell of a drop, just to turn up the heat; I'd been held hostage for a week by a river nymph. But that afternoon with Amelita in the honeymoon suite is something I will never forget. We drink May wine. We eat tiny little strawberries. She gets on all fours and insists I fuck her like a ram."

"Whoa!" I say, blushing.

Gramp is smiling. This is a memory he keeps like the pictures on the wall.

"We nap, we make love, we nap some more," Gramp says. "When I wake up, I am in a room with round windows and the room is rocking. That's when I realize I must have done a mind drop. I'm in her stateroom and we're out at sea. I'm so terrified, I pass out."

"And the next thing you wake up in the Catskills?" I ask.

"I wish," Gramp says. "The next thing, I wake up in the Colon Theater in Buenos Aires, and Caruso is bellowing at me. Thank the gods, I liked Donizetti. We're in cities in South America for six months: Rio, Montevideo, São Paulo. Wherever Amelita's booked we find a spot in the mountains or a really big park and I dig myself a ditch near a tree and sleep. I think, actually, that's what saved my life. But the trees on Sugarloaf Mountain aren't the trees in Bavaria. *Jackfruit. Palm trees.* It's not natural."

Gramp pours himself some more wine.

"Sometimes when I wake up, I can't remember my name," he says. "One morning, I see a joint on the little finger of my left hand is missing. A few weeks later, part of my ear lobe is gone. It doesn't take a lot of brains to figure out that the most vulnerable parts are the hanging bits. I start sleeping with my hand on my cock."

I remember Ben and the half-man forest god who wanted part of his penis.

"I think that might have to do with the gods down there," I tell my grandfather. "There's a forest god who's missing half his body parts so he tries to steal them. I saw him here once, in the woods."

"A half-man?" Gramp says. "I'm sorry I missed him. He's probably running around with my ear lobe. Where was I in this story?"

"South America," I say.

"Right," Gramp says. "The tour ends, but the war is still on, so we sail to New York City. I am now seriously concerned about my health. I tell Amelita I need to get to the mountains. Highmount is big with opera singers, so she wrangles us an invitation to the Catskills."

Gramp sighs.

"I'd been around spa mountain towns in Bavaria," he says. "The mountains were higher, but in Fleischmanns in 1916, you had a sense of Europe. You had the Grand Hotel in Highmount, 400 rooms and waiters in black tie; you had The St. Regis by Lake Switzerland, which looked like the hotels on Lake Como. The Fleischmanns family compound which had maybe six, seven buildings and of course a fantastic view of the mountains and valley, had just been sold and turned into a hotel. Amelita drives to the top of Belleayre Mountain which has an even more stupendous view and says, 'I'm gonna build here.' I say, 'I'm gonna sleep here' and find a cave. I wake up five years later and find Amelita has bought 180 acres and built an estate. And gotten herself a new husband."

He doesn't say anything for a while. I realize he's drifted off again.

"Gramp?" I say, touching his arm.

He snaps back.

"What, what?" he stammers.

"You were telling me about Amelita getting a new husband," I say. "So the thing Pop says about falling in love with a human messing up your life, that was true."

Gramp snorts.

"Your father suddenly cares about husbands? I find that unlikely."

"No," I say, "All the other stuff. Your health, the sleeping all the time, your, uh, missing fingers and things . . . "

"Minor," Gramp says. "Not even worth mentioning. Amelita and I had a great life. We weren't together every minute; she had her world, I had mine, but it worked. I'm not gonna lie, it wasn't perfect, I would have loved to have had a son with her . . . "

"Wait," I say, "That's not possible . . . "

Gramp looks amused.

"Yeah, that's what they want you to think," he says.

I'm having trouble believing this.

"It's not like two species? A cat and a dog?"

"No," Gramp says. "I'm not saying I've ever seen it, I just know, in Europe, there were old goats who said it could be done. The satyr has to want the child so much it consumes him; he has to be burning for it. And of course there are consequences. You anger the gods, there are always consequences."

This is all too weird.

"But why would the gods care?" I ask.

"It's an insult," Gramp says. "Fucking around with humans, that's fine. The summer and all its pleasures were created for us, after all. A ripe apple, a nineteen-year-old human – it's the same to them. But you have a child with a human, you're saying you find their species equal to us so of course the gods are pissed. Instead of the normal, 200 summer lifespan, the minute that child is born, the satyr's lifespan shrinks to a human's: seventy years. Maybe less, since you can also get their sicknesses. And there's no rebirth as a forest spirit or satyr; you go to the next world as a human – if they even have a next world."

"And you would have been willing to do that?" I say. "Lose like, two-thirds of your life?"

"Absolutely," Gramp says. "But Amelita wasn't into kids. Opera was her life and I respected that. She toured all over the world in winter, but I was sleeping then anyway. I was fine about the husband. We'd talked about that. Why should she be alone for months? And in the summer if Amelita wasn't around, there were the nymphs, one of whom was generous enough to give me a son. Your grandmother, Saris. Lovely creature. She had violet eyes, did your father ever tell you that? She died on this mountain, you know."

"Yeah," I said. "I know. Pop leaves her flowers."

Gramp looks pleased.

"That's good," he says. "It's important to remember."

He returns to his story.

"The home Amelita built for us here, she called it Sul Monte, a lot of it's gone but you can see for yourself how magnificent it was. She had a pool, a music studio, a guest house, a farm with cows. She didn't need 180 acres, she bought that for me: it was posted, no hunters or hikers, so I was protected. Amelita was a diva through and through. She named the animals for her favorite roles. Let's see if I can remember. The rooster was Don Basilio. The cows were Tosca, Butterfly, Zazà, and Mimi."

"So you don't have any bad feelings about getting involved with a human?" I say.

Gramp laughs.

"No, of course not," he says. "This was the woman I loved. Traveling might have messed me up, but I saw a world I would never have seen. And as your father conveniently forgets, if I'd never met Amelita and stayed with my colony in Europe, he never would have been born. You wouldn't exist."

"Why?" I ask.

"The wars," Gramp says. "Satyrs can't exist with that much hate. I like to think I would have been brave enough to try to get out, but who knows? World War One was bad: the fighting in the Argonne forest, the poison gases, the trenches desecrating the forests. It took out maybe a quarter of the satyrs in Europe. World War Two was worse. The areas around Auschwitz, Dachau, Bergen-Belsen, Treblinka; not one satyr is alive in those woods. You think we would have survived in Bavaria, a six-hour drive from Hitler and his ridiculous Eagle's Nest? I had a nephew, Leonid, who fell in love with a Jewish girl in Stuttgart. They had already shot her parents and brothers. When the Nazis came for her, Leonid knew what would happen, but he didn't want her to be alone.

He did a drop and died in her mind in the gas chamber at Auschwitz."

I never knew anything about family left behind in Europe.

"I'm sorry, Gramp," I say.

Gramp pats my shoulder.

"You have to live while you can, Danny," he says.

He's quiet for awhile, lost in thought.

"I wonder sometimes if Amelita's health was ruined because of me," he says. "Ten years after we came over, the doctors found a goiter. Did that happen because she had a satyr in her head for a year? It pressed on her larynx and ruined her voice. The upper range was gone. When she sang at the Budapest Opera House in 1930, they hissed at her. Can you imagine what that would be like for a woman who had been one of the greatest singers in the world?"

"When did Amelita die?" I ask.

Gramp looks at me, surprised.

"She's not dead," Gramp says. "She's in California. La Jolla. She went out for the husband's asthma. She's not in great health herself these days. I go out when I can to see her.

It comes back to me.

"Pop said you traveled," I say. "I just couldn't see how."

"There are always ways," Gramp says. "If you're willing to take the risk."

CHAPTER TWENTY-FIVE

Being squished between crates of cauliflower in a rickety old truck speeding down a highway is unnerving. The crates come at me no matter where I move, whenever the driver switches lanes. I had figured the slatted sides of the truck would allow in the healthful outdoor air, but looking out, when the driver gets on a road called the New York State Thruway, I'm not so sure. There are four lanes of vehicles, some of which are spewing black smoke. I've never been surrounded by so much machinery.

The truck, driven by a worker on the cauliflower farm near where Ben lives, is heading to a market called Hunts Point in a section of New York City called the Bronx. Where exactly that is, we don't know, but it doesn't matter. How big can New York be?

Ben was, of course, opposed to this trip, but Gramp had told me how to stay safe.

"All I have to do is get out in three days and keep it green," I told Ben. "I stick close to the trees which there are thousands of in New York. I'll be back before anyone knows I'm gone."

Now, looking out at a long truck with too many wheels to count, I'm not feeling so confident. I climb on top of the crates under cover of the tarp and repeat the incantation satyrs have used since trees flowered and vines bore grapes:

The world is large and the leaves fall,

Protect the satyr, far from the forest.

Then I force myself to think of the leaves rustling outside my cave in evening and will myself to sleep.

I'm startled awake by people shouting. Through the slats I see we're backing up to the bay of a brick building. A man with a clipboard is hollering to the driver. A moment later, the tarp is torn off and I'm exposed. I pull down my Yankees cap to make sure my horns are hidden. The man with the clipboard laughs.

"That's right, pal, whatever happens, hold on to the hat," Clipboard Man says.

I look at his hat. He's wearing the same cap that I am.

"Fuck the Dodgers," he says, in what I realize from his tone is one of his sacred invocations.

I bow my head.

"Fuck the Dodgers," I say, respectfully.

I would have thought Clipboard Man would be angry at me for sneaking onto his truck. But apparently in the Bronx, they don't care what you do as long as you're wearing the right hat.

"So you know where you are?" Clipboard Man asks.

"Not exactly," I say. "I need to get to get to NYU. In the Village."

"Were you planning on hoofing it?" Clipboard Man says.

I glance down at my sneakers, but the laces are tight.

"It's kind of a pain in the ass from here," Clipboard Man says. "You got the bus then the train. You know what? For a Yankees fan, I got a better idea."

An hour later, after a ride in another truck, I'm in Greenwich Village in front of a fruit and vegetable store with an awning that reads "Balducci's Produce." I've seen pictures of New York City in magazines, but standing in the street I'm in a sensory spin.

A couple fights; a firetruck careens across West Tenth Street with firemen hanging from the side and siren screaming; an ambulance, its own siren wailing, speeds up Greenwich Avenue. The noisiest place is a tall brick building called the Women's House of Detention. There are bars on the windows and the women behind them, bereft at being separated from their lovers, scream down to them on the sidewalk.

When you gettin' me out of here? Where's that scumbag lawyer? Where the fuck's my bail?

New York University, Clipboard Man has told me, is nearby, east on West Eighth Street, then south when I hit Waverly Place.

Eighth Street is crammed with so many wonders that eager as I am to find Diane, I want to look at everything. A store on the corner of the Avenue of the Americas and Eighth Street is selling the juice of the Orange Julius plant, which has such a divine fragrance that I stop and have one. It is a delicious juice, milky and sweet. I pass a half-dozen bookstores filled with more books than I could dream; a jewelry shop with turquoise and silver from far desert territories; clothing stores, including one selling furs of long dead animals. I stop and bow my head for the lives lost.

New York University, I was told, is on Waverly Place, op- posite Washington Square Park. I've eaten a lot of pictures of universities in magazines, so I know what to expect: grand, ivy-covered stone buildings and sprawling lawns; neatly groomed young people in plaid jackets or skirts with knee socks. But all I see is a row of tall, ugly buildings and hoards of young people in jeans. Nobody is wearing plaid.

I walk around, trying to pick up Diane's scent. It's im- possible. Hundreds of women pass by, many wearing Kiehl's Original Musk. Still, I wait outside NYU all afternoon, until they turn out the lights and lock the doors.

I'm discouraged and hungry. I go to a nearby shop called "Chock Full o'Nuts" and buy two sandwiches and a container of milk. They cost 35 cents for a sandwich and 15 cents for milk, proof that the rolls of twenties Ben stole for me for this trip will be more than enough. Then I go into Washington Square Park and sit down on a bench and eat. I immediately feel better. My sandwiches, cream cheese on walnut and rai- sin bread, are delicious. Washington Square seems to be the gathering place of the Village. Students are lounging about and tossing colored discs to one another. Two men are play- ing guitars around a large fountain in the middle of the park, singing a traditional beatnik song:

Hangman, hangman, slack your rope,
Slack it for a while,
For I think I see my mother coming . . .

I take my flute out of my jacket pocket and join in. The musicians smile at me. It's nice to be accepted by authentic beatniks. I am not happy about missing Diane, but if these few streets are all there is to NYU, I will certainly find her tomorrow.

I look around for a place to sleep. Many of the shrubs and trees in the park are sickly. But in the northeast corner there is a large English elm which probably put down its roots three hundred years ago. I lean close to its trunk and address it quietly and respectfully.

"I am Daniel, son of Jacob," I say. "I've traveled far from my home in the mountains and would be grateful for your hospitality."

Then I quickly climb up into the crook of two strong branches, high enough so no human will spot me. The branches of the elm wrap tenderly around me and I fall into a sweet, deep sleep, awakening only when I feel a noose tightening around my neck.

CHAPTER TWENTY-SIX

A young woman with coffee-colored skin is sitting on a branch above me. She wears a torn blouse and a long skirt, and even with a rope around my neck, I can't help noticing she's very pretty. She's also furious.

"What you doing in my tree, boy?" she asks.

"Sleeping," I manage to say.

I know the city has dangers, but this is worse than anything I imagined. She must be an angry tree spirit. I didn't know they could assume bodily form.

"You ask me before you climb up?" she says. "Or you just take what you want, like every other white boy?"

"Listen, I'm not from around here," I say. "If I did something to offend you, I'm sorry."

"You're sorry you hung me by the neck and made a spectacle of it?" the woman says. "I'm sorry too. Took me five minutes to die."

I'm horrified.

"That's awful," I say, "I would never do that."

"You're white, ain't ya?" the woman says and kicks me.

I go sailing out of the tree and hit the ground. My Yankees hat flies off my head and lands beside me. It's daylight. There is no rope around my neck. I look up. The woman is gone, but on a bench opposite me I see a middle-aged man in a rumpled suit with a newspaper and a cup of coffee, looking down at me. He seems mildly interested like I'm a bird that fell out of a nest, but he's not surprised. I guess it takes a lot to surprise a New Yorker.

"Nice horns, but the one on the right is a little lopsided," he says. "Hazing thing?"

I have no idea what he's talking about, but I play along.

"Yeah," I say, snatching my hat and putting it back on.

"How long were you up there?" the man asks.

"I don't know," I say. "I fell asleep and a girl with a rope tried to hang me. I mean, I dreamt she was going to hang me."

"Rose Butler," the man said. "She was a slave 150 years ago. It was in your orientation pack, remember? Nineteen years old, set fire to her owner's house and locked the family in. You were sleeping in a hanging tree, kid. They also buried paupers here. This whole park's full of poor, dead people."

"You know a lot about this place," I say, getting up.

"I teach history," the man says. "You sure you're not hurt? That was a big fall."

"I'm fine," I say, "Would you know what time it is?"

"A student with horns who's concerned about getting to class on time," the professor says. "This is even more astonishing than sleeping in a tree."

He checks his watch.

"Almost nine," he says. "If you have a class you'd better run."

I trot across the park to the buildings on University Place. Students are streaming in from all over. I stand in the middle of the block, scanning. Dozens of girls rush by. Then I spot Diane walking along the south side of the park carrying a book bag. My heart starts racing. I run over and step in front of her just as she's about to cross the street. She is not happy to see me.

"Danny," Diane says. "Oh, Christ. What are you doing here?"

Not the warmest welcome, but not unexpected either. I just have to break through.

"I came to New York to see you," I say. "I wanted to explain."

Diane is glaring at me.

"Explain being an asshole who attacks women?" Diane says. "No explanation necessary. It was obvious."

"No," I say. "It's not what you think. It's complicated. Look, can't you just give me a few minutes so we can talk?"

"I have a shrink appointment," Diane says. "Now would you get out of my fucking way?"

I don't move.

"Look, I didn't feel you up on purpose, I did it to save you," I say.

It comes out louder than I intended. Two students walking by turn around.

Diane lowers her voice.

"I know exactly what you did and I can't believe that now you've followed me to New York," she says. "You're obsessed and you're crazy. If you don't beat it, I'm calling the cops."

A few students are looking at us. I step out of Diane's way as she walks quickly across the street into a forbidding building of brick and concrete. It's no place for a creature of the forest, but I've got to go in.

I spot a sign for counseling services and follow it to a large room on the second floor, with armchairs and lots of magazines. From down a hall I hear a jumble of young, female voices.

"...fat....," "...mother....," "...fat...," "...mother...," "...fat... "

I slip into the hall. There are nearly a dozen closed doors. Halfway down the hall I pick up Diane's scent.

"Your eyelids are getting heavy, so heavy," I hear a man behind the door saying. " If you want to sleep, sleep."

I know what to do. It's dangerous, but I've got the solution. If I can get into Diane's head while she's sleeping I'll be able to explain everything.

I'm still unclear about how to get into someone's head; it's possible the person has to be yearning for you. But Pop has leapt into the heads of women he doesn't know who are simply lonely and neglected. Maybe all it takes for a woman to be receptive is to long for love in a general way. Ben didn't know how he got into Yvonne Rio's head. Gramp claimed he wasn't even awake when he fell into Galli-Curci's mind.

It's true that there is a door between me and Diane, but if a satyr can leap through someone's skull, how can a door matter? The important thing, I think, must be to concentrate very hard, to think of the power of love, then make a great leap.

I'm scared, but great love takes courage.

I close my eyes and concentrate on the love that has driven me to a dangerous city of steel and concrete. I picture my love blazing through the door like a shooting star.

The world goes dark.

I feel my hooves leave the ground and next thing I know, I have landed on my ass on a thick carpet.

"Oh, Christ!" I hear the shrink yell.

I open my eyes. Diane is lying asleep on a couch across the room from me. That doesn't seem right, it feels too far away. I feel a terror in the pit of my belly as the realization hits: I have landed in the wrong head. And now I'm hearing the shrink's thoughts.

"A satyr? With horns? What the fuck? Why did that pop into my head?"

I grab my Yankees cap and slap it back on my head. I've got to be calm. If I got in I can get out, but with this guy's thoughts rattling around, I can't get a firm footing. The room I'm in is a replica of the shrink's office, but the floor is rocking. It's making me ill. I hold on to the side of the shrink's chair to try to steady myself. Then I look out of the canopy of his lashes at Diane, concentrate, and send my love blazing to her.

An electric current shoots through me, lights up the room, and knocks me against the wall.

"Whoa!!!" the shrink yelps.

I see Diane stirring.

The floor is rocking. The shrink's thoughts are coming from all directions, bumping into each other.

" Stroke?" –" Brain bleed?" – " Double vision?"

He stands up, walks over to a window and checks his reflection.

"Face drooping? No. Arm weakness? No. Trouble speaking? Get her the fuck out."

The shrink returns to his chair and addresses Diane.

"In a few minutes, I am going to count to three. At three you will wake up. You will be relaxed and refreshed, as if you had a nice, long sleep. One, two. . . . "

"No way, not yet, I want out of here!" I yell.

"Three," the therapist says.

Diane sits up, dazed.

"Did it work?" Diane asks. "Was I out?"

I stare at Diane, concentrating my love as hard as I can.

I love you so much. I love you more than Gatsby loved Daisy. I love you with my mind and body, my heart and horns.

I focus and leap.

Another electrical charge makes the light in my room flicker, but it is much weaker, and so am I. These leaps take energy. I'm spent. Even if I can't make it into Diane's head, I try one more time to send her my thoughts.

Don't leave me, please don't leave me.

Then I pass out.

When I wake up, it's only me and the shrink. We're not in his office anymore; we're sitting on a sofa in a room with tall windows and shelves full of books. It's getting dark outside.

I'm panicking again, but I force myself to breathe slowly. Pop never talked about being stuck in anybody's mind. No, wait, that's exactly what Pop warned me about: you go into a human's mind and she likes you so much she won't let you out. I'll rest and get my strength back, then I'll be able to jump right out. It will probably be easier once he's asleep. Can I tell him to go to sleep? Do I have any influence over him? If I touch him can he feel it? Of course they've got to be able to feel it, why else would Pop go in?

I reach out my hand and touch the shrink's nose lightly, like a fly.

He swats it away and I feel it.

Now *that* is weird.

I lean close to him and whisper in his ear.

"You are sleepy, very sleepy. I am going to count to three and when I reach three, you are going to go right to sleep."

His thoughts sound like he is speaking.

"The hell I am. A satyr, what's that about? Or is it a faun? Never did know the difference. And why is he wearing clothes? Damn cute though; looks kind of like Sal Mineo with horns. When I saw "Exodus" he was so cool. Those eyes, that beautiful, petulant mouth. I wanted Sal Mineo. I wanted him to love me like he loved Jill Haworth. Take out your big thing and shove me up against the demarcation line, Sal, but watch out for the barbed wire . . . "

He's getting an erection. I see the outline against his pants. He unzips his fly and pulls out his dick. There's a drop of semen on the tip. Interesting how repulsive that is when it's not your own.

"I'm not Sal Mineo," I holler. "I'm a satyr who got into your head."

"A satyr? Why not? Fuck me, goat-boy! Fuck me like they did to Sal Mineo in "Exodus." You know that part when he says, 'The Nazis, they used me like a woman' . . . "

I know what he wants, but I'm not the guy who is going to give it to him. Still, sharing his thoughts is taking me places: loving men on a summer day holding hands in the sunshine like any other couple. I think of George hugging Dante.

"You don't want a satyr in your head," I tell the shrink. "You need someone real. A man who will love you for who you really are. And bring you flowers."

The shrink's hard-on wilts.

"I've always wanted someone to bring me flowers. Why do you have to be a woman to get them? The only way a man gets flowers is to drop dead. I've always been attracted to men. Why am I lying to myself? What the hell is so wrong with it?"

"Nothing," I say. "The important thing is love."

"Yeah and I love my horny Sal Mineo!"

Not good. I will be stuck in his head listening to college girls whine about their mothers, forever.

"Forget movie stars," I say. "Think about a man you know in real life."

"Chalmers. He asked me for drinks once, but I had to work. His forearms. So beefy. He grew up in Scotland. I know it's a cliché, but I think of him in a kilt . . . "

"You're going to close your eyes and go to sleep," I say. "A deep, deep sleep. You're going to dream of you and Chalmers, naked in bed. He has his arms around you. He loves you so much that every day he brings you flowers and sings you a song he's written just for you. A song so beautiful it calls you to him."

A moment later, I land with a thud on the shrink's floor, my hat beside me.

The shrink sleeps on, smiling.

I put on my hat, go to the door, and very quietly let myself out.

CHAPTER TWENTY-SEVEN

My legs are wobbly as I leave the apartment and it's hard to open the door that leads to the street. The position of the sun tells me it's mid-afternoon. I've been in a human's head for several hours and I feel like I may collapse. I need greenery.

The street I'm on is quiet, with three-story high brick houses and a few straggly trees. I walk to the closest, a skinny ginkgo biloba, introduce myself, and make my request.

"Might you spare me a few of your leaves?" I ask, "that I may renew myself?"

The tree rustles its leaves and I gently break off a dozen. They smell of dog piss, but they make me feel stronger. Looking down the street, I see the Women's House of Detention. I know where I am: Ninth Street, near the Avenue of the Americas, just one street away from where I arrived in the Village. I feel more confident. I'll just head back to Washington Square Park and wait for Diane to pass through again.

I pull my Yankees hat low on my head and find a bench on the opposite side of the park from the angry elm, near West 4th Street where chess players are hanging out. It's evening, hundreds of people rush by. My optimism evaporates. My sense of smell is so overwhelmed I doubt I could pick out Diane if she was standing behind me. This is my second day in the city, I've got one more day and I have no idea how to find Diane.

I'm so lost in thought that I don't realize a man in a corduroy cap and denim jacket, carrying a guitar case, has stopped in front of me.

"Hey," he says. "Ain't you the goat from Woodstock?"

The man sticks out his hand.

"Bob," he says. "Café Espresso. Remember?"

I'm too tired to be impressed by a big shot but not so tired I'm going to expose myself to a human.

"Danny," I say, shaking his hand. "I'm obviously not a goat."

Dylan laughs.

"I know what you are, man," he says. "I knew the minute I saw you. Mind if I sit?"

I shrug.

Dylan sits and lights up a fat, misshapen cigarette. It's marijuana, strong and sweet. Dylan takes a deep breath, holds it, and offers it to me.

"Thanks, but I don't smoke," I say.

"You sure?" Dylan says. "It'll take your mind off your troubles. Which, if you don't mind me sayin,' it looks like you got."

"It's okay," I say. "I'm good."

Dylan looks skeptical but says nothing. He takes a few more drags, then he stubs out the joint on the bottom of his boot and puts it in his pocket.

"So, what's going on, woman trouble?" Dylan asks. " 'Cause living in the woods, it can't be money trouble and it can't be career trouble and there's only one other trouble left."

I'm not sure how much I should tell a human, but I'm feeling beaten and alone. And musicians are supposed to be kindred spirits, so what's to lose?

"It's my girl," I say. "Well, actually, she's not exactly my girl. We had a fight, and now she won't talk to me."

"The one you were with in Woodstock?" Dylan says.

"Yeah," I say.

"I remember her," Dylan says, which seems unlikely, but is nice of him to say. "Cute."

"She goes to NYU," I say. "I tried to talk to her yesterday, and she told me to get lost. If I could just get her to listen I could straighten things out, but I don't even know where she lives."

"Did you look her up in the phone book?" Dylan asks.

I've never heard of that kind of book.

"No," I say.

Dylan laughs.

"Goat, we gotta get you out more," he says. "Phone books got addresses. And if there ain't a phone book handy you just ask the operator. You ever use a phone?"

I shake my head, embarrassed.

"No," I say. "I don't think she'd talk to me anyway."

"You know what? I could call her for you," Dylan says. "She's into music, right? I'll tell her you're a good guy, just come over and meet us at the Kettle and hear you out. And if she still hates your guts she'll get to hear some good music. What's her name?"

I'm torn between my desperation to see Diane and fear she'll humiliate me by telling Bob Dylan I'm a creep. Who am I kidding? I've got to see her.

"Diane LeVine," I say.

Dylan goes to a phone booth on the corner of West 4th Street. Ten minutes later, he's back.

"Tough chick," he says. "Made me sing, 'Hard Rain's Gonna Fall.' Says *maybe* she'll come. Bullshit. She's coming. C'mon."

I get up. Bob pulls his shirt collar up around his ears, pulls his cap down low and we turn south down MacDougal Street.

"By the way, the woman we're meeting up with is my girl-friend," Dylan says. "So don't say nothin' about Joanie in Woodstock, okay?"

I nod. Dylan seems to have a satyr's attitude toward love. And he's very comfortable around me. It would be wild if his father was one of those satyrs that Gramp talked about who mated with a human, though that was just legend. On the other hand, he is always wearing a hat. Maybe he's hiding something, too.

We walk down the crowded street. The Kettle, which is really named Kettle of Fish, is a run-down bar.

"Gets kind of crazy downstairs these days," Dylan says.

Dylan leads the way to a table up against the back wall where a pretty, dark-haired girl in a tunic and black tights is waiting. I recognize her. She's the woman on the cover of his album. She's friendly and down-to-earth. I like her right away.

"Suze," Dylan says, introducing us. "This here is Goat. He's a musician from Woodstock."

Dylan orders us drinks. I have some red wine, which I realize I've been parched for, and try to make conversation, but I'm distracted thinking about Diane. I keep checking the door and trying to look like I'm not checking the door. She walks in.

"That's her," I whisper to Dylan.

Diane is wearing a black turtleneck, black skirt, and black tights. She's looking around, trying to be cool, but when she sees Dylan I can see her lose it for a moment. Then she comes over. All I get for a hello is a brisk nod.

I'm so clutched up, it's tough to introduce everybody. But Dylan turns on the charm in a way I never would have guessed he could. He gives Diane a smile like he's thrilled to be seeing her.

"Hey, really happy to see you again," he says, taking her hand. "Great guy you've got here. *Great* musician."

Diane is melting a little. Maybe.

"Yeah," she says.

A skinny little guy with a goatee comes over to Dylan.

"They're ready for you downstairs," he says.

We go outside and head down a narrow staircase with a rickety iron rail to a basement club – The Gaslight.

"You got your pipes on you, right?" Dylan asks.

"How did you . . . ?" I start to ask.

"Goat," Dylan says.

The club is narrow, with stone and stucco walls and a hodgepodge of tables. When Dylan walks in there's a murmur of excitement. A waitress leads Diane and Suze and me to a round table near the stage. Dylan, on stage, is strapping on a guitar and harmonica, joking with another guitarist, stocky and bearded, who's near the microphone.

"Dave Van Ronk," Suze whispers. "Blues singer. Kind of runs the scene."

Speaking to the audience, Dylan seems shy. He doesn't make eye contact, he mumbles.

"Come out with an album this spring," he says. "Thought I'd play a few tunes that didn't make it. . . . old blues song . . . "

Once he starts singing, the shyness disappears:

Baby, please don't go,
Baby, please don't go,
Baby, please don't go back to New Orlean,
You gonna hurt me so.

It's a traditional song, but Dylan is making it his own; he's a guy who's hurting and trying to make it seem like he's not hurting, sometimes even making fun of his hurt. I glance over at Diane, and I can tell she feels the same way. Bob Dylan is a one-of-a-kind genius. We're hearing a song tonight that is never going to be sung exactly this way again. It's one-time only art, like the sunrise.

Dylan plays two songs he says never made the "Freewheelin'" album. He sings "Blowin' in the Wind," the song Diane and I listened to all summer. I wish I could take her hand. When Dylan finishes the song, the audience goes crazy.

Dylan smiles.

"Good friend of mine, fine flute player, is in town from Woodstock," he says. "He's never played New York City, but maybe we can get him up here."

He looks straight at me.

"Whadaya say, Goat?"

I can't believe this is happening. I'm petrified. Bob Dylan wants me to play in front of a room full of humans. If my hat slips, I'm finished. And what if I screw up? These aren't my friends back in the colony. But the audience is waiting and Diane is looking at me like now she's about to find out who I really am. I take my flute out of my jacket pocket and walk on stage.

Dylan leans towards me.

"What'll it be?" he says.

I'm so nervous I go blank.

"Your call," I say.

Dylan looks out at Diane, smiles mischievously, picks up his harmonica and starts playing the first few notes of the song I first heard when I found Diane; "Honey Just Allow Me One More Chance." That's the perfect song, all right . . . give me just one more chance, Diane, to get along with you. I pick it up. Dylan is so into the music, so sensitive, that my nerves disappear and it's like we've played together all our lives.

Diane is trying to look cool, but people in the audience are looking at her, wondering who the girl is that Bob Dylan is singing to, and I know she's getting off on it. At the bridge Dylan steps back, cuing me to take the lead. It's a fast beat for pipes, but a good one; it's a melody that gives a flute space to fly. When we're done, the room explodes in applause.

I smile and nod my head in thanks and start to walk off, but Dylan stops me.

"Okay, Goat," he says, "Go get 'em."

He walks off, leaving me alone on the stage.

They say that when you are about to die, your life flashes before you. What flashes before me now is the music of my life: the Lorenz Hart song I sang to Diane when we went to Crump's Castle; the aria that made my grandfather fall in love with Galli-Curci and follow her across the sea. Or should

I play it safe and go with a beatnik song that a crowd that loves Bob Dylan would like?

Appear muse, goddamn it. Materialize and guide me.

Out in the audience I see a woman who looks like Melena, smiling at me. What did Melena say? Play from the heart. What the audience might prefer no longer matters. Perfection no longer matters.

I'm going with "Stay With Me," the song that keeps going through my head and refuses to go away. I wish there were someone to accompany me so I could sing to Diane, but if the feelings are powerful enough the music will carry the words.

I bring the flute to my lips and play, building to the closing verse.

I'll be strong
I'll be wild
For a touch of your hand, for a glimpse of that smile
'Cause I know, I just know
You're the one.
So when dark comes tonight
Hold me close, make it right
Greet the stars, sing the sun
Stay with me.

When I am done, the room is dead quiet for a moment.

"They hated it," I think.

Then there is stomping and shouting and applause. I look for the woman who resembled Melena, but I can no longer find her. Dylan steps up to the mike.

"Goat," he says to the crowd. "You heard him here first."

And to me.

"Great tune, Goat. We should do something with it."

I walk off stage and go back to Diane who is finally smiling at me.

"That was really good, Danny," she says.

I am so happy I might be my own song. We say our good-byes and walk up the stairs to MacDougal. It's drizzling and foggy. The streetlights, illuminating the fog, are making everything softer. It's become a magic night. I don't want to ruin it by saying the wrong thing.

I stand on the sidewalk, not sure what to do.

Diane doesn't seem to know what to do either. Dylan and the music have moved me out of the monster zone, but I'm not the guy she hung out with all summer either.

"So," I say. "Do you think we could sit somewhere out of the rain and talk?"

"We could go to a café," she says. "There's the Rienzi across the street. Or the Reggio."

I look across the street.

"They look crowded," I say. "Can't we go to your place?"

Diane gives me a skeptical look

"I'll sit on the other side of the room," I say. "I just need to explain.

Diane seems to be considering it.

"You promise not to try anything?" she asks.

"Diane we were friends all summer," I say. "Did I ever do anything you didn't want me to do?"

"You're kidding, right?" Diane says. "Feeling me up when I was knocked out? The mermaids?"

"The pool wasn't my idea, it was a prank," I say. "Well, not a prank exactly. It's a long story. I can't tell you with people all around."

Diane leads us west, through Sheridan Square, to a white brick building on Christopher Street where a man in uniform stands guard.

"I know, doorman building, very bourgeois," Diane says, though I haven't said a word. "My father insisted."

We get into an elevator, which makes me nauseous, and get off on the eighth floor. The apartment has large windows that overlook the Village. The furniture looks new, but there's a grimy poster on the wall about a World Congress of women in Russia and another about a march on Washington for jobs and freedom. Diane gestures for me to take an armchair near the window and sits down opposite on the couch. Then she jumps up, nervous.

"I really need to smoke," she says. "How about you? Want some weed?"

I didn't smoke with Dylan, but I sure need something now. Maybe it will calm me down.

Diane opens the window, takes a small bag of marijuana from a desk drawer and rolls a fat joint. A sweet smell fills the room. Diane takes two long drags and passes it to me.

I take a breath and breathe it in deeply the way she did. It's scratchy and thick. I cough violently.

Diane is annoyed.

"Don't tell me you never smoked dope," she says.

"Not really," I manage to say.

"Weird, for a musician," Diane says. "Okay, take a little less and inhale it slower. Then hold it in as long as you can."

I try it again. It's less irritating this time.

"Better," I say. "But I don't feel anything."

"It takes a while," Diane says.

I take another hit and pass it back across the room to her.

She inhales.

"So," she says. "Start explaining. And it better be good."

There is a speech I've rehearsed a million times, but it has gone out of my head.

"Where do you want me to start?" I ask.

"How about feeling me up on the mountain when I was knocked out cold?"

"Okay," I say. "But I didn't mean to feel you up. I don't even like that expression."

Diane glares at me.

I try again.

"Look," I say. "I did touch you, but it wasn't the way you think. You came tumbling down the mountain and I was afraid you were going over. I grabbed you and when I saw you up close, you were so beautiful I just wanted to touch you. It sounds awful when I say it like this, I knew I shouldn't, but I couldn't stop myself. And then you woke up and screamed."

"You were wearing *horns*," Diane says. "And when you and your creep friends went after those girls in the pool you were wearing horns again. What is that, some sort of sick, horn-wearing, woman-molesting club?"

Her tone is angry, but the marijuana seems to be calming me down.

"That wasn't my idea," I say. "It was my friend's. He thought somebody was keeping the women there against their will and we could save them."

Diane looks disgusted.

"Oh Christ, Danny, that is so lame," she says. "Save some synchronized swimmers who are just trying to make a living? By tearing off their clothes? And grown men running around in horns? I know the papers said it was a prank but it's a step away from rape. You're pretending to be what, the devil? You think it's okay to grab and terrorize women? What kind of sick crap is that?"

Something in me snaps. *Sick?* That's not what it was at all. That's not who *I* am at all. I am a satyr. I adore women. The marijuana must have just taken me to another plane because for the first time in my life, I am seeing things clearly:

You can't have a relationship if the person you love doesn't know who you really are. It's trying to hide what I am from Diane that's caused all these problems. She needs to know, like the woman who loved my grandfather.

I take off my hat.

Diane gasps.

"I'm not a devil Diane, I'm a satyr," I say. "I venerate women."

Diane's gone pale.

"This is bad weed," she says. "Somebody cut it with acid. I'm seeing things."

I go to Diane and kneel in front of her.

"It's not bad weed," I say. "I know it's a shock, but I'm real. My horns are real. Touch them."

"I'm tripping," she says. "I'm really scared. I need to come down."

I've got to calm her down.

"Please don't be scared," I say. "I don't want you to be scared. I know it's a shock, but my horns are real. You wanted to study a lost race, I'm a lost race."

I take Diane's wrist, gently.

"Please," I say. "Touch them."

I guide Diane's hand to a horn. She touches the base where it meets my scalp.

"They're attached," she says, more to herself than me.

I let go of her hand.

"They're part of me, Diane," I say. "As much as your fingers are part of you."

"A birth defect," Diane says. "A bony growth. Some medical thing that looks like horns."

"No," I say. "This is *not* a birth defect. It's not something you're seeing because you're high. I'm a satyr, my father is a satyr, my grandfather is a satyr. We're just like you. Except we have horns and hooves and sleep all winter."

"Hooves too?" Diane says, weakly.

That might have been too much.

"Forget the hooves," I say. "It's more like really bony feet. We have funny-looking feet."

"This is some heavy weed," Diane says.

She closes her eyes and sits back, trying to slow her breathing. A few minutes later, she opens her eyes.

"Look," she says. "Let's say it's not the grass – which I know it is. Let's say you've really got these weird things growing out of your head. I could see it, this satyr fantasy, going through life like that. That could definitely fuck you up. But I know that's not what's going on and if I weren't so stoned, I could prove it. You're walking around with horns stuck to your head."

The marijuana must be affecting her differently. I'm not getting through and the horns are freaking her out. I put my hat back on.

"Damn it, Diane, forget the horns," I say. "I love you! I loved you the minute I saw you on the mountain. And I know, before this thing at the pool you loved me, too. You wouldn't have given yourself to me the way you did, if you didn't. We're meant to be together. Like Gatsby and Daisy."

"*What?*" Diane says.

I can't believe a person who reads so much doesn't know what I'm talking about.

"The book, "The Great Gatsby,"" I say. "You know. Gatsby and Daisy are separated for five years, but then he finds her and she realizes she has always loved him."

If Diane was high a moment ago, she's come down fast.

"He finds her and he's so possessive she can't stand him," she says. "Then he's shot dead. And she's *relieved*."

I can't believe what I'm hearing.

"No, no," I say, "That can't be how it ends . . . "

"Oh Christ, of course it is," Diane says. "Didn't you even finish it? What am I even doing, talking to a crazy person about a book? I am never smoking grass again. Will you just leave?"

This isn't happening. This can't be happening.

"But what about this summer?" I say, "What happened between us? That night in your car?"

"The car?" Diane asks, as if she doesn't remember.

"At the ski slope," I say.

Diane stands up.

"I never knew anybody who lived in the mountains year-round," she says. "You were exotic. You weren't even going to college. We had some fun, we made out, that was *it*."

Now my reality is starting to break up. I showed Diane my mountain. I played her the most beautiful songs I knew. I've traveled to a city of steel and concrete that's making me sick. This is the woman I'm risking my life for?

"That's what you thought of me?" I manage to say. "An *exotic*?"

"Danny," Diane says. "Until you showed up I didn't think of you at *all*."

She goes to the door and opens it.

"I think you better go," she says.

The marijuana must be adding to this dream-like feeling, but even with this sense of unreality, I know exactly who I am: I am satyr, proud member of an ancient race. I am here to exult in my being and the joys of love and summer. If it is my destiny to adore one woman and she does not love me in return, by the gods, I will find another woman and love again.

"Goodbye, Diane," I say.

Chapter Twenty-Eight

I felt strong telling Diane goodbye, but back on the street the pain of what just happened hits me. Diane was in shock because she did not know horned men existed, I think; she'll be better once she gets used to the idea.

Then I realize what I'm doing and stop. Enough with made-up stories. I believed in Gatsby, but Gatsby doesn't wind up with Daisy; he winds up dead. I loved Diane, but she never cared for me the way I wanted to believe. None of that was real. What's real is grass and the mountains and the nymph mark on my chest and Ben and Pop. And Thalia, who was sweet to me even when I was hung up on someone else.

I've got to get back home and quickly. Gramp told me I would be okay if I spent no more than three days in the city, but I think I've been exposed to more steel and trucks and concrete than he figured on. I've got to get someplace green.

I walk back to Washington Square Park. The chess corner is deserted except for a man with long, filthy hair who is stretched out on a bench under a blanket of newspapers. You don't need a satyr's sense of smell to pick up this guy's stink. Then again am I that much better? Alone in New York City, with the woman I loved throwing me out and no place to go.

I look for another spot to regain my strength. A tree would be safest but after my experience with the angry ghost, I don't want to risk it. Who knows how many people they hung in Washington Square? I see a bench not far from the fountain and crawl under it. The grass is patchy and littered, too grimy to eat, but at least it is grass. I rub my face in it and feel better. Tomorrow I will find the bus the city people take to the country and go home.

I drift off. A great stench fills my nostrils, I feel someone patting my pockets. I open my eyes. It's the homeless guy. Around him a crowd of dead people in ragged clothing are holding their noses.

"Yucchhh!" "Uuughhh." "Disgusting."

The sight of the dead freezes me. The homeless man finds my wallet and sprints off into the night. I roll out from under the bench and start after him, but I am still half asleep and I fall. My hat falls, too. I snatch it up. The dead are staring.

"You're a satyr?" a dead guy with powerful arms asks. "I thought that was a myth."

"Are you sickly?" an old man asks worriedly. "Because we're already crowded."

A pregnant woman turns on him.

"What are you, an idiot?" she says. "When was the last time they buried anyone here?"

"A Siamese cat, last week," the old man says. "A writer snuck it in."

This is not good. These may not be malevolent spirits, but the dead talk when they cannot sleep and often that is because the earth is poisoned.

And two dead men coming at me from the corner near the hanging tree are definitely evil. They've got nooses around their necks trailing rope. The taller man takes off his noose and swings it in my direction.

I run. The rope hits my shoulder. I leap out of the park and across the street. Turning around, I see the noose men hit an invisible wall and fall to the ground. Washington Square Park must be their prison.

I stand in the street trying to catch my breath. Normally I leap as easily as I breathe, but now I am panting. I sit down on a stoop, then check my pockets for money. I have 58 cents. A bus to the mountains has to be more than this. If I could get back to the food market I might be able to ride a truck home, but the Bronx is a great distance from the Village. I don't have the strength to get there.

Then I remember: Pop's friend, Noah, lives in New York. There are too many Yablonskys to find his street in the phone book, but he has a business address: 1619 Broadway near 50th Street.

He won't be there till morning. But there is probably a park for me to sleep on the way. I walk north. I don't see a single tree. I have a feeling that the city might have changed since my grandfather was here in 1916.

Times Square is astonishing. Even though it's the middle of the night, food shops and movie theaters are open. One even advertises a film about woodland creatures: "Nymphs Gone Wild." Flashing signs illuminate the night: advertisements for Admiral TV and Trans World Airlines; a portrait of a man on the side of a building blowing real smoke rings into the air.

Hundreds of people jam the street. Women in high heels and very tight skirts approach men seductively, even going into the street when their cars stop, asking if they would like to have some fun. It's a courting ritual in which the female is the aggressor.

A young woman in a low-cut blouse walks up to me. Her skin is sallow, there are purple bruises on her arms, and she has been badly scratched on the inside of one elbow. I have a feeling it has been a long time since she had a glass of milk. She would also be prettier without so much paint on her face, but of course, I greet her respectfully.

"Good evening, Ethereal Creature," I say.

"Let me guess, first time in the city?" she says.

I nod.

"Blow job, five bucks; straight up, ten; fifty, you get me all night," she says.

Now I get it. This woman thinks she has to pay someone to make love to her. No satyr would ever denigrate a woman that way.

"Listen," I say, "You don't know me, but I know something about this. You're a woman, you deserve love. You don't need to do this."

"Save it for church, asshole," the woman says.

A skinny man in maroon pants, a dark shirt, a dark green jacket and a wide-brimmed purple hat walks over.

"You bothering the lady?" the man asks. "You bothering the lady, I'll fix your pretty face."

He flashes a knife.

This city is worse than I ever imagined – this man is ready to cut me. I walk quickly away, down 42nd Street, looking for a place to hide. I see a narrow opening between buildings and squeeze through to an alley.

The alley is filthy with human feces and broken bottles, but I spot a partly opened window at shoulder height. I pull myself up and look through. No one is inside.

I wiggle through, falling onto rolls of fabric.

The only light is coming from red exit lights which make the room look washed in blood. The smells are ammonia-like and harsh. I try to identify what's inside: paint, turpentine, alcohol, perhaps glue. Human smells, male and female, young and mature, drift in also, but they are at least a few hours old.

My eyes adjust to the light. I seem to be in an artisan's workshop. I see worktables, hammers and nails, a table with a saw, sheets of plywood. It's not a good place to sleep.

I find a door and walk into another room. Across from me, exactly my height, is an open metal coffin studded with pro-truding nails, the height and shape of a man. It's so bizarre I stare at it a long time. Then it hits me: the coffin is a murder tool. When closed, it will send spikes through a man's body. I lean against the wall, willing myself not to faint.

I force myself to look up and down the hall. As far as I can see in the blood red light there are machines designed to tor-ture and maim and kill: a set of large metal blades at the end of a wooden platform, with a bucket just beneath the blade. Pincers and daggers. The metal outline of a boot, with bolts to pierce the heel.

I run as fast as I can through the hall. It opens into a large room that is filled with animals. Not living animals. Diane had called my horns a deformity. Now, all around me are creatures who really are deformed. A calf with two heads. A kitten with an extra paw. A dog with an eye in the middle of its head. A human nine inches tall with blackened skin and a topknot of black hair.

I spin around, looking for a way to get out.

There's another room up ahead, where I see the outline of a tree. I doubt it will be living but maybe it will lead to an exit.

I run into the room. The light here, thank the gods, is pleasant, like a clear morning in the mountains. There's a replica of a beautiful forest glade with flowers and a lily pond. I breathe a sigh of relief. Next to the pond is a river nymph, obviously fake, a life-sized replica like the ones stores use to display clothes. It's a ridiculous fake, with short, cropped hair and a green gown so coarse no nymph would wipe her hands on it, but the satyr who is reaching out to touch her. . . . oh shit . . .

The satyr is real. He has horns exactly like mine and a lower body with hair like mine and small, rugged hooves. He's Pop's friend Seth, taken to New York City and stuffed.

I back away, overwhelmed by terror.

Then the feeling turns even more powerfully to fury. Fury at the stupidity of humans who can't accept anyone who doesn't look like them; who force satyrs to hide; who murder and display and gawk.

I am not deformed. I am not a freak. I am a satyr, sacred of the mountains. And we honor our dead.

I break off the branches of the trees around Seth and stack them at his feet. I pick up two stones and rub them together and make a fire. I remove my stupid hat and stand in front of Seth, holding a burning branch. Then I recite the holy words:

"Precious creature of the forest, you lived in joy and celebration and abundance. No flower went unnoticed, no nymph nor wine nor summer moon ignored. Return to the spirits of the mountains, drink with your brothers, delight with the nymphs. You were loved."

I kneel and light the fire. I watch Seth turn into a great flame. The fire spreads to the plastic nymph beside him, who begins melting. An alarm sounds. I'm sick of hiding and creeping through back alleys. I put my hat back on, find my way to the entrance, kick out a display window, and walk out into the street. I'm going home.

CHAPTER TWENTY-NINE

I'm back on 42nd Street. The sun is coming up and the streets are finally quiet, but the horror house has made me sick. I lean against the wall and puke. When I stand and wipe my mouth with my hand, I see blood. It's too early for Noah to be at work, but I need to make it to his building while I still can.

I walk back to Broadway and turn north. It is difficult to keep going. At 46th Street I see a man wearing two jackets sleeping beside a building. Nobody pays any attention to him. I sit down beside the man to rest for a few minutes. When I open my eyes the streets are much busier. I wouldn't mind sleeping here the rest of my life, but I have to get to Noah. I drag myself up, repeating the address in my head:

1619 Broadway. 1619 Broadway.

The sidewalk is getting steeper. I pass 48th Street, then 49th. Then I see 1619, an ornate, narrow building of black marble and gold – the Brill Building. Inside, visitors are being stopped by a guard.

"Eighth floor, Room 809," he tells me, when I ask for Noah Yablonsky. "Elevator C."

A mechanical box is dangerous, but I'm in no condition to climb. I get in the box and touch a light with the number eight. The contact makes me dizzy.

Pressing a buzzer for Yablonsky Public Relations makes me even dizzier. I lean against the door for support and when it opens, I collapse. Breathing takes strength and I do not have it. I am dying in a city of concrete and steel, which I came to by choice. What shame I will bring on my line.

When I open my eyes Noah is squatting on the floor next to me.

"Danny?" Noah is saying. "Can you hear me?"

I need to speak, but I can't.

Noah turns to a young woman who's staring down at me.

"You know the health food store on 47th?" Noah says. "I need you to get there as fast as you can and get all the fresh-squeezed carrot and spinach juice you can carry."

When I wake up, the girl is gone and Noah is next to me with a large container and a straw.

"Sip," he says.

I drink a half cup of spinach juice, then manage to sit up and lean against the wall. There are, I realize, long, large leaves stuffed under my shirt. A potted plant, stripped half-bare, sits across the room.

"Malabar chestnut," Noah says. "Not exactly native to the Catskills, but it's all I had. You feel better?"

"A little," I say.

"I'm guessing you were down here chasing that girl who screamed at you at the pool," Noah says. "Now I'm going to ask you something and I need you to be straight with me: did you have sex with her?"

I laugh.

"Yeah, right," I say.

"Did you?" Noah asks.

"No," I say.

"Well, there's a relief," Noah says. "Did you go into her head?"

"Not hers, her shrink's," I say.

Noah passes me a big container of carrot juice.

"Drink it all," he says.

I get down as much as I can.

"Okay," Noah says. "We're gonna get you home. You think you can walk? We'll make better time than a taxi. It's just two blocks."

"I'll try," I say.

Outside, I'm not so sure. The fumes of the traffic hit me and I feel dizzy. But it's starting to feel personal, this attack of concrete and steel, and if it's going to get me, I want to go out standing.

I put my arm around Noah's shoulder and we walk across 50th Street. Brick and steel buildings are blocking out the sky. The city is a blur. We cross the Avenue of the Americas which is far noisier and crowded here than it was in the Village.

We go through the side door of a very big building. A man in a blue uniform takes one look at me and rushes over. From somewhere in the building, I hear the music of a large orchestra and the echoing sound of dozens of feet, stomping rhythmically. Then we're in an enormous theater, with a ceiling taller than a three-story building and acres of empty chairs. Noah and the man in the uniform dump me in a padded chair and disappear. I know I'm having visions because I see deer on a great stage, each with a tall rack of antlers, standing on their hind legs like humans and dancing. They're pulling a sleigh carrying a fat man in a red suit and their feet make a deafening noise as they hit the floor. It's gaudy and loud and crude. My eyes focus. The dancers are human women, wearing fawn-colored tights.

Noah is huddling with a man sitting a few rows from the stage.

The man shouts an order.

"Reindeer, fifteen minutes! Santa, elves, places!"

A tall woman, with fake antlers on her head and a red, glowing ball over her nose, walks over to Noah, her shiny, fake hooves clacking.

"What the hell's going on, Noah?" she says. "It's an NBC special. I'm Rudolph."

Then she sees me and stops. I've got puke stains on my clothes, my face is smudged with smoke. I have a bad feeling that I smell.

"Oh no," she says.

She walks to me and kneels down and I smell it: carnation, rose, peach, bergamot, musk, moss, amber, sandalwood.

It comes back in a rush: green eyes, the perfume, a beautiful woman turning a Rodgers & Hart song into a lullaby. The one about the shortest day of the year, which has the longest night of the year . . .

"And the longest night," my mother sang, "Is the shortest night with you."

I had pictured our reunion a million times: she was a beautiful nymph, so lovely that when she touched down, the trees bowed. She'd find me when I was with my friends and clutch me to her and everyone would see that I had a mother too, and how much I was loved. The stupid stories I'd told myself: that she'd regretted her actions almost as soon as she left me, but the winds had carried her away and stranded her somewhere in a far territory. That the gods kept her away from me, but one day she would break through. That when she sat with me on Venerable Mother's Day she would not be able to keep from touching me and stroking my hair.

And none of that was ever real.

My mother is a human. She was not imprisoned in a far territory, she was in a city three hours away. She could have come back anytime. Instead, she's in a ridiculous costume, wearing fake antlers and a big red nose.

"*Mom?*" I say. "You left me for *this?*"

My mother doesn't move, she is just staring at me.

Noah speaks.

"He's sick, Gloria," Noah says. "He needs his mother."

My mother reaches out and touches my face like I'm something that could break.

"He's beautiful," she says. "Why are they always so damn beautiful?"

She kneels down and puts her arms around me. The dizziness stops, I feel stronger. It's not a myth, it's real, I can feel it, the transfusing power of a mother's love.

"My baby," my mother says and starts to cry. "I'm sorry baby. I'm so sorry."

I pass out. When I wake up, I'm lying in the back seat of a car with my head in my mother's lap. The windows are open and I smell trees. The car stops briefly, and I see a sign for Woodstock. Then we are moving again. My mother is looking down at me, smiling.

"You had a good, long sleep," she says. "You feel better?"

"Yeah," I say. "I can sit, I think."

I sit up, trying to adjust to this. My mother, next to me. My mother, human. Noah driving, my mother with me in the mountains.

"West Hurley, Ashokan," my mother says, looking out the window. "My God, this road brings me back."

Then she turns back to me.

"Noah says you came to New York looking for a girl," she says.

The pain of it, Diane in her apartment telling me to get out, comes back.

"Yeah," I say. "She thought I was a freak."

My mother looks like someone has insulted her too.

"You know that's not true, right?" she says.

There's a lump in my throat. I know it's not true, but the look on Diane's face when she saw my horns, the memory of Seth stuffed in a museum, have risen up and overtaken me.

"You're part of an ancient and special race," my mother says. "It's just hard for humans to believe."

"You believed it," I say.

"Yeah," she says. "And I handled it great, huh? Dumped you when you were two weeks old. A wonderful reflection of the human race."

I don't know what to say. My mother looks out the window.

"I get if you hate me," she says. "When it comes to you, I hate me."

"I don't hate you," I say.

My mother turns back to me.

"Well let's say if there have been times you're really pissed at me, I get it," she says.

I reach for her hand. I've got my mother. *My* mother. I just want to be next to her and breathe her in. Carnation, rose, peach, bergamot, musk, moss, amber, sandalwood . . .

"Your scent?" I say.

My mother looks confused for a moment, then laughs.

"Oh right," she says. "That great nose. L'Air du Temps. Your father said after we'd been together, he could smell it on himself for days. You think you can drink something?"

"Yeah," I say.

I take a huge drink of carrot juice. We pass Boiceville, then Mt. Tremper. The forests are thicker. I breathe them in: maple and pine and hemlock.

"Noah," I say. "Is there somewhere around here where I could go into the woods?"

Noah turns onto a smaller road, then a dirt road which dead ends at a forest. I open the door and get out.

"Shall I come with you?" my mother asks.

"No," I say. "I need to do this myself."

CHAPTER THIRTY

The woods are dotted with white and purple aster, silverrod, goldenrod and desiccated leaves; the bittersweet fragrance, stronger in September, of the flowering and the gone.

I turn to the thickest part of the forest and bow my head respectfully.

Thank you for making me a satyr –

Then I stop.

Is that what I am, with a human mother? Was I ever? I have the hooves and the horns; I have a satyr father and a satyr grandfather, but am I still sacred to the mountains? I left the mountains for the love of a human girl and fouled myself on city pavement and steel. Perhaps the mountains no longer wish to nurture me.

But I left for love, like my grandfather. And I revere the mountains. Perhaps, finally, what I am is for me to decide. I bow my head and give thanks to the earth and the flowers and the trees: not like a young goat, like a satyr fully grown, who will take risks for love, and perhaps fail, and is not afraid to see things as they are.

Thank you for making me a satyr. Thank you for the abundance of summer. May I never squander a ray of sun nor fail to delight in the glory of a flower and never, ever decline the gift of love from a lady.

Then I lie down on the forest floor, arms outstretched, absorbing it into me.

"All good?" Noah asks, when I return.

"Yeah," I say.

He heads back to the main road and I turn to my mother.

"Now," I say, "Tell me everything."

She doesn't look happy. She looks, kind of, like she's been called up before a group of angry, old goats. But she also looks like she's been expecting this.

"Okay," she says. "Well, as you probably figured out, I grew up in the mountains too. My family had a hotel, near Fleischmanns. It was okay in the summer when the city people came up; then it was fun. But in the winter, which you never see, it was death: bare trees, depressing short days, freezing. The only good thing about winter was the hotel shut down and we got to go to the city."

"There was a small group of Jews who lived in Fleischmanns year-round. For us, New York was the mother ship. We'd take day trips into Manhattan; my father would drop my mother off at Macy's to go shopping; I would go with my father to Katz's, a deli on the lower east side. I didn't see a lot of my father; his whole life was work, hanging out with him was a big deal. So, we'd sit in Katz's, my father would have a pastrami on rye, I'd have a turkey sandwich with these huge French fries and a Dr. Brown's black cherry soda."

"The best part of the day was the afternoon when we'd go to a Broadway show. Great shows: "Damn Yankees," "Guys & Dolls," "The Boys from Syracuse." You know how you see something and you just know it's what you're meant to do? That's how it was with me and the theater. I saw these showgirls doing a nightclub number in "Guys & Dolls." They were so glamorous in their white mink stoles and fishnet stockings. And that was it, I had to be a Broadway dancer. My parents hated the idea. But my last year in high school, my father died and my mother was overwhelmed trying to keep the hotel going. I just headed down to New York."

My mother pauses.

"Would you like a little more carrot juice?" she asks.

"Yes, thank you," I say. "Keep going."

"I was lucky," my mother says. "I got work fast. First clubs, which was just tits and glitz, then touring companies, then, finally, Broadway. The chorus, but who cares? Then this jerk drops me in a lift and I break my arm in two places. I don't have any money, so I come back to the mountains. It was April, an unusually early spring. As much as I hated the Catskills in winter, I loved it in spring. The grass was so fresh like it was the first grass in the history of the world. And the mountains . . . there was a back road behind Fleischmanns, Red Kill Road. The view was so beautiful that even as a kid, it made me ache. It made me lonely and happy at the same time. I was maybe seven years old. It was so beautiful I didn't want to be alone in it, I wanted to be with a guy who loved me. How can a seven-year-old even think about that? But I did."

I don't think it's strange. It's the knowledge every satyr has of what makes life fulfilling: *It's an afternoon in summer. Make it perfect. Be with me.* My mother just had it young and ached for one person. Like me.

"My mother had a vase with a nymph and satyr on it and when I was growing up, I'd read stories about them," my mother says. "One of the farmers swore he saw a horned man one night in the apple orchard. But he also had a still in that orchard. Anyway, it was spring. Every day, I'd climb up the mountain and do scales, because I liked the sound of my voice up there. One day I thought I heard another girl mimicking me, but when I looked around, no one was there."

"Nymphs," I say.

"They could be real bitches," my mother says. "Another time, I went up the mountain wearing a straw hat with a long green ribbon. A breeze blows it off. I try to find it, but it's gone. A few minutes later the most attractive man I have ever seen comes strolling out of the woods wearing my hat and grins at me."

"Pop," I say.

My mother nods.

"I've seen a lot of good-looking men," my mother says. "I'm in show business, right? I had a scene once with Marlon Brando. That man could charm a snake. But your father had something I had never experienced. That grin: it was so playful, so confident, so fucking . . . *male.* He had this magnetism. I look at him and I know right away what he is; I didn't think I was losing my mind, I just accepted it. He stands there for a few minutes, waiting. Then, when I smile, he gets down on one knee, and he says – I remember it exactly – 'Ethereal Creature, it's an afternoon in summer. Make it perfect. Be with me.' And that was that."

My mother looks the way Gramp did, talking about Amelita.

"After that, we were always together," my mother says. "The nymphs were not happy about it. Your father had been a very popular guy. And losing him to a human really outraged them. The satyrs weren't thrilled either. Being with one woman was something that just was not done. They were also very superstitious; they thought that just saying my name out loud would curse the colony. *'Angering the gods.'* We didn't care. We didn't want to be around anyone else. I'd spend the night with your father, then slip off before dawn to the hotel. Or tell my mother I was visiting friends. And then, you came along."

I'm realizing something: Gramp said if a satyr really wanted a child with a human and was willing to give up his normal lifespan, he could make it happen. That means Pop must have really wanted me. All the time I was hung up on my mother, I was probably the most wanted, best-loved goat on the mountain.

"Mom," I say, though the word still feels weird, "Did Pop tell you if he had a baby with you he would be giving up over half his life?"

My mother looks shocked.

"*What?*" she says.

"It's like a trade-off," I say. "If a satyr has a baby with a human he gets the life cycle of a human. Pop's father told me. "

My mother looks stunned.

"No, no, he never said that," she says. "I don't think I would have gone through with it if he'd said that. Not my beautiful Jake."

She looks so upset that I feel I should stop asking questions, but this is something I need to know.

"But he did ask you if you wanted a baby, right?" I say.

My mother looks away.

"Yes of course," my mother says.

"And what did you say?" I ask.

She turns back to me.

"I said yes," she says. "And in that moment, I really meant it. Being with your father, it was like nothing else existed. I didn't think about New York, I didn't think about dancing. It was like it was going to be summer for the rest of our lives. And it happened so fast, much, much faster than a regular pregnancy."

"But where did you have me?" I say.

"In the woods," my mother says. "One of the nymphs, the Greek, Melena – one of the nice ones – delivered you. You were so perfect. Beautiful long eyelashes, black curls plastered to your head, little onyx hooves. I never knew I could love anything the way I loved you."

A million feelings are fighting inside me. Sadness, anger, love, confusion.

"But you left," I say.

"Yeah," my mother says. "The rotten part of your mother. When I held you, when I nursed you for the first time, I swore I would never let you go. But it became obvious very quickly that being a mother was the opposite of summer of love in the woods. You needed my attention every minute. If I put you down, even to run outside to go to the bathroom, you howled. Your father was no help. In his world babies were women's work. The second night, when you were screaming, he said, 'I can't take this' and went off with his friends. Five days in, I thought, 'I don't know how much of this I can take either.'"

"But it wouldn't have been forever," I say. "In three months, I would have been able to take care of myself."

"That's what your father said and I guess it would have been true if you were all satyr," my mother says. "But how could we tell? You had hooves, but you had my blood too. Human children take years to be independent. I loved you but years . . . I knew I would never be able to do that. Then two weeks after you're born, I find out that my manager has been trying to get ahold of me. I was up for a part in L.A. . Your father was furious that I was even considering it, but it was the kind of chance you don't turn down. I broke the news to my mother that there were satyrs in the Catskills and one of them had given me a baby. With hooves."

I try to picture that.

"What did she do?" I ask.

"She passed out," my mother says. "The next day I left."

She's sounding so matter of fact about this.

"But why didn't you take me?" I say.

"I was going to a city in an airplane," my mother says. "Either of those could have killed you. You had no immunity to metals or machines; once when I was wearing a watch and picked you up, you broke out in a rash. You needed the mountains. I thought about coming back, but your father had been so angry when I left. Then it was November and the long sleep. Then . . . "

My mother doesn't speak for a few moments.

"This is the hardest part," she says. "I want to say I was guilty and afraid to face everyone and the longer I stayed away, the guiltier I got. Which is true. My mother would bring me pictures when she came to New York. You were so sweet, I'd tell myself okay, after this job, this audition, I'll go back. But the truth, the shitty rotten truth, is that I was twenty-six when I had you and I didn't want to be a mother. I didn't want to live in a dying resort town where they torched hotels at the end of the season. I wanted to live in a big city. I wanted to be a movie star.

I remember Ann-Margret and "Bye Bye Birdie."

"Did you get to be a star?" I ask.

My mother laughs.

"You think there are a lot of movie stars playing reindeer at Radio City? My part got cut and I ended up back in New York in the chorus. I got what I deserved, huh?"

"It's okay, Mom," I say, and I mean it. "I have you now. The other mothers don't stick around much anyway."

My mother laughs.

"You're a sweet boy, Danny," she says.

We're higher in the mountains now. I realize I have another question.

Mom," I say. "What about my nymph mark?"

My mother looks puzzled.

"Your what?" she asks.

"The apple on my chest. My birthmark. Like Pop's lilac blossom. We all have them."

She still doesn't understand.

"Can I see it?" she asks.

I pull up my shirt.

My mother looks at it, then laughs.

"Melena," she says. "She was an artist. She must have done it after I left so you'd fit in. People call New York The Big Apple. She knew I'd end up there."

"She gave me your mark," I say.

My mother smiles.

"She was always one step ahead of everybody else," she says. "I'd love to see her. Has she been around?"

"She died," I say. "This summer. Just before I came to New York."

My mother's smile disappears.

"Oh," my mother says. "I'm so sorry. Too late again."

We climb the steep hill up Route 28 to Highmount, descend into Fleischmanns, then make the sharp turn onto the country road leading past Lake Switzerland. The season is over, the rowboats gone, the hotels closed. The mountains are tranquil, returned to the locals and the satyrs.

Noah drives past the Halcott Center post office and the creamery and the Grange Hall, then takes a right on Elk Creek Road, pulling up in front of The Maplewood House.

Pop, who has been pacing the lawn, comes running down with Bernie and Artie. Mrs. Belinsky follows. Her eyes are red and puffy like she has been crying.

Pop hugs me to him.

"Are you okay?" Pop asks.

"I'm good," I say. "Really."

My mother gets out.

"Hi Ma," she says to Mrs. Belinsky and I suddenly get it: why Mrs. Belinsky hugged me so tight, why she stuffed me full of food, why she was sad when I was sad.

My mother turns to Pop, "Hey Jake," she says.

Pop could do anything. He could be polite for the sake of Mrs. Belinsky; he could explode; he could tell my mother she is dead to him. But I can sense, under the tough guy face he's trying to wear as he looks at my mother, something else is going on.

"Hey Gloria," Pop says.

So?" Mrs. Belinksy says to her daughter. "You coming or going?"

My mother looks over at Pop, then at Noah.

"You don't have to be back in the city till four tomorrow," Noah says.

"I guess maybe I'll spend the night," my mother says and you would have to be a very stupid goat, considering the way she and Pop are eying one another, not to know where.

Maybe next summer The Maplewood House will go up in flames at the end of the season and the Belinsky family will give up the hotel business and sell building supplies. Maybe the humans will feel so liberated by their free love pills they won't need satyrs. Things change, but a love that gives you only one season is still love. I tuck Diane away in a tender place.

Noah, Mom, Pop, me and the Belinsky family, *my* family, head to the kitchen. Mrs. Belinsky, with Mom helping, sets out a huge spread ending with every sweet in the pantry: lemon cake, chocolate babka, Linzer tarts sticky with jam. Artie takes the Yankees hat from my head and puts it on his own. Pop takes off his hat too. We sit together around the big table in the kitchen, drinking tea, laughing at Mom's stories about being a dancing reindeer, heaping great spoons of heavy cream on our cake. The gods, I think, have been kind.

I excuse myself, go outside and take out my pipes. When I get to Crump's Castle, Thalia is sitting on the stone wall, smiling.

I walk to her and drop to one knee.

"Ethereal Creature, it's an afternoon in summer," I say. "Make it perfect. Be with me."

ACKNOWLEDGMENTS

Although I have yet to spot a satyr in the Catskills, I know their territory well. I grew up in a small hotel much like Danny's in the late 1950s and early 1960s and the hotels and hangouts in the novel are, for the most part, real.

Bob Dylan was known to drop by the Café Espresso in Woodstock. The Hotel Mathes in Fleischmanns was locally famous for its bar with port-hole views into the pool. In the evenings, glamorous New York City women strolled Main Street in tight, Marilyn Monroe-inspired wiggle dresses and mink stoles while the men did their best to emulate Rat Pack cool.

Memory, however, takes you only so far. In creating this book, I am indebted to local historians and experts.

Thanks to John Duda, Trustee of the Greater Fleischmanns Museum of Memories, for taking me through decades of Fleischmanns history and tracking down early photos of Crump's Castle. To Diane Galusha, the President of the

Historical Society of the Town of Middletown, who walked me around Highmount, showing me where Lorenz Hart and Richard Rodgers once studied. To Steve Meinstein, whose family ran a hotel in Fleischmanns, and his wife June, who were invaluable in recreating the mood of the town in the 1960s. To Bob Byer, musician and one-time trombone player at the Concord Hotel, for leading me through the labyrinth backstage.

Scents, wildlife and woodlands are important in a satyr's life. Thanks to Erik Eckholm, long-time birdwatcher and a former New York Times colleague, for setting me straight about Catskills bird song. To Lisa Wadler, Susan Moseman and Caity Moseman Wadler for information about native flowers. To my brothers, Martin Wadler and David Wadler, and my cousins, Jason Wadler and Steven Wadler, for information about the deep woods and trails. Thank you to Christopher J. McKelvey, Section Chief of the Mined Land Section Division of Mineral Resources, New York State Department of Environmental Conservation, for familiarizing me with the topography. And apologies, as well. I took nearly as many liberties with caves as I did with satyrs.

Thanks to American classical composer John Craton, who has written about Amelita Galli-Curci, and tried to track down that singer's perfume. We both failed, so I invoked poetic license and gave the soprano "L 'Heure Bleue," introduced in 1912. Thanks also to the contributors of the fragrantica.com site for the wealth of information on scents.

Thank you to my first readers and consultants: Lewis Grossberger, Susan Beth Pfeffer, J. Stephen Sheppard, Roz Warren, Leslie Wells, Dinitia Smith, and Gioia Diliberto. Thank you to my copyeditor, Nancy Wartik.

Thank you to my agent, Joy Harris, for tirelessly searching for a publisher for the story of a lovelorn satyr who believes everything he reads.

And finally, thank you to my grandmother, Gussie Belinsky Wadler, a Russian immigrant who, with her sons, Bernie, Artie, and Hymie, ran a bedraggled little hotel called The Maplewood House in the Catskills Mountains, where the music from the P.A. system echoed off the mountains.

It was magic.

—Joyce Wadler

New York City, March 2025

ABOUT THE AUTHOR

Joyce Wadler is an award-winning New York City humorist and journalist who created and wrote the "I Was Misinformed" humor column for The New York Times, where she was a reporter for 15 years. She now writes a humor column on Substack.

Joyce was the New York correspondent for The Washington Post, a contributing editor for New York Magazine and Rolling Stone, and a staff reporter at New York City's three major newspapers. Her books include "My Breast," her memoir about breast cancer, which she later adapted as a CBS television movie, "Cured, My Ovarian Cancer Story," and "Liaison," the true story of the diplomat spy and the Chinese opera star whose affair inspired the play, "M. Butterfly."

Joyce's many awards include The National Society of Newspaper Columnists First Place Award for Humor, the Silurians Press Club Award for Commentary/ Editorial, The New York Press Club Award for Humor, The New York

Newspaper Publishers Association Award for column writing, and Columbia University's prestigious Mike Berger Award for Feature Writing.

Joyce grew up in the Catskills and lives in Greenwich Village. But in summer, she always returns to the mountains.

For more information, go to joycewadler.com